A Journey in Other Worlds
A Romance of the Future

by

John Jacob Astor

A Journey in Other Worlds
A Romance of the Future
by John Jacob Astor

Copyright © 2024

All Rights reserved.

No part of this publication may be reproduced, stored in a retrieval system, or transmitted in any form or by any means, electronic, mechanical, photocopying or Otherwise, without the written permission of the publisher.
The author/editor asserts the moral right to be identified as the author/editor of this work.

ISBN: 978-93-62765-54-3

Published by

DOUBLE 9 BOOKS

2/13-B, Ansari Road
Daryaganj, New Delhi – 110002
info@double9books.com
www.double9books.com
Tel. 011-40042856

This book is under public domain

ABOUT THE AUTHOR

John Jacob Astor was an American business entrepreneur, real estate developer, investor, author, lieutenant colonel in the Spanish-American War, and a prominent member of the Astor family. He died in the early hours of April 15, 1912, when the Titanic sank. Astor was the richest passenger on the RMS Titanic and was regarded to be one of the world's wealthiest persons at the time, with a net worth of approximately $87 million (equal to $2.75 billion in 2023) when he perished. John Jacob Astor IV was an American business entrepreneur, real estate developer, investor, author, lieutenant colonel in the Spanish-American War, and a prominent member of the Astor family. He died in the early hours of April 15, 1912, when the Titanic sank. Astor was the richest passenger on the RMS Titanic and was regarded to be one of the world's wealthiest persons at the time, with a net worth of approximately $87 million (equal to $2.75 billion in 2023) when he perished.

CONTENTS

PREFACE 9

BOOK I
CHAPTER I
JUPITER 10
CHAPTER II
ANTECEDENTAL 16
CHAPTER III
PRESIDENT BEARWARDEN'S SPEECH 18
CHAPTER IV
PROF. CORTLANDT'S HISTORICAL SKETCH OF THE WORLD 24
CHAPTER V
DR. CORTLANDT'S HISTORY CONTINUED 32
CHAPTER VI
FAR-REACHING PLANS 44
CHAPTER VII
HARD AT WORK 51
CHAPTER VIII
GOOD-BYE 58

BOOK II
CHAPTER I
THE LAST OF THE EARTH 64
CHAPTER II
SPACE AND MARS 69
CHAPTER III
HEAVENLY BODIES 75
CHAPTER IV
PREPARING TO ALIGHT 80

CHAPTER V
　　EXPLORATION AND EXCITEMENT...83
CHAPTER VI
　　MASTODON AND WILL-O'-THE WISPS...87
CHAPTER VII
　　AN UNSEEN HUNTER..94
CHAPTER VIII
　　SPORTSMEN'S REVERIES...99
CHAPTER IX
　　THE HONEY OF DEATH..105
CHAPTER X
　　CHANGING LANDSCAPES...111
CHAPTER XI
　　A JOVIAN NIAGARA..116
CHAPTER XII
　　HILLS AND VALLEYS...123
CHAPTER XIII
　　NORTH-POLAR DISCOVERIES..131
CHAPTER XIV
　　THE SCENE SHIFTS..137

BOOK III
CHAPTER I
　　SATURN..144
CHAPTER II
　　THE SPIRIT'S FIRST VISIT...149
CHAPTER III
　　DOUBTS AND PHILOSOPHY..157
CHAPTER IV
　　A PROVIDENTIAL INTERVENTION..162
CHAPTER V
　　AYRAULT'S VISION...166
CHAPTER VI
　　A GREAT VOID AND A GREAT LONGING...................................170
CHAPTER VII
　　THE SPIRIT'S SECOND VISIT...179

CHAPTER VIII
  CASSANDRA AND COSMOLOGY 185
CHAPTER IX
  DOCTOR CORTLANDT SEES HIS GRAVE 195
CHAPTER X
  AYRAULT 201
CHAPTER XI
  DREAMLAND TO SHADOWLAND 205
CHAPTER XII
  SHEOL 210
CHAPTER XIII
  THE PRIEST'S SERMON 214
CHAPTER XIV
  HIC ILLE JACET 217
CHAPTER XV
  MOTHER EARTH 223

PREFACE

The protracted struggle between science and the classics appears to be drawing to a close, with victory about to perch on the banner of science, as a perusal of almost any university or college catalogue shows. While a limited knowledge of both Greek and Latin is important for the correct use of our own language, the amount till recently required, in my judgment, has been absurdly out of proportion to the intrinsic value of these branches, or perhaps more correctly roots, of study. The classics have been thoroughly and painfully threshed out, and it seems impossible that anything new can be unearthed. We may equal the performances of the past, but there is no opportunity to surpass them or produce anything original. Even the much-vaunted "mental training" argument is beginning to pall; for would not anything equally difficult give as good developing results, while by learning a live matter we kill two birds with one stone? There can be no question that there are many forces and influences in Nature whose existence we as yet little more than suspect. How much more interesting it would be if, instead of reiterating our past achievements, the magazines and literature of the period should devote their consideration to what we do NOT know! It is only through investigation and research that inventions come; we may not find what we are in search of, but may discover something of perhaps greater moment. It is probable that the principal glories of the future will be found in as yet but little trodden paths, and as Prof. Cortlandt justly says at the close of his history, "Next to religion, we have most to hope from science."

BOOK I

CHAPTER I
JUPITER

Jupiter--the magnificent planet with a diameter of 86,500 miles, having 119 times the surface and 1,300 times the volume of the earth--lay beneath them.

They had often seen it in the terrestrial sky, emitting its strong, steady ray, and had thought of that far-away planet, about which till recently so little had been known, and a burning desire had possessed them to go to it and explore its mysteries. Now, thanks to APERGY, the force whose existence the ancients suspected, but of which they knew so little, all things were possible.

Ayrault manipulated the silk-covered glass handles, and the Callisto moved on slowly in comparison with its recent speed, and all remained glued to their telescopes as they peered through the rushing clouds, now forming and now dissolving before their eyes. What transports of delight, what ecstatic bliss, was theirs! Men had discovered and mastered the secret of apergy, and now, "little lower than the angels," they could soar through space, leaving even planets and comets behind.

"Is it not strange," said Dr. Cortlandt, "that though it has been known for over a century that bodies charged with unlike electricities attract one another, and those charged with like repel, no one thought of utilizing the counterpart of gravitation? In the nineteenth century, savants and Indian jugglers performed experiments with their disciples and masses of inert matter, by causing them to remain without visible support at some distance from the ground; and while many of these, of course, were quacks, some were on the right track, though they did not push their research."

President Bearwarden and Ayrault assented. They were steering for an apparently hard part of the planet's surface, about a degree and a half north of its equator.

"Since Jupiter's axis is almost at right angles to the plane of its orbit," said the doctor, "being inclined only about one degree and a half, instead of twenty-three and a half, as was the earth's till nearly so recently, it will be possible for us to have any climate we wish, from constantly warm at the equator to constantly cool or cold as we approach the poles, without being troubled by extremes of winter and summer."

Until the Callisto entered the planet's atmosphere, its five moons appeared like silver shields against the black sky, but now things were looking more terrestrial, and they began to feel at home. Bearwarden put down his note-book, and Ayrault returned a photograph to his pocket, while all three gazed at their new abode. Beneath them was a vast continent variegated by chains of lakes and rivers stretching away in all directions except toward the equator, where lay a placid ocean as far as their telescopes could pierce. To the eastward were towering and massive mountains, and along the southern border of the continent smoking volcanoes, while toward the west they saw forests, gently rolling plains, and table-lands that would have satisfied a poet or set an agriculturist's heart at rest. "How I should like to mine those hills for copper, or drain the swamps to the south!" exclaimed Col. Bearwarden. "The Lake Superior mines and the reclamation of the Florida Everglades would be nothing to this."

"Any inhabitants we may find here have so much land at their disposal that they will not need to drain swamps on account of pressure of population for some time," put in the doctor.

"I hope we may find some four-legged inhabitants," said Ayrault, thinking of their explosive magazine rifles. "If Jupiter is passing through its Jurassic or Mesozoic period, there must be any amount of some kind of game." Just then a quiver shook the Callisto, and glancing to the right they noticed one of the volcanoes in violent eruption. Smoke filled the air in clouds, hot stones and then floods of lava poured from the crater, while even the walls of the hermetically sealed Callisto could not arrest the thunderous crashes that made the interior of the car resound.

"Had we not better move on?" said Bearwarden, and accordingly they went toward the woods they had first seen. Finding a firm strip of land between the forest and an arm of the sea, they gently grounded the Callisto, and not being altogether sure how the atmosphere of their new abode would suit terrestrial lungs, or what its pressure to the square inch might be, they cautiously opened a port-hole a crack, retaining their hold upon it with its screw. Instantly there was a rush and a whistling sound as of escaping steam, while in a few moments their barometer stood at thirty-six inches, whereupon they closed the opening.

"I fancy," said Dr. Cortlandt, "we had better wait now till we become accustomed to this pressure. I do not believe it will go much higher, for the window made but little resistance when we shut it."

Finding they were not inconvenienced by a pressure but little greater than that of a deep coal-mine, they again opened the port, whereupon their barometer showed a further rise to forty-two, and then remained stationary. Finding also that the chemical composition of the air suited them, and that they had no difficulty in breathing, the pressure being the same as that sustained by a diver in fourteen feet of water, they opened a door and emerged. They knew fairly well what to expect, and were not disturbed by their new conditions. Though they had apparently gained a good deal in weight as a result of their ethereal journey, this did not incommode them; for though Jupiter's volume is thirteen hundred times that of the earth, on account of its lesser specific gravity, it has but three hundred times the mass- -i. e., it would weigh but three hundred times as much. Further, although a cubic foot of water or anything else weighs 2.5 as much as on earth, objects near the equator, on account of Jupiter's rapid rotation, weigh one fifth less than they do at the poles, by reason of the centrifugal force. Influenced by this fact, and also because they were 483,000,000 miles from the sun, instead of 92,000,000 as on earth, they had steered for the northern limit of Jupiter's tropics. And, in addition to this, they could easily apply the apergetic power in any degree to themselves when beyond the limits of the Callisto, and so be attracted to any extent, from twice the pull they receive from gravitation on earth to almost nothing.

Bearwarden and Ayrault shouldered their rifles, while Dr. Cortlandt took a repeating shot-gun with No. 4 shot, and, having also some hunting-knives and a sextant, all three set out in a northwesterly direction. The ground was rather soft, and a warm vapor seemed to rise from it. To the east the sky was veiled by dense clouds of smoke from the towering volcanoes, while on their left the forest seemed to extend without limit. Clumps of huge ferns were scattered about, and the ground was covered with curious tracks.

"Jupiter is evidently passing through a Carboniferous or Devonian period such as existed on earth, though, if consistent with its size, it should be on a vastly larger scale," said the doctor. "I never believed in the theory," he continued, "that the larger the planet the smaller should be its inhabitants, and always considered it a makeshift, put forward in the absence of definite knowledge, the idea being apparently that the weight of very large creatures would be too great for their strength. Of the fact that mastodons and creatures far larger than any now living on earth existed there, we have absolute proof, though gravitation must have been practically the same then as now."

Just here they came upon a number of huge bones, evidently the remains of some saurian, and many times the size of a grown crocodile. On passing a growth of most luxuriant vegetation, they saw a half-dozen sacklike objects, and drawing nearer noticed that the tops began to swell, and at the same time became lighter in colour. Just as the doctor was about to investigate one of them with his duck-shot, the enormously inflated tops of the creatures collapsed with a loud report, and the entire group soared away. When about to alight, forty yards off, they distended membranous folds in the manner of wings, which checked their descent, and on touching the ground remained where they were without rebound.

"We expected to find all kinds of reptiles and birds," exclaimed the doctor. "But I do not know how we should class those creatures. They seem to have pneumatic feet and legs, for their motion was certainly not produced like that of frogs."

When the party came up with them the heads again began to swell.

"I will perforate the air-chamber of one," said Col. Bearwarden, withdrawing the explosive cartridge from the barrel of his rifle and substituting one with a solid ball. "This will doubtless disable one so that we can examine it."

Just as they were about to rise, he shot the largest through the neck. All but the wounded one, soared off, while Bearwarden, Ayrault, and Cortlandt approached to examine it more closely.

"You see," said Cortlandt, "this vertebrate--for that is as definitely as we can yet describe it--forces a great pressure of air into its head and neck, which, by the action of valves, it must allow to rush into its very rudimentary lower extremities, distending them with such violence that the body is shot upward and forward. You may have noticed the tightly inflated portion underneath as they left the ground."

While speaking he had moved rather near, when suddenly a partially concealed mouth opened, showing the unmistakable tongue and fangs of a serpent. It emitted a hissing sound, and the small eyes gleamed maliciously.

"Do you believe it is a poisonous species?" asked Ayrault.

"I suspect it is," replied the doctor; "for, though it is doubtless able to leap with great accuracy upon its prey, we saw it took some time to recharge the upper air-chamber, so that, were it not armed with poison glands, it would fall an easy victim to its more powerful and swifter contemporaries, and would soon become extinct."

"As it will be unable to spring for some time," said Bearwarden, "we might as well save it the disappointment of trying," and, snapping the used shell from his rifle, he fired an explosive ball into the reptile, whereupon about half the body disappeared, while a sickening odour arose. Although the sun was still far above the horizon, the rapidity with which it was descending showed that the short night of less than five hours would soon be upon them; and though short it might be very dark, for they were in the tropics, and the sun, going down perpendicularly, must also pass completely around the globe, instead of, as in northern latitudes on earth in summer, approaching the horizon obliquely, and not going far below it. A slight and diffused sound here seemed to rise from the ground all about them, for which they could not account. Presently it became louder, and as the sun touched the horizon, it poured forth in prolonged strains. The large trumpet-shaped lilies, reeds, and heliotropes seemed fairly to throb as they raised their anthem to the sky and the setting sun, while the air grew dark with clouds of birds that gradually alighted on the ground, until, as the chorus grew fainter and gradually ceased, they flew back to their nests. The three companions had stood astonished while this act was played. The doctor then spoke:

"This is the most marvellous development of Nature I have seen, for its wonderful divergence from, and yet analogy to, what takes place on earth. You know our flowers offer honey, as it were, as bait to insects, that in eating or collecting it they may catch the pollen on their legs and so carry it to other flowers, perhaps of the opposite sex. Here flowers evidently appeal to the sense of hearing instead of taste, and make use of birds, of which there are enormous numbers, instead of winged insects, of which I have seen none, one being perhaps the natural result of the other. The flowers have become singers by long practice, or else, those that were most musical having had the best chance to reproduce, we have a neat illustration of the 'survival of the fittest.' The sound is doubtless produced by a shrinking of the fibres as the sun withdraws its heat, in which case we may expect another song at sunrise, when the same result will be effected by their expanding."

Searching for a camping-place in which to pass the coming hours, they saw lights flitting about like will-o'-the-wisps, but brighter and intermittent.

"They seem to be as bright as sixteen-candle-power lamps, but the light is yellower, and appears to emanate from a comparatively large surface, certainly nine or ten inches square," said the doctor.

They soon gave up the chase, however, for the lights were continually moving and frequently went out. While groping in the growing darkness, they came upon a brown object about the size of a small dog and close to the ground. It flew off with a humming insect sound, and as it did so it showed the brilliant phosphorescent glow they had observed.

"That is a good-sized fire-fly," said Bearwarden. "Evidently the insects here are on the same scale as everything else. They are like the fire-flies in Cuba, which the Cubans are said to put into a glass box and get light enough from to read by. Here they would need only one, if it could be induced to give its light continuously."

Having found an open space on high ground, they sat down, and Bearwarden struck his repeater, which, for convenience, had been arranged for Jupiter time, dividing the day into ten hours, beginning at noon, midnight being therefore five o'clock.

"Twenty minutes past four," said he, "which would correspond to about a quarter to eleven on earth. As the sun rises at half-past seven, it will be dark about three hours, for the time between dawn and daylight will, of course, be as short as that we have just experienced between sunset and night."

"If we stay here long," said the doctor, "I suppose we shall become accustomed, like sailors, to taking our four, or in this case five, hours on duty, and five hours off."

"Or," added Ayrault, "we can sleep ten consecutive hours and take the next ten for exploring and hunting, having the sun for one half the time and the moons for the other."

Bearwarden and Cortlandt now rolled themselves in their blankets and were soon asleep, while Ayrault, whose turn it was to watch till the moons rose--for they had not yet enough confidence in their new domain to sleep in darkness simultaneously--leaned his back against a rock and lighted his pipe. In the distance he saw the torrents of fiery lava from the volcanoes reflected in the sky, and faintly heard their thunderous crashes, while the fire-flies twinkled unconcernedly in the hollow, and the night winds swayed the fernlike branches. Then he gazed at the earth, which, but little above the horizon, shone with a faint but steady ray, and his mind's eye ran beyond his natural vision while he pictured to himself the girl of his heart, wishing that by some communion of spirits he might convey his thoughts to her, and receive hers. It was now the first week of January on earth. He could almost see her house and the snow-clad trees in the park, and knew that at that hour she was dressing for dinner, and hoped and believed that he was in her heart. While he thus mused, one moon after another rose, each at a different phase, till three were at once in the sky. Adjusting the electric protection-wires that were to paralyze any creature that attempted to come within the circle, and would arouse them by ringing a bell, he knocked the ashes from his pipe, rolled himself in a blanket, and was soon asleep beside his friends.

CHAPTER II
ANTECEDENTAL

"Come in!" sounded a voice, as Dr. Cortlandt and Dick Ayrault tapped at the door of the President of the Terrestrial Axis Straightening Company's private office on the morning of the 21st of June, A. D. 2000. Col. Bearwarden sat at his capacious desk, the shadows passing over his face as April clouds flit across the sun. He was a handsome man, and young for the important post he filled--being scarcely forty--a graduate of West Point, with great executive ability, and a wonderful engineer. "Sit down, chappies," said he; "we have still a half hour before I begin to read the report I am to make to the stockholders and representatives of all the governments, which is now ready. I know YOU smoke," passing a box of Havanas to the professor.

Prof. Cortlandt, LL. D., United States Government expert, appointed to examine the company's calculations, was about fifty, with a high forehead, greyish hair, and quick, grey eyes, a geologist and astronomer, and altogether as able a man, in his own way, as Col. Bearwarden in his. Richard Ayrault, a large stockholder and one of the honorary vice-presidents in the company, was about thirty, a university man, by nature a scientist, and engaged to one of the prettiest society girls, who was then a student at Vassar, in the beautiful town of Poughkeepsie.

"Knowing the way you carry things in your mind, and the difficulty of rattling you," said Cortlandt, "we have dropped in on our way to hear the speech that I would not miss for a fortune. Let us know if we bother you."

"Impossible, dear boy," replied the president genially. "Since I survived your official investigations, I think I deserve some of your attention informally."

"Here are my final examinations," said Cortlandt, handing Bearwarden a roll of papers. "I have been over all your figures, and testify to their accuracy in the appendix I have added."

So they sat and chatted about the enterprise that interested Cortlandt and Ayrault almost as much as Bearwarden himself. As the clock struck eleven, the president of the company put on his hat, and, saying au revoir to his friends, crossed the street to the Opera House, in which he was to read a report that would be copied in all the great journals and heard over thousands of miles of wire in every part of the globe. When he arrived, the vast building was already filled with a distinguished company, representing the greatest intelligence, wealth, and powers of the world. Bearwarden went in by the stage entrance, exchanging greetings as he did so with officers of the company and directors who had come to hear him. Cortlandt and Ayrault entered by the regular door, the former going to the Government representatives' box, the latter to join his fiancee, Sylvia Preston, who was there with her mother. Bearwarden had a roll of manuscript at hand, but so well did he know his speech that he scarcely glanced at it. After being introduced by the chairman of the meeting, and seeing that his audience was all attention, he began, holding himself erect, his clear, powerful voice making every part of the building ring.

CHAPTER III
PRESIDENT BEARWARDEN'S SPEECH

"To the Bondholders and Stockholders of the Terrestrial Axis Straightening Company and Representatives of Earthly Governments.

"GENTLEMEN: You know that the objects of this company are, to straighten the axis of the earth, to combine the extreme heat of summer with the intense cold of winter and produce a uniform temperature for each degree of latitude the year round. At present the earth's axis--that is, the line passing through its centre and the two poles--is inclined to the ecliptic about twenty-three and a half degrees. Our summer is produced by the northern hemisphere's leaning at that angle towards the sun, and our winter by its turning that much from it. In one case the sun's rays are caused to shine more perpendicularly, and in the other more obliquely. This wabbling, like that of a top, is the sole cause of the seasons; since, owing to the eccentricity of our orbit, the earth is actually fifteen hundred thousand miles nearer the sun during our winter, in the northern hemisphere, than in summer. That there is no limit to a planet's inclination, and that inclination is not essential, we have astronomical proof. Venus's axis is inclined to the plane of her orbit seventy-five degrees, so that the arctic circle comes within fifteen degrees of the equator, and the tropics also extend to latitude seventy-five degrees, or within fifteen degrees of the poles, producing great extremes of heat and cold.

"Venus is made still more difficult of habitation by the fact that she rotates on her axis in the same time that she revolves about the sun, in the same way that the moon does about the earth, so that one side must be perpetually frozen while the other is parched.

"In Uranus we see the axis tilted still further, so that the arctic circle descends to the equator. The most varied climate must therefore prevail during its year, whose length exceeds eighty-one of ours.

"The axis of Mars is inclined about twenty-eight and two thirds degrees to the plane of its orbit; consequently its seasons must be very similar to ours, the extremes of heat and cold being somewhat greater.

"In Jupiter we have an illustration of a planet whose axis is almost at right angles to the plane of its orbit, being inclined but about a degree and a half. The hypothetical inhabitants of this majestic planet must therefore have perpetual summer at the equator, eternal winter at the poles, and in the temperate regions everlasting spring. On account of the straightness of the axis, however, even the polar inhabitants--if there are any--are not oppressed by a six months' night, for all except those at the VERY pole have a sunrise and a sunset every ten hours--the exact day being nine hours, fifty five minutes, and twenty-eight seconds. The warmth of the tropics is also tempered by the high winds that must result from the rapid whirl on its axis, every object at the equator being carried around by this at the rate of 27,600 miles an hour, or over three thousand miles farther than the earth's equator moves in twenty-four hours.

"The inclination of the axis of our own planet has also frequently considerably exceeded that of Mars, and again has been but little greater than Jupiter's at least, this is by all odds the most reasonable explanation of the numerous Glacial periods through which our globe has passed, and of the recurring mild spells, probably lasting thousands of years, in which elephants, mastodons, and other semi-tropical vertebrates roamed in Siberia, some of which died so recently that their flesh, preserved by the cold, has been devoured by the dogs of modern explorers.

"It is not to be supposed that the inclining of the axes of Jupiter, Venus, the Earth, and the other planets, is now fixed; in some cases it is known to be changing. As long ago as 1890, Major-Gen. A. W. Drayson, of the British Army, showed, in a work entitled Untrodden Ground in Astronomy and Geology, that, as a result of the second rotation of the earth, the inclination of its axis was changing, it having been 23° 28' 23" on January 1, 1750, 23° 27' 55.3" on January 1, 1800, and 23° 27' 30.9" on January 1, 1850; and by calculation one hundred and ten years ago showed that in 1900 (one hundred years ago) it would be 23° 27' 08.8". This natural straightening is, of course, going on, and we are merely about to anticipate it. When this improvement was mooted, all agreed that the EXTREMES of heat and cold could well be spared. 'Balance those of summer against those of winter by partially straightening the axis; reduce the inclination from twenty-three degrees, thirty minutes, to about fifteen degrees, but let us stop there,' many said. Before we had gone far, however, we found it would be best to make the work complete. This will reclaim and make productive the vast areas of Siberia and the northern part of this continent, and will do much for the antarctic regions; but there will still be change in temperature; a wind blowing towards the equator will always be colder than one blowing from it, while the slight eccentricity of the orbit will supply enough change to awaken recollections of seasons in our eternal spring.

"The way to accomplish this is to increase the weight of the pole leaving the sun, by increasing the amount of material there for the sun to attract, and to lighten the pole approaching or turning towards the sun, by removing some heavy substance from it, and putting it preferably at the opposite pole. This shifting of ballast is most easily accomplished, as you will readily perceive, by confining and removing water, which is easily moved and has a considerable weight. How we purpose to apply these aqueous brakes to check the wabbling of the earth, by means of the attraction of the sun, you will now see.

"From Commander Fillmore, of the Arctic Shade and the Committee on Bulkheads and Dams, I have just received the following by cable telephone: 'The Arctic Ocean is now in condition to be pumped out in summer and to have its average depth increased one hundred feet by the dams in winter. We have already fifty million square yards of windmill turbine surface in position and ready to move. The cables bringing us currents from the dynamos at Niagara Falls are connected with our motors, and those from the tidal dynamos at the Bay of Fundy will be in contact when this reaches you, at which moment the pumps will begin. In several of the landlocked gulfs and bays our system of confining is so complete, that the surface of the water can be raised two hundred feet above sea-level. The polar bears will soon have to use artificial ice. Perhaps the cheers now ringing without may reach you over the telephone.'"

The audience became greatly interested, and when the end of the telephone was applied to a microphone the room fairly rang with exultant cheers, and those looking through a kintograph (visual telegraph) terminating in a camera obscura on the shores of Baffin Bay were able to see engineers and workmen waving and throwing up their caps and falling into one another's arms in ecstasies of delight. When the excitement subsided, the president continued:

"Chairman Wetmore, of the Committee on Excavations and Embankments in Wilkesland and the Antarctic Continent, reports: 'Two hundred and fifty thousand square miles are now hollowed out and enclosed sufficiently to hold water to an average depth of four hundred feet. Every summer, when the basin is allowed to drain, we can, if necessary, extend our reservoir, and shall have the best season of the year for doing work until the earth has permanent spring. Though we have comparatively little water or tidal power, the earth's crust is so thin at this latitude, on account of the flattening, that by sinking our tubular boilers and pipes to a depth of a few thousand feet we have secured so terrific a volume of superheated steam that, in connection with our wind turbines, we shall have no difficulty in raising half a cubic mile of water a minute to our enclosure, which is but little above sea-level, and into which, till the pressure increases, we can fan or blow the water, so that it can be full three weeks after our longest day, or, since the present unimproved arrangement gives the indigenes but one day and night a year, I will add the 21st day of December.

"'We shall be able to find use for much of the potential energy of the water in the reservoir when we allow it to escape in June, in melting some of the accumulated polar ice-cap, thereby decreasing still further the weight of this pole, in lighting and warming ourselves until we get the sun's light and heat, in extending the excavations, and in charging the storage batteries of the ships at this end of the line. Everything will be ready when you signal "Raise water."'"

"Let me add parenthetically," said Bearwarden, "that this means of obtaining power by steam boilers sunk to a great depth is much to be commended; for, though the amount of heat we can withdraw is too small to have much effect, the farther towards the centre our globe can be cooled the deeper will the water of the oceans be able to penetrate--since it is its conversion into steam that prevents the water from working its way in farther--and the more dry land we shall have."

"You see," the president continued, "the storage capacity at the south pole is not quite as great as at the north, because it is more difficult to excavate a basin than to close the exits of one that already exists, which is what we have done in the arctic. The work is also not so nearly complete, since it will not be necessary to use the southern reservoir for storing weight for six months, or until the south pole, which is now at its maximum declination from the sun, is turned towards it and begins to move away; then, by increasing the amount of matter there, and at the same time lightening the north pole, and reversing the process every six months, we decrease the speed at which the departing pole leaves the sun and at which the approaching pole advances. The north pole, we see, will be a somewhat more powerful lever than the south for working the globe to a straight position, but we may be sure that the latter, in connection with the former, will be able to hold up its end." [The building here fairly shook with applause, so that, had the arctic workers used the microphone, they might have heard in the enthusiastic uproar a good counterpart of their own period.]

"I only regret," the president continued, "that when we began this work the most marvellous force yet discovered--apergy--was not sufficiently understood to be utilized, for it would have eased our labours to the point of almost eliminating them. But we have this consolation: it was in connection with our work that its applicability was discovered, so that had we and all others postponed our great undertaking on the pretext of waiting for a new force, apergy might have continued to lie dormant for centuries. With this force, obtained by simply blending negative and positive electricity with electricity of the third element or state, and charging a body sufficiently with this fluid, gravitation is nullified or partly reversed, and the earth repels the body with the same or greater power than that with which it still attracts or attracted it, so that it may be suspended or caused to move away into space. Sic itur ad astra, we may say. With this force and everlasting spring before us, what may we not achieve? We may some day be able to visit the planets, though many may say that, since the axes of most of those we have considered are more inclined than ours, they would rather stay here. 'Blessed are they that shall inherit the earth,'" he went on, turning a four-foot globe with its axis set vertically and at right angles to a yellow globe labelled "Sun"; and again waxing eloquent, he added: "We are the instruments destined to bring about the accomplishment of that prophecy, for never in the history of the world has man reared so splendid a monument to his own genius as he will in straightening the axis of the planet.

"No one need henceforth be troubled by sudden change, and every man can have perpetually the climate he desires. Northern Europe will again luxuriate in a climate that favoured the elephants that roamed in northern Asia and Switzerland. To produce these animals and the food they need, it is not necessary to have great heat, but merely to prevent great cold, half the summer's sun being absorbed in melting the winter's accumulation of ice.

"When the axis has reached a point at which it inclines but about twelve degrees, it will become necessary to fill the antarctic reservoir in June and the Arctic Ocean in December, in order to check the straightening, since otherwise it might get beyond the perpendicular and swing the other way. When this motion is completely arrested, I suggest that we blow up the Aleutian Isles and enlarge Bering Strait, so as to allow what corresponds to the Atlantic Gulf Stream in the Pacific to enter the Arctic Archipelago, which I have calculated will raise the average temperature of that entire region about thirty degrees, thereby still further increasing the amount of available land.

"Ocean currents, being the result of the prevailing winds, which will be more regular than at present, can be counted upon to continue practically as they are. It may not be plain to you why the trade winds do not blow towards the equator due south and north, since the equator has much the same effect on air that a stove has in the centre of a room, causing an ascending current towards the ceiling, which moves off in straight lines in all directions on reaching it, its place being taken by cold currents moving in opposite directions along the floor. Picture to yourselves the ascending currents at the equator moving off to the poles from which they came. As they move north they are continually coming to parts of the globe having smaller circles of latitude than those they have left, and therefore not moved forward as rapidly by the earth's daily rotation as the latitudes nearer the equator. The winds consequently run ahead of the surface, and so move east of north--the earth turning towards the east--while the heavier colder surface currents, rushing towards the equator to take the place of the ascending column, coming from regions where the surface whirls comparatively slowly to those where it is rotating faster, are continually left behind, and so move southwest; while south of the equator a corresponding motion results. Though this is not the most exact explanation, it may serve to make the action clear. I will add, that if any one prefers a colder or a warmer climate than that of the place in which he lives, he need only go north or south for an hour; or, if he prefers his own latitude, he can rise a few thousand feet in the air, or descend to one of the worked-out coal-mines which are now used as sanitariums, and secure his object by a slight change of altitude. Let us speed the departure of racking changes and extremes of climate, and prepare to welcome what we believe prevails in paradise--namely, everlasting spring."

Appended to the address was the report of the Government Examining Committee, which ran: "We have critically examined the Terrestrial Axis Straightening Company's figures and calculations, also its statements involving natural philosophy, physics, and astronomy, all of which we find correct, and hereby approve.

[Signed]

"For the Committee:
"HENRY CHELMSFORD CORTLANDT,
"Chairman."

The Board of Directors having ratified the acts of its officers, and passed congratulatory resolutions, the meeting adjourned sine die.

CHAPTER IV
PROF. CORTLANDT'S HISTORICAL SKETCH OF THE WORLD

IN A. D. 2000

Prof. Cortlandt, preparing a history of the times at the beginning of the great terrestrial and astronomical change, wrote as follows: "This period--A.D. 2000--is by far the most wonderful the world has as yet seen. The advance in scientific knowledge and attainment within the memory, of the present generation has been so stupendous that it completely overshadows all that has preceded. All times in history and all periods of the world have been remarkable for some distinctive or characteristic trait. The feature of the period of Louis XIV was the splendour of the court and the centralization of power in Paris. The year 1789 marked the decline of the power of courts and the evolution of government by the people. So, by the spread of republican ideas and the great advance in science, education has become universal, for women as well as for men, and this is more than ever a mechanical age.

"With increased knowledge we are constantly coming to realize how little we really know, and are also continually finding manifestations of forces that at first seem like exceptions to established laws. This is, of course, brought about by the modifying influence of some other natural law, though many of these we have not yet discovered.

"Electricity in its varied forms does all work, having superseded animal and manual labour in everything, and man has only to direct. The greatest ingenuity next to finding new uses for this almost omnipotent fluid has been displayed in inducing the forces of Nature, and even the sun, to produce it. Before describing the features of this perfection of civilization, let us review the steps by which society and the political world reached their present state.

"At the close of the Franco-Prussian War, in 1871, Continental Europe entered upon the condition of an armed camp, which lasted for nearly half a century. The primary cause of this was the mutual dislike and jealousy of France and Germany, each of which strove to have a larger and better equipped national defence than the other. There were also many other causes, as the ambition of the Russian Czar, supported by his country's vast though imperfectly developed resources and practically unlimited supply of men, one phase of which was the constant ferment in the Balkan Peninsula, and another Russia's schemes for extension in Asia; another was the general desire for colonies in Africa, in which one Continental power pretty effectually blocked another, and the latent distrust inside the Triple Alliance. England, meanwhile, preserved a wise and profitable neutrality.

"These tremendous sacrifices for armaments, both on land and water, had far-reaching results, and, as we see it now, were clouds with silver linings. The demand for hardened steel projectiles, nickel-steel plates, and light and almost unbreakable machinery, was a great incentive to improvement in metallurgy while the necessity for compact and safely carried ammunition greatly stimulated chemical research, and led to the discovery of explosives whose powers no obstacle can resist, and incidentally to other more useful things.

"Further mechanical and scientific progress, however, such as flying machines provided with these high explosives, and asphyxiating bombs containing compressed gas that could be fired from guns or dropped from the air, intervened. The former would have laid every city in the dust, and the latter might have almost exterminated the race. These discoveries providentially prevented hostilities, so that the 'Great War,' so long expected, never came, and the rival nations had their pains for nothing, or, rather, for others than themselves.

"Let us now examine the political and ethnological results. Hundreds of thousands, of the flower of Continental Europe were killed by overwork and short rations, and millions of desirable and often--unfortunately for us--undesirable people were driven to emigration, nearly all of whom came to English-speaking territory, greatly increasing our productiveness and power. As, we have seen, the jealousy of the Continental powers for one another effectually prevented their extending their influence or protectorates to other continents, which jealousy was considerably aided by the small but destructive wars that did take place. High taxes also made it more difficult for the moneyed men to invest in colonizing or development companies, which are so often the forerunners of absorption; while the United States, with her coal--of which the Mediterranean states have scarcely any--other resources, and low taxes, which, though necessary, can be nothing but an evil, has been able to expand naturally as no other nation ever has before.

"This has given the English-speakers, especially the United States, a free hand, rendering enforcement of the Monroe doctrine easy, and started

English a long way towards becoming the universal language, while all formerly unoccupied land is now owned by those speaking it.

"At the close of our civil war, in 1865, we had but 3,000,000 square miles, and a population of 34,000,000. The country staggered beneath a colossal debt of over $4,000,000,000, had an expensive but essentially perishable navy, and there was an ominous feeling between the sections. The purchase of Alaska in 1867, by which we added over half a million square miles to our territory, marked the resumption of the forward march of the United States. Twenty-five years later, at the presidential campaign of 1892, the debt had been reduced to $900,000,000, deducting the sinking fund, and the charge for pensions had about reached its maximum and soon began to decrease, though no one objected to any amount of reward for bona fide soldiers who had helped to save the country. The country's wealth had also enormously increased, while the population had grown to 65,000,000. Our ancestors had, completed or in building, a navy of which no nation need be ashamed; and, though occasionally marred by hard times, there was general prosperity.

"Gradually the different States of Canada--or provinces, as they were then called--came to realize that their future would be far grander and more glorious in union with the United States than separated from it; and also that their sympathy was far stronger for their nearest neighbours than for any one else. One by one these Northern States made known their desire for consolidation with the Union, retaining complete control of their local affairs, as have the older States. They were gladly welcomed by our Government and people, and possible rivals became the best of friends. Preceding and also following this, the States of Mexico, Central America, and parts of South America, tiring of the incessant revolutions and difficulties among themselves, which had pretty constantly looked upon us as a big brother on account of our maintenance of the Monroe doctrine, began to agitate for annexation, knowing they would retain control of their local affairs. In this they were vigorously supported by the American residents and property-holders, who knew that their possessions would double in value the day the United States Constitution was signed.

"Thus, in the first place, by the encouragement of our people, and latterly, apparently, by its own volition, the Union has increased enormously in power, till it now embraces 10,000,000 square miles, and has a free and enlightened population of 300,000,000. Though the Union established by Washington and his contemporaries has attained such tremendous proportions, its growth is by no means finished; and as a result of modern improvements, it is less of a journey now to go from Alaska to the Orinoco than it was for the Father of his Country to travel from New York or Philadelphia to the site of the city named in his honour.

"Adequate and really rapid transportation facilities have done much to bind the different parts of the country together, and to rub off the edges of local prejudice. Though we always favour peace, no nation would think of opposing the expressed wishes of the United States, and our moral power for good is tremendous. The name Japhet means enlargement, and the prophecy seems about to be literally fulfilled by these his descendants. The bankrupt suffering of so many European Continental powers had also other results. It enabled the socialists--who have never been able to see beyond themselves--to force their governments into selling their colonies in the Eastern hemisphere to England, and their islands in the Western to us, in order to realize upon them. With the addition of Canada to the United States and its loss to the British Empire, the land possessions of the two powers became about equal, our Union being a trifle the larger. All danger of war being removed by the Canadian change, a healthful and friendly competition took its place, the nations competing in their growth on different hemispheres. England easily added large areas in Asia and Africa, while the United States grew as we have seen. The race is still, in a sense, neck-and-neck, and the English-speakers together possess nearly half the globe. The world's recent rate of progress would have been impossible without this approximation to a universal language. The causes that checkmated the Continental powers have ceased to exist. Many millions of men whose principal thought had been to destroy other members of the race became producers, but it was then too late, for the heavy armaments had done their work.

"Let us now glance at the times as they are, and see how the business of life is transacted. Manhattan Island has something over 2,500,000 inhabitants, and is surrounded by a belt of population, several miles wide, of 12,000,000 more, of which it is the focus, so that the entire city contains more than 14,500,000 souls. The several hundred square miles of land and water forming greater New York are perfectly united by numerous bridges, tunnels, and electric ferries, while the city's great natural advantages have been enhanced and beautified by every ingenious device. No main avenue in the newer sections is less than two hundred feet wide, containing shade and fruit trees, a bridle-path, broad sidewalks, and open spaces for carriages and bicycles. Several fine diagonal streets and breathing-squares have also been provided in the older sections, and the existing parks have been supplemented by intermediate ones, all being connected by parkways to form continuous chains.

"The hollow masts of our ships--to glance at another phase en passant--carry windmills instead of sails, through which the wind performs the work, of storing a great part of the energy required to run them at sea, while they are discharging or loading cargo in port; and it can, of course, work to better advantage while they are stationary than when they are running before it. These turbines are made entirely of light metal, and fold when not in use, so that only the frames are visible. Sometimes these also fold and are housed, or wholly disappear within the mast. Steam-boilers are also placed at the foci of huge concave mirrors, often a hundred feet in diameter, the required heat being supplied by the sun, without smoke, instead of by bulky and dirty coal. This discovery gave commercial value to Sahara and other tropical deserts, which are now desirable for mill-sites and for generating power, on account of the directness with which they receive the sun's rays and their freedom from clouds. Mile after mile Africa has been won for the uses of civilization, till great stretches that were considered impassible are as productive as gardens. Our condensers, which compress, cool, and rarefy air, enabling travellers to obtain water and even ice from the atmosphere, are great aids in desert exploration, removing absolutely the principal distress of the ancient caravan. The erstwhile 'Dark Continent' has a larger white population now than North America had a hundred years ago, and has this advantage for the future, that it contains 11,600,000 square miles, while North America has less than 9,000,000. Every part of the globe will soon sustain about as large and prosperous a population as the amount of energy it receives from the sun and other sources will warrant; public debts and the efficiency of the governments being the variable elements.

"The rabbits in Australia, and the far more objectionable poisonous snakes in South America and India, have been exterminated by the capture of a few dozen of the creatures in the infested districts, their inoculation with the virus similar to the murus tiphi, tuberculosis or any other contagious-germ complaint to which the species treated was particularly susceptible, and the release of these individuals when the disease was seen to be taking hold. The rabbits and serpents released at once returned to their old haunts, carrying the plague far and wide. The unfortunate rabbits were greatly commiserated even by the medicos that wielded the death-dealing syringe; but, fortunately for themselves, they died easily. The reptiles, perhaps on account of the wider distribution of the nerve centres, had more lingering but not painful deaths, often, while in articulo mortis, leaving the holes with which they seemed to connect their discomfort, and making a final struggle along the ground, only to die more quickly as a result of their exertions. We have applied this also to the potato-bug, locust, and other insect pests, no victim being too small for the ubiquitous, subtle germ, which, properly cultivated and utilized, has become one of man's best friends.

"We have microbe tests that show us as unmistakably whether the germs of any particular disease--like malaria, typhoid, or scarlet fever--are present in the air, as litmus-paper shows alkalinity of a solution. We also inoculate as a preventive against these and almost all other germ diseases, with the same success that we vaccinate for smallpox.

"The medicinal properties of all articles of food are so well understood also, that most cures are brought about simply by dieting. This, reminds me of the mistakes perpetrated on a friend of mine who called in Dr. Grave-Powders, one of the old-school physicians, to be treated for insomnia and dyspepsia. This old numskull restricted his diet, gave him huge doses of medicine, and decided most learnedly that he was daily growing worse. Concluding that he had but a short time to live, my friend threw away the nauseating medicines, ate whatever he had a natural desire for, and was soon as well as ever--the obvious moral of which is, that we can get whatever treatment we need most beneficially from our food. Our physicians are most serious and thoughtful men. They never claim to be infallible, but study scientifically to increase their knowledge and improve the methods of treatment. As a result of this, fresh air, regular exercise for both sexes, with better conditions, and the preservation of the lives of children that formerly died by thousands from preventable causes, the physique, especially of women, is wonderfully improved, and the average longevity is already over sixty.

"Our social structure, to be brief, is based on science, or the conservation of energy, as the Greek philosophers predicted. It was known to them that a certain amount of power would produce only a certain amount of work--that is, the weight of a clock in descending or a spring in uncoiling returns theoretically the amount of work expended in raising or coiling it, and in no possible way can it do more. In practice, on account of friction, etc., we know it does less. This law, being invariable, of course limits us, as it did Archimedes and Pythagoras; we have simply utilized sources of power that their clumsy workmen allowed to escape. Of the four principal sources--food, fuel, wind, and tide--including harnessed waterfalls, the last two do by far the most work. Much of the electrical energy in every thunderstorm is also captured and condensed in our capacious storage batteries, as natural hygeia in the form of rain was and is still caught in our country cisterns. Every exposed place is crowned by a cluster of huge windmills that lift water to some pond or reservoir placed as high as possible. Every stiff breeze, therefore, raises millions of tons of water which operate hydraulic turbines as required. Incidentally these storage reservoirs, by increasing the surface exposed to evaporation and the consequent rainfall, have a very beneficial effect on the dry regions in the interior of the continent, and in some cases have almost superseded irrigation. The windmill and dynamo thus utilize bleak mountain-tops that, till their discovery, seemed to be but indifferent successes in Dame Nature's domain. The electricity generated by these, in connection with that obtained by waterfalls, tidal dynamos, thunderstorms, chemical action, and slow-moving quadruple-expansion steam engines, provides the power required to run our electric ships and water-spiders, railways, and stationary and portable motors, for heating the cables laid along the bottom of our canals to prevent their freezing in winter, and for almost every conceivable purpose. Sometimes a man has a windmill on his roof for light and heat; then, the harder the wintry blasts may blow the brighter and warmer becomes the house, the current passing through a storage battery to make it more steady. The operation of our ordinary electric railways is very simple: the current is taken from an overhead, side, or underneath wire, directly through the air, without the intervention of a trolley, and the fast cars, for they are no longer run in trains, make five miles a minute. The entire weight of each car being used for its own traction, it can ascend very steep grades, and can attain high speed or stop very quickly.

"Another form is the magnetic railway, on which the cars are wedge-shaped at both ends, and moved by huge magnets weighing four thousand tons each, placed fifty miles apart. On passing a magnet, the nature of the electricity charging a car is automatically changed from positive to negative, or vice versa, to that of the magnet just passed, so that it repels while the next attracts. The successive magnets are charged oppositely, the sections being divided halfway between by insulators, the nature of the electricity in each section being governed by the charge in the magnet. To prevent one kind of electricity from uniting with and neutralizing that in the next section by passing through the car at the moment of transit, there is a "dead stretch" of fifty yards with rails not charged at all between the sections. This change in the nature of the electricity is repeated automatically every fifty miles, and obviates the necessity of revolving machinery, the rails aiding communication. "Magnetism being practically as instantaneous as gravitation, the only limitations to speed are the electrical pressure at the magnets, the resistance of the air, and the danger of the wheels bursting from centrifugal force. The first can seemingly be increased without limit; the atmospheric resistance is about to be reduced by running the cars hermetically sealed through a partial vacuum in a steel and toughened glass tube; while the third has been removed indefinitely by the use of galvanized aluminum, which bears about the same relation to ordinary aluminum that steel does to iron, and which has twice the tensile strength and but one third the weight of steel. In some cases the rails are made turned in, so that it would be impossible for a car to leave the track without the road-bed's being totally demolished; but in most cases this is found to be unnecessary, for no through line has a curve on its vast stretches with a radius of less than half a mile. Rails, one hundred and sixty pounds to the yard, are set in grooved steel ties, which in turn are held by a concrete road-bed consisting of broken stone and cement, making spreading rails and loose ballast impossible. A large increase in capital was necessary for these improvements, the elimination of curves being the most laborious part, requiring bridges, cuttings, and embankments that dwarf the Pyramids and would have made the ancient Pharaohs open their eyes; but with the low rate of interest on bonds, the slight cost of power, and great increase in business, the venture was a success, and we are now in sight of further advances that will enable a traveller in a high latitude moving west to keep pace with the sun, and, should he wish it, to have unending day."

CHAPTER V
DR. CORTLANDT'S HISTORY CONTINUED

"In marine transportation we have two methods, one for freight and another for passengers. The old-fashioned deeply immersed ship has not changed radically from the steam and sailing vessels of the last century, except that electricity has superseded all other motive powers. Steamers gradually passed through the five hundred-, six hundred-, and seven hundred-foot-long class, with other dimensions in proportion, till their length exceeded one thousand feet. These were very fast ships, crossing the Atlantic in four and a half days, and were almost as steady as houses, in even the roughest weather.

"Ships at this period of their development had also passed through the twin and triple screw stage to the quadruple, all four together developing one hundred and forty thousand indicated horse-power, and being driven by steam. This, of course, involved sacrificing the best part of the ship to her engines, and a very heavy idle investment while in port. Storage batteries, with plates composed of lead or iron, constantly increasing in size, had reached a fair state of development by the close of the nineteenth century.

"During the second decade of the twentieth century the engineers decided to try the plan of running half of a transatlantic liner's screws by electricity generated by the engines for driving the others while the ship was in port, this having been a success already on a smaller scale. For a time this plan gave great satisfaction, since it diminished the amount of coal to be carried and the consequent change of displacement at sea, and enabled the ship to be worked with a smaller number of men. The batteries could also, of course, be distributed along the entire length, and placed where space was least valuable.

"The construction of such huge vessels called for much governmental river and harbour dredging, and a ship drawing thirty-five feet can now enter New York at any state of the tide. For ocean bars, the old system of taking the material out to sea and discharging it still survives, though a jet of water from force-pumps directed against the obstruction is also often employed with quick results. For river work we have discovered a better method. All the mud is run back, sometimes over a mile from the river bank, where it is used as a fertilizer, by means of wire railways strung from poles. These wire cables combine in themselves the functions of trolley wire and steel rail, and carry the suspended cars, which empty themselves and return around the loop for another load. Often the removed material entirely fills small, saucer-shaped valleys or low places, in which case it cannot wash back. This improvement has ended the necessity of building jetties.

"The next improvement in sea travelling was the 'marine spider.' As the name shows, this is built on the principle of an insect. It is well known that a body can be carried over the water much faster than through it. With this in mind, builders at first constructed light framework decks on large water-tight wheels or drums, having paddles on their circumferences to provide a hold on the water. These they caused to revolve by means of machinery on the deck, but soon found that the resistance offered to the barrel wheels themselves was too great. They therefore made them more like centipeds with large, bell-shaped feet, connected with a superstructural deck by ankle-jointed pipes, through which, when necessary, a pressure of air can be forced down upon the enclosed surface of water. Ordinarily, however, they go at great speed without this, the weight of the water displaced by the bell feet being as great as that resting upon them. Thus they swing along like a pacing horse, except that there are four rows of feet instead of two, each foot being taken out of the water as it is swung forward, the first and fourth and second and third rows being worked together. Although, on account of their size, which covers several acres, they can go in any water, they give the best results on Mediterraneans and lakes that are free from ocean rollers, and, under favourable conditions, make better speed than the nineteenth-century express trains, and, of course, going straight as the crow flies, and without stopping, they reach a destination in considerably shorter time.

"Some passengers and express packages still cross the Atlantic on 'spiders,' but most of these light cargoes go in a far pleasanter and more rapid way. The deep-displacement vessels, for heavy freight, make little better speed than was made by the same class a hundred years ago. But they are also run entirely by electricity, largely supplied by wind, and by the tide turning their motors, which become dynamos while at anchor in any stream. They therefore need no bulky boilers, engines, sails, or coal-bunkers, and consequently can carry unprecedentedly large cargoes with comparatively small crews. The officers on the bridge and the men in the crow's nest--the way to which is by a ladder INSIDE the mast, to protect the climber from the weather--are about all that is needed; while disablement is made practically impossible, by having four screws, each with its own set of automatically lubricating motors.

"This change, like other labour-saving appliances, at first resulted in laying off a good many men, the least satisfactory being the first to go; but the increase in business was so great that the intelligent men were soon reemployed as officers at higher rates of pay and more interesting work than before, while they as consumers were benefited as much as any one else by the decreased cost of production and transportation.

"With a view to facilitating interchange still further, our Government has gradually completed the double coast-line that Nature gave us in part. This was done by connecting islands separated from shore by navigable water, and leaving openings for ingress and exit but a few hundred yards wide. The breakwaters required to do this were built with cribbing of incorrodible metal, affixed to deeply driven metallic piles, and filled with stones along coasts where they were found in abundance or excess. This, while clearing many fields and improving them for cultivation, provided just the needed material; since irregular stones bind together firmly, and, while also insoluble, combine considerable bulk with weight. South of Hatteras, where stones are scarce, the sand dredged from parts of the channel was filled into the crib, the surface of which has a concave metallic cover, a trough of still water being often the best barrier against the passage of waves. This double coast-line has been a great benefit, and propelled vessels of moderate draught can range in smooth water, carrying very full loads, from Labrador to the Orinoco. The exits are, of course, protected by a line of cribbing a few hundred feet to seaward.

"The rocks have been removed from all channels about New York and other commercial centres, while the shallow places have been dredged to a uniform depth. This diminishes the dangers of navigation and considerably decreases the speed with which the tides rush through. Where the obstructions consisted of reefs surrounded by deep water, their removal with explosives was easy, the shattered fragments being allowed to sink to the bottom and remain there beneath the danger line.

"Many other great works have also been completed. The canals at Nicaragua have been in operation many years, it having been found best to have several sizes of locks, and to use the large ones only for the passage of large vessels. The improved Erie and Champlain Canals also enable ships four hundred feet long to reach New York from the Great Lakes via the Hudson River.

"For flying, we have an aeroplane that came in when we devised a suitable motor power. This is obtained from very light paper-cell batteries that combine some qualities of the primary and secondary type, since they must first be charged from a dynamo, after which they can supply full currents for one hundred hours--enough to take them around the globe--while partly consuming the elements in the cells. The power is applied through turbine screws, half of which are capable of propelling the flat deck in its inclined position at sufficient speed to prevent its falling. The moving parts have ball bearings and friction rollers, lubrication being secured automatically, when required, by a supply of vaseline that melts if any part becomes hot. All the framing is of thin but very durable galvanized aluminum, which has superseded steel for every purpose in which weight is not an advantage, as in the permanent way on railways. The air ships, whose length varies from fifty to five hundred feet, have rudders for giving a vertical or a horizontal motion, and several strengthening keels that prevent leeway when turning. They are entirely on the principle of birds, maintaining themselves mechanically, and differing thus from the unwieldy balloon. Starting as if on a circular railway, against the wind, they rise to a considerable height, and then, shutting off the batteries, coast down the aerial slope at a rate that sometimes touches five hundred miles an hour. When near the ground the helmsman directs the prow upward, and, again turning on full current, rushes up the slope at a speed that far exceeds the eagle's, each drop of two miles serving to take the machine twenty or thirty; though, if the pilot does not wish to soar, or if there is a fair wind at a given height, he can remain in that stratum of the atmosphere by moving horizontally. He can also maintain his elevation when moving very slowly, and though the headway be entirely stopped, the descent is gradual on account of the aeroplane's great spread, the batteries and motors being secured to the under side of the deck.

"The motors are so light that they develop two horse power for every pound of their weight; while, to keep the frames thin, the necessary power is obtained by terrific speed of the moving parts, as though a steam engine, to avoid great pressure in its cylinders, had a long stroke and ran at great piston speed, which, however, is no disadvantage to the rotary motion of the electric motor, there being no reciprocating cranks, etc., that must be started and stopped at each revolution.

"To obviate the necessity of gearing to reduce the number of revolutions to those possible for a large screw, this member is made very small, and allowed to revolve three thousand times a minute, so that the requisite power is obtained with great simplicity of mechanism, which further decreases friction. The shafts, and even the wires connecting the batteries with the motors, are made large and hollow. Though the primary battery pure and simple, as the result of great recent advances in chemistry, seems to be again coming up, the best aeroplane batteries are still of the combination-storage type. These have been so perfected that eight ounces of battery yield one horse power for six hours, so that two pounds of battery will supply a horse power for twenty-four hours; a small fifty-horse-power aeroplane being therefore able to fly four days with a battery weight of but four hundred pounds.

"Limestone and clarified acid are the principal parts of these batteries. It was known long ago that there was about as much imprisoned solar energy in limestone as in coal, but it was only recently that we discovered this way of releasing and using it.

"Common salt plays an important part in many of our chemical reactions. By combining it with limestone, and treating this with acid jelly, we also get good results on raising to the boiling-point.

"However enjoyable the manly sport of yachting is on water, how vastly more interesting and fascinating it is for a man to have a yacht in which he can fly to Europe in one day, and with which the exploration of tropical Africa or the regions about the poles is mere child's play, while giving him so magnificent a bird's-eye view! Many seemingly insoluble problems are solved by the advent of these birds. Having as their halo the enforcement of peace, they have in truth taken us a long step towards heaven, and to the co-operation and higher civilization that followed we shall owe much of the success of the great experiment on Mother Earth now about to be tried.

"Another change that came in with a rush upon the discovery of a battery with insignificant weight, compact form, and great capacity, was the substitution of electricity for animal power for the movement of all vehicles. This, of necessity brought in good roads, the results obtainable on such being so much greater than on bad ones that a universal demand for them arose. This was in a sense cumulative, since the better the streets and roads became, the greater the inducement to have an electric carriage. The work of opening up the country far and near, by straightening and improving existing roads, and laying out new ones that combine the solidity of the Appian Way with the smoothness of modern asphalt, was largely done by convicts, working under the direction of State and Government engineers. Every State contained a horde of these unprofitable boarders, who, as they formerly worked, interfered with honest labour, and when idle got into trouble. City streets had been paved by the municipality; country roads attended to by the farmers, usually very unscientifically. Here was a field in which convict labour would not compete, and an important work could be done. When once this was made the law, every year showed improvement, while the convicts had useful and healthful occupation.

"The electric phaetons, as those for high speed are called, have three and four wheels, and weigh, including battery and motor, five hundred to four thousand pounds. With hollow but immensely strong galvanically treated aluminum frames and pneumatic or cushion tires, they run at thirty-five and forty miles an hour on country roads, and attain a speed over forty on city streets, and can maintain this rate without recharging for several days. They can therefore roam over the roads of the entire hemisphere, from the fertile valley of the Peace and grey shores of Hudson Bay, to beautiful Lake Nicaragua, the River Plate, and Patagonia, improving man by bringing him close to Nature, while they combine the sensations of coasting with the interest of seeing the country well.

"To recharge the batteries, which can be done in almost every town and village, two copper pins attached to insulated copper wires are shoved into smooth-bored holes. These drop out of themselves by fusing a small lead ribbon, owing to the increased resistance, when the acid in the batteries begins to 'boil,' though there is, of course, but little heat in this, the function of charging being merely to bring about the condition in which part of the limestone can be consumed, the batteries themselves, when in constant use, requiring to be renewed about once a month. A handle at the box seat turns on any part of the attainable current, for either going ahead or reversing, there being six or eight degrees of speed for both directions, while the steering is done with a small wheel.

"Light but powerful batteries and motors have also been fitted on bicycles, which can act either as auxiliaries for hill-climbing or in case of head wind, or they can propel the machine altogether.

"Gradually the width of the streets became insufficient for the traffic, although the elimination of horses and the consequent increase in speed greatly augmented their carrying capacity, until recently a new system came in. The whole width of the avenues and streets in the business parts of the city, including the former sidewalks, is given up to wheel traffic, an iron ridge extending along the exact centre to compel vehicles to keep to the right. Strips of nickel painted white, and showing a bright phosphorescence at night, are let into the metal pavement flush with the surface, and run parallel to this ridge at distances of ten to fifteen feet, dividing each half of the avenue into four or five sections, their width increasing as they approach the middle. All trucks or drays moving at less than seven miles an hour are obliged to keep in the section nearest the building line, those running between seven and fifteen in the next, fifteen to twenty-five in the third, twenty-five to thirty-five in the fourth, and everything faster than that in the section next the ridge, unless the avenue or street is wide enough for further subdivisions. If it is wide enough for only four or less, the fastest vehicles must keep next the middle, and limit their speed to the rate allowed in that section, which is marked at every crossing in white letters sufficiently large for him that runs to read. It is therefore only in the wide thoroughfares that very high speed can be attained. In addition to the crank that corresponds to a throttle, there is a gauge on every vehicle, which shows its exact speed in miles per hour, by gearing operated by the revolutions of the wheels.

"The policemen on duty also have instantaneous kodaks mounted on tripods, which show the position of any carriage at half- and quarter-second intervals, by which it is easy to ascertain the exact speed, should the officers be unable to judge it by the eye; so there is no danger of a vehicle's speed exceeding that allowed in the section in which it happens to be; neither can a slow one remain on the fast lines.

"Of course, to make such high speed for ordinary carriages possible, a perfect pavement became a sine qua non. We have secured this by the half-inch sheet of steel spread over a carefully laid surface of asphalt, with but little bevel; and though this might be slippery for horses' feet, it never seriously affects our wheels. There being nothing harder than the rubber ties of comparatively light drays upon it--for the heavy traffic is carried by electric railways under ground--it will practically never wear out.

"With the application of steel to the entire surface, car-tracks became unnecessary, ordinary wheels answering as well as those with flanges, so that no new tracks were laid, and finally the car companies tore up the existing ones, selling them in many instances to the municipalities as old iron. Our streets also need but little cleaning; neither is the surface continually indented, as the old cobble-stones and Belgian blocks were, by the pounding of the horses' feet, so that the substitution of electricity for animal power has done much to solve the problem of attractive streets.

"Scarcely a ton of coal comes to Manhattan Island or its vicinity in a year. Very little of it leaves the mines, at the mouths of which it is converted into electricity and sent to the points of consumption by wire, where it is employed for all uses to which fuel was put, and many others. Consequently there is no smoke, and the streets are not encumbered with coal-carts; the entire width being given up to carriages, etc. The ground floors in the business parts are used for large warehouses, trucks running in to load and unload. Pedestrians therefore have sidewalks level with the second story, consisting of glass floors let into aluminum frames, while all street crossings are made on bridges. Private houses have a front door opening on the sidewalk, and another on the ground level, so that ladies paying visits or leaving cards can do so in carriages. In business streets the second story is used for shops. In place of steel covering, country roads have a thick coating of cement and asphalt over a foundation of crushed stone, giving a capital surface, and have a width of thirty-three feet (two rods) in thinly settled districts, to sixty-six feet (four rods) where the population is greater. All are planted with shade and fruit trees, while the wide driveways have one or two broad sidewalks. The same rule of making the slow-moving vehicles keep near the outside prevails, though the rate of increase in speed on approaching the middle is more rapid than in cities, and there is usually no dividing ridge. On reaching the top of a long and steep hill, if we do not wish to coast, we convert the motors into dynamos, while running at full speed, and so change the kinetic energy of the descent into potential in our batteries. This twentieth-century stage-coaching is one of the delights to which we are heirs, though horses are still used by those that prefer them.

"We have been much aided in our material progress by the facility with which we obtain the metals. It was observed, some time ago, that when artesian and oil wells had reached a considerable depth, what appeared to be drops of lead and antimony came up with the stream. It finally occurred to a well-borer that if he could make his drill hard enough and get it down far enough, keeping it cool by solidified carbonic acid during the proceeding, he would reach a point at which most of the metals would be viscous, if not actually molten, and on being freed from the pressure of the crust they would expand, and reach the surface in a stream. This experiment he performed near the hot geysers in Yellowstone Park, and what was his delight, on reaching a depth scarcely half a mile beyond his usual stopping-place, to be rewarded by a stream of metal that heralded its approach by a loud explosion and a great rush of superheated steam! It ran for a month, completely filling the bed of a small, dried-up river, and when it did stop there were ten million tons in sight. This proved the feasibility of the scheme, and, though many subsequent attempts were less successful, we have learned by experience where it is best to drill, and can now obtain almost any metal we wish.

"'Magnetic eyes' are of great use to miners and Civil engineers. These instruments are something like the mariner's compass, with the sensitiveness enormously increased by galvanic currents. The 'eye,' as it were, sees what substances are underground, and at what distances. It also shows how many people are in an adjoining room--through the magnetic properties of the iron in their blood--whether they are moving, and in what directions and at what speed they go. In connection with the phonograph and concealed by draperies, it is useful to detectives, who, through a registering attachment, can obtain a record of everything said and done.

"Our political system remains with but little change. Each State has still two United States Senators, though the population represented by each representative has been greatly increased, so that the Senate has grown numerically much more than the House. It is the duty of each member of

Congress to understand the conditions existing in every other member's State or district, and the country's interest always precedes that of party. We have a comprehensive examination system in the civil service, and every officeholder, except members of the Cabinet, retains his office while efficiently performing his duty, without regard to politics. The President can also be re-elected any number of times. The Cabinet members, as formerly, usually remain in office while he does, and appear regularly in Congress to defend their measures.

"The really rapid transit lines in New York are underground, and have six tracks, two being used for freight. At all stations the local tracks rise several feet towards the street and slope off in both directions, while the express tracks do this only at stations at which the faster trains stop. This gives the passengers a shorter distance to descend or rise in the elevators, and the ascent before the stations aids the brakes in stopping, while the drop helps the motors to start the trains quickly in getting away.

"Photography has also made great strides, and there is now no difficulty in reproducing exactly the colours of the object taken.

"Telephones have been so improved that one person can speak in his natural voice with another in any part of the globe, the wire that enables him to hear also showing him the face of the speaker though he be at the antipodes. All telephone wires being underground and kept by themselves, they are not interfered with by any high-tension electric-light or power wires, thunderstorms, or anything else.

"Rain-making is another subject removed from the uncertainties, and has become an absolute science. We produce clouds by explosions in the atmosphere's heights and by surface air forced by blowers through large pipes up the side of a mountain or natural elevation and there discharged through an opening in the top of a tower built on the highest part. The aëriduct is incased in a poor heat-conductor, so that the air retains its warmth until discharged, when it is cooled by expansion and the surrounding cold air. Condensation takes place and soon serves to start a rain.

"Yet, until the earth's axis is straightened, we must be more or less dependent on the eccentricities of the weather, with extremes of heat and cold, droughts and floods, which last are of course largely the result of several months' moisture held on the ground in the form of snow, the congestion being relieved suddenly by the warm spring rains.

"Medicine and surgery have kept pace with other improvements-- inoculation and antiseptics, as already seen, rendering most of the germ diseases and formerly dreaded epidemics impotent; while through the potency of electrical affinity we form wholesome food-products rapidly, instead of having to wait for their production by Nature's slow processes.

"The metric system, now universal, superseded the old-fashioned arbitrary standards, so prolific of mistakes and confusion, about a century ago.

"English, as we have seen, is already the language of 600,000,000 people, and the number is constantly increasing through its adoption by the numerous races of India, where, even before the close of the last century, it was about as important as Latin during the greatness of Rome, and by the fact that the Spanish and Portuguese elements in Mexico and Central and South America show a constant tendency to die out, much as the population of Spain fell from 30,000,000 to 17,000,000 during the nineteenth century. As this goes on, in the Western hemisphere, the places left vacant are gradually filled by the more progressive Anglo-Saxons, so that it looks as if the study of ethnology in the future would be very simple.

"The people with cultivation and leisure, whose number is increasing relatively to the population at each generation, spend much more of their year in the country than formerly, where they have large and well-cultivated country seats, parts of which are also preserved for game. This growing custom on the part of society, in addition to being of great advantage to the out-of-town districts, has done much to save the forests and preserve some forms of game that would otherwise, like the buffalo, have become extinct.

"In astronomy we have also made tremendous strides. The old-fashioned double-convex lens used in telescopes became so heavy as its size grew, that it bent perceptibly from its own weight, when pointed at the zenith, distorting the vision; while when it was used upon a star near the horizon, though the glass on edge kept its shape, there was too much atmosphere between it and the observed object for successful study. Our recent telescopes have, therefore, concave plate-glass mirrors, twenty metres in diameter, like those used for converging the sun's rays in solar engines, but with curves more mathematically exact, which collect an immense amount of light and focus it on a sensitive plate or on the eye of the observer, whose back is turned to the object he is studying. An electrical field also plays an important part, the electricity being as great an aid to light as in the telephone it is to sound. With these placed generally on high mountain peaks, beyond the reach of clouds, we have enormously increased the number of visible stars, though there are still probably boundless regions that we cannot see. These telescopes have several hundred times the power of the largest lenses of the nineteenth century, and apparently bring Mars and Jupiter, when in opposition, within one thousand and ten thousand miles, respectively, so that we study their physical geography and topography; and we have good maps of Jupiter, and even of Saturn, notwithstanding their distance and atmospheric envelopes, and we are able to see the disks of third-magnitude stars.

"It seems as if, when we wish any particular discovery or invention, in whatever field, we had but to turn our efforts in its direction to obtain our desire. We seem, in fact, to have awakened in the scenes of the Arabian Nights; yet the mysterious genius which we control, and which dims Aladdin's lamp, is the gift of no fairy godmother sustained by the haze of dreams, but shines as the child of science with fadeless and growing splendour, and may yet bring us and our little planet much closer to God.

"We should indeed be happy, living as we do at this apex of attained civilization, with the boundless possibilities of the future unfolding before us, on the horizon of which we may fairly be said to stand.

"We are freed from the rattling granite pavement of only a century ago, which made the occupant of an omnibus feel like a fly inside of a drum; from the domination of our local politics by ignorant foreigners; and from country roads that either filled the eyes, lungs, and hair of the unfortunates travelling upon them with dust, or, resembling ploughed and fertilized fields, saturated and plastered them with mud. These miseries, together with sea-sickness in ocean travelling, are forever passed, and we feel that 'Excelsior!' is indeed our motto. Our new and increasing sources of power have so stimulated production and manufacturing that poverty or want is scarcely known; while the development of the popular demand, as a result of the supplied need, is so great that there is no visible limit to the diversification of industry or the possibilities of the arts.

"It may seem strange to some that apparently so disproportionate a number of inventions have been made in the last century. There are several reasons. Since every discovery or advance in knowledge increases our chance of obtaining more, it becomes cumulative, and our progress is in geometric instead of arithmetical ratio. Public interest and general appreciation of the value of time have also effectively assisted progress. At the beginning of each year the President, the Governors of the States, and the Mayors of cities publish a prospectus of the great improvements needed, contemplated, and under way within their jurisdiction--it may be planning a new boulevard, a new park, or an improved system of sewers; and at the year's end they issue a resume of everything completed, and the progress in everything else; and though there is usually a great difference between the results hoped for and those attained, the effect is good. The newspapers publish at length the recommendations of the Executives, and also the results obtained, and keep up public interest in all important matters.

"Free to delve in the allurement and fascination of science, emancipated man goes on subduing Nature, as his Maker said he should, and turning her giant forces to his service in his constant struggle to rise and become more like Him who gave the commandments and showed him how he should go.

"Notwithstanding our strides in material progress, we are not entirely content. As the requirements of the animal become fully supplied, we feel a need for something else. Some say this is like a child that cries for the moon, but others believe it the awakening and craving of our souls. The historian narrates but the signs of the times, and strives to efface himself; yet there is clearly a void, becoming yearly more apparent, which materialism cannot fill. Is it some new subtle force for which we sigh, or would we commune with spirits? There is, so far as we can see, no limit to our journey, and I will add, in closing, that, with the exception of religion, we have most to hope from science."

CHAPTER VI
FAR-REACHING PLANS

Knowing that the rectification of the earth's axis was satisfactorily begun, and that each year would show an increasing improvement in climate, many of the delegates, after hearing Bearwarden's speech, set out for their homes. Those from the valley of the Amazon and the eastern coast of South America boarded a lightning express that rushed them to Key West at the rate of three hundred miles an hour. The railroad had six tracks, two for through passengers, two for locals, and two for freight. There they took a "water-spider," six hundred feet long by three hundred in width, the deck of which was one hundred feet above the surface, which carried them over the water at the rate of a mile a minute, around the eastern end of Cuba, through Windward Passage, and so to the South American mainland, where they continued their journey by rail.

The Siberian and Russian delegates, who, of course, felt a keen interest in the company's proceedings, took a magnetic double-ender car to Bering Strait. It was eighteen feet high, one hundred and fifty feet long, and had two stories. The upper, with a toughened glass dome running the entire length, descended to within three feet of the floor, and afforded an unobstructed view of the rushing scenery. The rails on which it ran were ten feet apart, the wheels being beyond the sides, like those of a carriage, and fitted with ball bearings to ridged axles. The car's flexibility allowed it to follow slight irregularities in the track, while the free, independent wheels gave it a great advantage in rounding curves over cars with wheels and axle in one casting, in which one must slip while traversing a greater or smaller arc than the other, except when the slope of the tread and the centrifugal force happen to correspond exactly. The fact of having its supports outside instead of underneath, while increasing its stability, also enabled the lower floor to come much nearer the ground, while still the wheels were large. Arriving in just twenty hours, they ran across on an electric ferry-boat, capable of carrying several dozen cars, to East Cape, Siberia, and then, by running as far north as possible, had a short cut to Europe.

The Patagonians went by the all-rail Intercontinental Line, without change of cars, making the run of ten thousand miles in forty hours. The

Australians entered a flying machine, and were soon out of sight; while the Central Americans and members from other States of the Union returned for the most part in their mechanical phaetons.

"A prospective improvement in travelling," said Bearwarden, as he and his friends watched the crowd disperse, "will be when we can rise beyond the limits of the atmosphere, wait till the earth revolves beneath us, and descend in twelve hours on the other side."

"True," said Cortlandt, "but then we can travel westward only, and shall have to make a complete circuit when we wish to go east."

A few days later there was a knock at President Bearwarden's door, while he was seated at his desk looking over some papers and other matters. Taking his foot from a partly opened desk drawer where it had been resting, he placed it upon the handle of a handsome brass-mounted bellows, which proved to be articulating, for, as he pressed, it called lustily, "Come in!" The door opened, and in walked Secretary of State Stillman, Secretary of the Navy Deepwaters, who was himself an old sailor, Dr. Cortlandt, Ayrault, Vice-President Dumby, of the T. A. S. Co., and two of the company's directors.

"Good-morning," said Bearwarden, as he shook hands with his visitors. "Charmed to see you." "That's a great invention," said Secretary Stillman, examining the bellows. "We must get Congress to make an appropriation for its introduction in the department buildings in Washington. You have no idea how it dries my throat to be all the time shouting, 'Come in!'"

"Do you know, Bearwarden," said Secretary Deepwaters, "I'm afraid when we have this millennium of climate every one will be so well satisfied that our friend here (pointing to Secretary Stillman with his thumb) will have nothing to do."

"I have sometimes thought some of the excitement will be gone, and the struggle of the 'survival of the fittest' will become less problematical," said Bearwarden.

"The earth seems destined to have a calm old age," said Cortlandt, "unless we can look to the Cabinet to prevent it."

"This world will soon be a dull place. I wish we could leave it for a change," said Ayrault. "I don't mean forever, of course, but just as people have grown tired of remaining like plants in the places in which they grew. Alan has been a caterpillar for untold ages; can he not become the butterfly?"

"Since we have found out how to straighten the axis," said Deepwaters, "might we not go one better, and improve the orbit as well?--increase the difference between aphelion and perihelion, and give those that still like a changing climate a chance, while incidentally we should see more of the world--I mean the solar system--and, by enlarging the parallax, be able to measure the distance of a greater number of fixed stars. Put your helm hard down and shout 'Hard-a-lee!' You see, there is nothing simpler. You keep her off now, and six months hence you let her luff."

"That's an idea!" said Bearwarden. "Our orbit could be enough like that of a comet to cross the orbits of both Venus and Mars; and the climatic extremes would not be inconvenient. The whole earth being simultaneously warmed or cooled, there would be no equinoctials or storms resulting from changes on one part of the surface from intense heat to intense cold; every part would have a twelve-hour day and night, and none would be turned towards or from the sun for six months at a time; for, however eccentric the orbit, we should keep the axis absolutely straight. At perihelion there would simply be increased evaporation and clouds near the equator, which would shield those regions from the sun, only to disappear again as the earth receded.

"The only trouble," said Cortlandt, "is that we should have no fulcrum. Straightening the axis is simple enough, for we have the attraction of the sun with which to work, and we have but to increase it at one end while decreasing it at the other, and change this as the poles change their inclination towards the sun, to bring it about. If a comet with a sufficiently large head would but come along and retard us, or opportunely give us a pull, or if we could increase the attraction of the other planets for us, or decrease it at times, it might be done. If the force, the control of which was discovered too late to help us straighten the axis, could be applied on a sufficiently large scale; if apergy----"

"I have it!" exclaimed Ayrault, jumping up. "Apergy will do it. We can build an airtight projectile, hermetically seal ourselves within, and charge it in such a way that it will be repelled by the magnetism of the earth, and it will be forced from it with equal or greater violence than that with which it is ordinarily attracted. I believe the earth has but the same relation to space that the individual molecule has to any solid, liquid, or gaseous matter we know; and that, just as molecules strive to fly apart on the application of heat, this earth will repel that projectile when electricity, which we are coming to look upon as another form of heat, is properly applied. It must be so, and it is the manifest destiny of the race to improve it. Man is a spirit cursed with a mortal body, which glues him to the earth, and his yearning to rise, which is innate, is, I believe, only a part of his probation and trial."

"Show us how it can be done," shouted his listeners in chorus.

"Apergy is and must be able to do it," Ayrault continued. "Throughout Nature we find a system of compensation. The centripetal force is offset by the centrifugal; and when, according to the fable, the crystal complained of its hard lot in being unable to move, while the eagle could soar through the upper air and see all the glories of the world, the bird replied, 'My life is but for a moment, while you, set in the rock, will live forever, and will see the last sunrise that flashes upon the earth.'

"We know that Christ, while walking on the waves, did not sink, and that he and Elijah were carried up into heaven. What became of their material bodies we cannot tell, but they were certainly superior to the force of gravitation. We have no reason to believe that in miracles any natural law was broken, or even set aside, but simply that some other law, whose workings we do not understand, became operative and modified the law that otherwise would have had things its own way. In apergy we undoubtedly have the counterpart of gravitation, which must exist, or Nature's system of compensation is broken. May we not believe that in Christ's transfiguration on the mount, and in the appearance of Moses and Elias with him--doubtless in the flesh, since otherwise mortal eyes could not have seen them--apergy came into play and upheld them; that otherwise, and if no other modification had intervened, they would have fallen to the ground; and that apergy was, in other words, the working principle of those miracles?"

"May we not also believe," added Cortlandt, "that in the transfiguration Christ's companions took the substance of their material bodies--the oxygen, hydrogen, nitrogen, and carbon--from the air and the moisture it contained; for, though spiritual bodies, be their activity magnetic or any other, could of course pass the absolute cold and void of space without being affected, no mortal body could; and that in the same manner Elijah's body dissolved into air without the usual intervention of decomposition; for we know that, though matter can easily change its form, it can never be destroyed."

All assented to this, and Ayrault continued: "If apergy can annul gravitation, I do not see why it should not do more, for to annul it the repulsion of the earth that it produces must be as great as its attraction, unless we suppose gravitation for the time being to be suspended; but whether it is or not, does not affect the result in this case, for, after the apergetic repulsion is brought to the degree at which a body does not fall, any increase in the current's strength will cause it to rise, and in the case of electro-magnets we know that the attraction or repulsion has practically no limit. This will be of great advantage to us," he continued, "for if a projectile could move away from the earth with no more rapid acceleration than that with which it approaches, it would take too long to reach the nearest planet, but the maximum repulsion being at the start by reason of its proximity to the earth--for apergy, being the counterpart of gravitation, is subject to Newton's and Kepler's laws--the acceleration of a body apergetically charged will be greatest at first. Two inclined planes may have the same fall, but a ball will reach the bottom of one that is steepest near the top in less time than on any other, because the maximum acceleration is at the start. We are all tired of being stuck to this cosmical speck, with its monotonous ocean, leaden sky, and single moon that is useless more than half the time, while its size is so microscopic compared with the universe that we can traverse its great circle in four days. Its possibilities are exhausted; and just as Greece became too small for the civilization of the Greeks, and as reproduction is growth beyond the individual, so it seems to me that the future glory of the human race lies in exploring at least the solar system, without waiting to become shades."

"Should you propose to go to Mars or Venus?" asked Cortlandt.

"No," replied Ayrault, "we know all about Mars; it is but one seventh the size of the earth, and as the axis is inclined more than ours, it would be a less comfortable globe than this; while, as our president here told us in his T. A. S. Company's report, the axis of Venus is inclined to such a degree that it would be almost uninhabitable for us. It would be as if colonists tried to settle Greenland, or had come to North America during its Glacial period. Neither Venus nor Mars would be a good place now."

"Where should you propose to go?" asked Stillman.

"To Jupiter, and, if possible, after that to Saturn," replied Ayrault; "the former's mean distance from the sun is 480,000,000 miles; but, as our president showed us, its axis is so nearly straight that I think, with its internal warmth, there will be nothing to fear from cold. Though, on account of the planet's vast size, objects on its surface weigh more than twice as much as here, if I am able to reach it by means of apergy, the same force will enable me to regulate my weight. Will any one go with me?"

"Splendid!" said Bearwarden. "If Mr. Dumby, our vice-president, will temporarily assume my office, nothing will give me greater pleasure."

"So will I go, if there is room for me," said Cortlandt. "I will at once resign my place as Government expert, and consider it the grandest event of my life."

"If I were not afraid of leaving Stillman here to his own devices, I'd ask for a berth as well," said Deepwaters.

"I am afraid," said Stillman, "if you take any more, you will be overcrowded."

"Modesty forbids his saying," said Deepwaters, "that it wouldn't do for the country to have all its eggs in one basket."

"Are you not afraid you will find the surface hot, or even molten?" asked Vice-President Dumby. "With its eighty-six thousand five hundred mile diameter, the amount of original internal heat must have been terrific."

"No," said Cortlandt, "it cannot be molten, or even in the least degree luminous, for, if it were, its satellites would be visible when they enter its shadow, whereas they entirely disappear."

"I do not believe Jupiter's surface is even perceptibly warm," said Bearwarden. "We know that Algol, known to the ancients as the 'Demon Star,' and several other variable stars, are accompanied by a dark companion, with which they revolve about a common centre, and which periodically obscures part of their light. Now, some of these non-luminaries are nearly as large as our sun, and, of course, many hundred times the size of Jupiter. If these bodies have lost enough heat to be invisible, Jupiter's surface at least must be nearly cold."

"In the phosphorescence of seawater," said Cortlandt, "and in other instances in Nature, we find light without heat, and we may soon be able to produce it in the arts by oxidizing coal without the intervention of the steam engine; but we never find any considerable heat without light."

"I am convinced," said Bearwarden, "that we shall find Jupiter habitable for intelligent beings who have been developed on a more advanced sphere than itself, though I do not believe it has progressed far enough in its evolution to produce them. I expect to find it in its Palaeozoic or Mesozoic period, while over a hundred years ago the English astronomer, Chambers, thought that on Saturn there was good reason for suspecting the presence of snow."

"What sort of spaceship do you propose to have?" asked the vice-president.

"As you have to pass through but little air," said Deepwaters, "I should suggest a short-stroke cylinder of large diameter, with a flat base and dome roof, composed of aluminum, or, still better, of glucinum or beryllium as it is sometimes called, which is twice as good a conductor of electricity as aluminum, four times as strong, and is the lightest of all known metals, having a specific gravity of only two, which last property will be of great use to you, for of course the more weight you have to propel the more apergetic repulsion you will have to develop."

"I will get some drawing-paper I left outside in my trap," said Ayrault, "when with your ideas we may arrive at something definite," saying which, he left the room.

"He seems very cynical in his ideas of life and the world in general," said Secretary Stillman, "for a man of his age, and one that is engaged."

"You see," replied Bearwarden, "his fiancee is not yet a senior, being in the class of two thousand and one at Vassar, and so cannot marry him for a year. Not till next June can this sweet girl graduate come forth with her mortar-board and sheepskin to enlighten the world and make him happy. That is, I suspect, one reason why he proposed this trip."

CHAPTER VII
HARD AT WORK

In a few moments Ayrault returned with pencils, a pair of compasses, and paper.

"Let us see, in the first place," said Deepwaters, "how long the journey will take. Since a stone falls 16.09 feet the first second, and + 64 feet the next, it is easy to calculate at what rate your speed would increase with the repulsion twice that of the ordinary traction. But I think this would be too slow. It will be best to treble or quadruple the apergetic charge, which can easily be done, in which case your speed will exceed the muzzle-velocity of a projectile from a long-range gun, in a few seconds. As the earth's repulsion decreases, the attraction of mars and Jupiter will increase, and, there being no resistance, your gait will become more and more rapid till it is necessary to reverse the charge to avoid being dashed to pieces or being consumed like a falling star by the friction in passing through Jupiter's atmosphere. You can be on the safe side by checking your speed in advance. You must, of course, be careful to avoid collisions with meteors and asteroids but if you do, they will be of use to you, for by attracting or repelling them you can change your course to suit yourself, and also theirs in inverse ratio to their masses. Jupiter's moons will be like head and stern lines in enabling you to choose the part of the surface on which you wish to land. With apergy it is as essential to have some heavy body on which to work, within range, as to have water about a ship's propellers. Whether, when apergy is developed, gravitation is temporarily annulled, or reversed like the late attraction of a magnet when the current is changed, or whether it is merely overpowered, in which case your motion will be the resultant of the two, is an unsettled and not very important point; for, though we know but little more of the nature of electricity than was known a hundred years ago, this does not prevent our producing and using it."

"Jupiter, when in opposition," he continued, "is about 380,000,000 miles from us, and it takes light, which travels at the rate of 190,000 miles a second, just thirty-four minutes to reach the earth from Jupiter. If we suppose the average speed of your ship to be one-five-hundredth as great, it will take you just eleven days, nineteen hours and twenty minutes to make the journey. You will have a fine view of Mars and the asteroids, and when 1,169,000 miles from Jupiter, will cross the orbit of Callisto, the fifth moon in distance from the giant planet. That will be your best point to steer by."

"I think," said Ayrault, "as that will be the first member of Jupiter's system we pass, and as it will guide us into port, it would be a good name for our ship, and you must christen her if we have her launched."

"No, no," said Deepwaters, "Miss Preston must do that; but we certainly should have a launch, for you might have to land in the water, and you must be sure the ship is tight."

"Talking of tight ships," said Bearwarden, passing a decanter of claret to Stillman, "may remind us that it is time to splice the 'main brace.' There's a bottle of whisky and some water just behind you," he added to Deepwaters, "while three minutes after I ring this bell," he said, pressing a button and jerking a handle marked '8,' "the champagne cocktails will be on the desk."

"I see you know his ways," said Stillman to Bearwarden, drooping his eyes in Deepwaters's direction.

"Oh, yes, I've been here before," replied Deepwaters. "You see, we navy men have to hustle now-a-days, and can't pass our time in a high-backed chair, talking platitudes."

At this moment there was a slight rumbling, and eight champagne cocktails, with the froth still on, and straws on a separate plate, shot in and landed on a corner of the desk.

"Help yourselves, gentlemen," said Bearwarden, placing them on a table; "I hope we shall find them cold."

"Do you know," said Deepwaters to Ayrault, while rapidly making his cocktail disappear, "the Callisto's cost with its outfit will be very great, especially if you use glucinum, which, though the ideal metal for the purpose, comes pretty high? I suggest that you apply to Congress for an appropriation. This experiment comes under the 'Promotion of Science Act,' and any bill for it would certainly pass."

"No, indeed," replied Ayrault; "the Callisto trip will be a privilege and glory I would not miss, and building her will be a part of it. I shall put in everything conducive to success, but will come to the Government only for advice."

"I will send a letter to all our ambassadors and consuls," said Stillman, "to telegraph the department anything they may know or learn that will be of use in adjusting the batteries, controlling the machine, or anything else, and will turn over to you in a succinct form all information that may be relevant, for without such sorting you would be overwhelmed."

"And I," said Deepwaters, "will order the commanders of our vessels to give you a farewell salute at starting, and to pick you up in case you fail. When you have demonstrated the suitability of apergy," he continued, "and the habitability of Jupiter and Saturn--,which, with their five and eight moons, respectively, and rings thrown in, must both be vastly superior to our little second-rate globe--we will see what can be done towards changing our orbit, and if we cannot swing a little nearer to our new world or worlds. Then we'll lower, or rather raise, the boats in the shape of numerous Callistos, and have a landing-party ready at each opposition, while a man or two can be placed in charge of each projectile to bring it back in ballast. Thus we may soon have regular interplanetary lines."

"As every place seems to have been settled from some other," said Cortlandt, "I do not see why, with increased scientific facilities, history should not repeat itself, and this be the point from which to colonize the solar system; for, for the present at least, it would seem that we could not get beyond that."

"As it will be quite an undertaking to change the orbit," said Deepwaters, "we shall have time meanwhile to absorb or run out all inferior races, so that we shall not make the mistake of extending the Tower of Babel."

"He is putting on his war-paint," said Stillman, "and will soon want a planet to himself."

"I see no necessity for even changing the orbit," said Bearwarden, "except for the benefit of those that remain. If this attempt succeeds, it can doubtless be repeated. An increase in eccentricity would merely shorten the journey, if aphelion always coincided with opposition, which it would not."

"Let us know how you are getting on," said Deepwaters to Ayrault, "and be sure you have the Callisto properly christened. Step lively there, landlubbers!" he called to Stillman; "I have an appointment at Washington at one, and it is now twenty minutes past twelve. We can lunch on the way."

Ayrault immediately advertised for bids for the construction of a glucinum cylinder twenty-five feet in diameter, fifteen feet high at the sides, with a domed roof, bringing up the total height to twenty-one feet, and with a small gutter about it to catch the rain on Jupiter or any other planet they might visit. The sides, roof, and floor were to consist of two sheets, each one third of an inch thick and six inches apart, the space between to be filled with mineral wool, as a protection against the intense cold of space. There were also to be several keels and supports underneath, on which the car should rest. Large, toughened plate-glass windows were to be let into the roof and sides, and smaller ones in the floor, all to be furnished with thick shades and curtains. Ayrault also decided to have it divided into two stories, with ceilings six and a half to seven and a half feet high, respectively, with a sort of crow's nest or observatory at the top; the floors to be lattice-work, like those in the engine-room of a steamer, so that when the carpets were rolled up they should not greatly obstruct the view. The wide, flat base and the low centre of gravity would, he saw, be of use in withstanding the high winds that he knew often prevailed on Jupiter.

As soon as possible he awarded the contract, and then entering his smart electric trap, steered for Vassar University along what was the old post-road--though its builders would not have recognized it with its asphalt surface, straightened curves, and easy grades--to ask his idol to christen the Callisto when it should be finished.

Starting from the upper end of Central Park, he stopped to buy her a bunch of violets, and then ran to Poughkeepsie in two hours.

Sylvia Preston was a lovely girl, with blue eyes, brown hair, and perfect figure, clear white skin, and just twenty. She was delighted to see him, and said she would love to christen the Callisto or do anything else that he wished. "But I am so sorry you are going away," she went on. "I hate to lose you for so long, and we shall not even be able to write."

"Why couldn't we be married now," he asked, "and go to Jupiter for our honeymoon?"

"I'm afraid, dear," she answered, "you would be sorry a few years hence if I didn't take my degree; and, besides, as you have asked those other men, there wouldn't be room for me."

"We could have made other arrangements," he replied, "had I been able to persuade you to go."

"Won't you dine with us at Delmonico's this evening, and go to the play?" she asked. "Papa has taken a box."

"Of course I will," he said, brightening up. "What are you going to wear?"

"Oh, I suppose something light and cool, for it's so hot," she answered.

"I'll go now, so as to be ready," he said, getting up and going towards the door to which Sylvia followed him.

A man in livery stood at the step of the phaeton. Ayrault got in and turned on the current, and his man climbed up behind.

On turning into the main road Ayrault was about to increase his speed, when Sylvia, who had taken a short cut appeared at the wayside carrying her hat in one hand and her gloves in the other.

"I couldn't let you go all by yourself," she said. "The fact is, I wanted to be with you."

"You are the sweetest thing that ever lived, and I'll love you all my days," he said, getting down and helping Sylvia to the seat beside him. "What a nuisance this fellow behind is!" he continued--referring to the groom--"for, though he is a Russian, and speaks but little English, it is unpleasant to feel he is there."

"You'll have to write your sweet nothings, instead of saying them," Sylvia replied.

"For you to leave around for other girls to see," answered Ayrault with a smile.

"I don't know what your other girls do," she returned, "but with me you are safe."

Ayrault fairly made his phaeton spin, going up the grades like a shot and down like a bird. On reaching New York, he left Sylvia at her house, then ran his machine to a florist's, where he ordered some lilies and roses, and then steered his way to his club, where he dressed for dinner. Shortly before the time he repaired to Delmonico's--which name had become historical, though the founders themselves were long dead--and sat guard at a table till Sylvia, wearing his flowers and looking more beautiful than any of them, arrived with her mother and father, and Bearwarden, whom they knew very well.

"How are the exams getting on, Miss Preston?" Bearwarden asked.

"Pretty well," she replied, with a smile. "We had English literature yesterday, and natural history the day before. Next week we have chemistry and philosophy."

"What are you taking in natural history?" asked Bearwarden, with interest.

"Oh, principally physical geography, geology, and meteorology," she replied. "I think them entrancing."

"It must be a consolation," said Ayrault, "when your best hat is spoiled by rain, to know the reason why. Your average," he continued, addressing Sylvia, "was ninety in the semi-annuals, and I haven't a doubt that the finals will maintain your record for the year."

"Don't be too sure," she replied. "I have been loafing awfully, and had to engage a 'grind' as a coach."

After dinner they went to the play, where they saw a presentation of Society at the Close of the Twentieth Century, which Sylvia and Ayrault enjoyed immensely.

A few days after the Delmonico dinner, while Bearwarden, Cortlandt, and Ayrault sat together discussing their plans, the servant announced Ayrault's family physician, Dr. Tubercle Germiny, who had been requested to call.

"Delighted to see you, doctor," said Ayrault, shaking hands. "You know Col. Bearwarden, our President, and Dr. Cortlandt--an LL. D., however, and not a medico."

"I have had the pleasure," replied Dr. Germiny, shaking hands with both.

"As you may be aware, doctor," said Ayrault, when they were seated, "we are about to take a short trip to Jupiter, and, if time allows, to Saturn. We have come to you, as one familiar with every known germ, for a few precautionary suggestions and advice concerning our medicine-chest."

"Indeed!" replied Dr. Germiny, "a thorough knowledge of bacteriology is the groundwork of therapeutics. It is practically admitted that every ailment, with the exception of mechanical injuries, is the direct result of a specific germ; and even in accidents and simple fractures, no matter what may be the nature of the bruise, a micro-organism soon announces its presence, so that if not the parent, it is the inseparable companion, in fact the shadow, of disease. Now, though not the first cause in this instance, it has been indubitably proved, that much of the effect, the fever and pain, are produced and continued by the active, omnipresent, sleepless sperm. Either kill the micrococcus or heal the wound, and you are free from both. It being, therefore, granted that the ills of life are in the air, we have but to find the peculiar nature of the case in hand, its habits, tastes, and constitution, in order to destroy it. Impoverish the soil on which it thrives, before its arrival, if you can foresee the nature of the inoculation to which you will be exposed, by a dilute solution of itself, and supply it only with what it particularly dislikes. For an already established tubercle requiring rapid action of the blood, such as may well exist among the birds and vertebrates of Jupiter and Saturn, I suggest a hypodermic rattlesnake injection, while hydrocyanic acid and tarantula saliva may also come in well. The combinations that so long destroyed us have already become our panacea."

"I see you have these poisons at your fingers' ends," said Ayrault, "and we shall feel the utmost confidence in the remedies and directions you prescribe."

They found that, in addition to their medicine-chest, they would have to make room for the following articles, and also many more: six shot-guns (three double-barrel 12-bores, three magazine 10-bores,) three rifles, three revolvers; a large supply of ammunition (explosive and solid balls), hunting-knives, fishing-tackle, compass, sextant, geometrical instruments, canned food for forty days, appliance for renewing air, clothing, rubber boots, apergetic apparatus, protection-wires, aneroid barometer, and kodaks.

CHAPTER VIII
GOOD-BYE

At last the preparations were completed, and it was arranged that the Callisto should begin its journey at eleven o'clock A. M., December 21st--the northern hemisphere's shortest day.

Though six months' operations could hardly be expected to have produced much change in the inclination of the earth's axis, the autumn held on wonderfully, and December was pronounced very mild. Fully a million people were in and about Van Cortlandt Park hours before the time announced for the start, and those near looked inquiringly at the trim little air-ship, that, having done well on the trial trip, rested on her longitudinal and transverse keels, with a battery of chemicals alongside, to make sure of a full power supply.

The President and his Cabinet--including, of course, the shining lights of the State and Navy Departments--came from Washington. These, together with Mr. and Mrs. Preston, and a number of people with passes, occupied seats arranged at the sides of the platform; while sightseers and scientists assembled from every part of the world.

"There's a ship for you!" said Secretary Stillman to the Secretary of the Navy. "She'll not have to be dry-docked for barnacles, neither will the least breeze make the passengers sick." "That's all you landlubbers think of," replied Deepwaters. "I remember one of the kings over in Europe said to me, as he introduced me to the queen: 'Your Secretary of State is a great man, but why does he always part his hair in the middle?'

"'So that it shall not turn his head,' I replied.

"'But with so gallant and handsome an officer as you to lean upon,' he answered, 'I should think he could look down on all the world.' Whereupon I asked him what he'd take to drink."

"Your apology is accepted," replied Secretary Stillman.

Cortlandt also came from Washington, where, as chief of the Government's Expert Examiners Board, he had temporary quarters. Bearwarden sailed over the spectators' heads in one of the Terrestrial Axis Straightening Company's flying machines, while Ayrault, to avoid the crowd, had come to the Callisto early, and was showing the interior arrangements to Sylvia, who had accompanied him. She was somewhat piqued because at the last moment he had not absolutely insisted on carrying her off, or offered, if necessary, to displace his presidential and Doctor-of-Laws friends in order to make room.

"You will have an ideal trip," she said, looking over some astronomical star-charts and photographic maps of Jupiter and Saturn that lay on the table, with a pair of compasses, "and I hope you won't lose your way."

"I shall need no compass to find my way back," replied Ayrault, "if I ever succeed in leaving this planet; neither will star-charts be necessary, for you will be a magnet stronger than any compass, and, compared with my star, all others are dim."

"You should write a book," said Sylvia, "and put some of those things in it." She was wearing a bunch of forget-me-nots and violets that she had cut from a small flower-garden of potted plants Ayrault had sent her, which she had placed in her father's conservatory.

At this moment the small chime clock set in the Callisto's wood-work rang out quarter to eleven. As the sounds died away, Sylvia became very pale, and began to regret in her womanly way that she had allowed her hero to attempt this experiment.

"Oh," she said, clinging to his arm, "it was very wrong of me to let you begin this. I was so dazzled by the splendour of your scheme when I heard it, and so anxious that you should have the glory of being the first to surpass Columbus, that I did not realize the full meaning. I thought, also, you seemed rather ready to leave me," she added gently, "and so said little; you do not know how it almost breaks my heart now that I am about to lose you. It was quixotic to let you undertake this journey."

"An undertaker would have given me his kind offices for one even longer, had I remained here," replied Ayrault. "I cannot live in this humdrum world without you. The most sustained excitement cannot even palliate what seems to me like unrequited love."

"O Dick!" she exclaimed, giving him a reproachful glance, "you mustn't say that. You know you have often told me my reason for staying and taking my degree was good. My lot will be very much harder than yours, for you will forget me in the excitement of discovery and adventure; but I--what can I do in the midst of all the old associations?"

"Never mind, sweetheart," he said, kissing her hand, "I have seemed on the verge of despair all the time."

Seeing that their separation must shortly begin, Ayrault tried to assume a cheerful look; but as Sylvia turned her eyes away they were suspiciously moist.

Just one minute before the starting-time Ayrault took Sylvia back to her mother, and, after pressing her hand and having one last long look into her--or, as he considered them, HIS--deep-sea eyes, he returned to the Callisto, and was standing at the foot of the telescopic aluminum ladder when his friends arrived. As all baggage and impedimenta had been sent aboard and properly stowed the day before, the travellers had not to do but climb to and enter by the second-story window. It distressed Bearwarden that the north pole's exact declination on the 21st day of December, when the axis was most inclined, could not be figured out by the hour at which they were to start, so as to show what change, if any, had already been brought about, but the astronomers were working industriously, and promised that, if it were finished by midnight, they would telegraph the result into space by flash-light code.

Raising his hat to his fiancee and his prospective parents-in-law, Ayrault followed them up. To draw in and fold the ladder was but the work of a moment. As the clocks in the neighbouring steeples began to strike eleven, Ayrault touched the switch that would correspond to the throttle of an engine, and the motors began to work at rapidly increasing speed. Slowly the Callisto left her resting-place as a Galatea might her pedestal, only, instead of coming down, she rose still higher.

A large American flag hanging from the window, which, as they started, fluttered as in a southern zephyr, soon began to flap as in a stiff breeze as the car's speed increased. With a final wave, at which a battery of twenty-one field-pieces made the air ring with a salute, and the multitude raised a mighty cheer, they drew it in and closed the window, sealing it hermetically in order to keep in the air that, had an opening remained, would soon have become rarefied.

The Callisto was going straight up

Sylvia had waved her handkerchief with the utmost enthusiasm, in spite of the sadness at her heart. But she now had other use for it in trying to hide her tears. The Callisto was still going straight up, with a speed already as great as a cannon ball's, and was almost out of sight. The multitude then began to disperse, and Sylvia returned to her home.

Let us now follow the Callisto. The earth and Jupiter not being exactly in opposition, as they would be if the sun, the earth, and Jupiter were in line, with the earth between the two, but rather as shown in the diagram, the Callisto's journey was considerably more than 380,000,000 miles, the mean opposition distance. As they wished to start by daylight--i. e., from the side of the earth turned towards the sun--they could not steer immediately for Jupiter, but were obliged to go a few hundred miles in the direction of the sun, then change their course to something like a tangent to the earth, and get their final right direction in swinging near the moon, since they must be comparatively near some material object to bring apergy into play.

The maximum power being turned on, the projectile shot from the earth with tremendous and rapidly increasing speed, by the shortest course--i. e., a straight line--so that for the present it was not necessary to steer.

Until beyond the limits of the atmosphere they kept the greatest apergetic repulsion focused on the upper part of their cylinder, so that its point went first, and they encountered least possible resistance. Looking through the floor windows, therefore, the travellers had a most superb view. The air being clear, the eastern border of North America and the Atlantic were outlined as on a map, the blue of the ocean and brownish colour of the land, with white snow-patches on the elevations, being very marked. The Hudson and the Sound appeared as clearly defined blue ribbons, and between and around the two they could see New York. They also saw the ocean dotted for miles with points in which they recognized the marine spiders and cruisers of the North Atlantic squadron, and the ships on the home station, which they knew were watching them through their glasses.

"I see," said Cortlandt, "that Deepwaters has been as good as his word, and has his ships on the watch to rescue us in case we fail."

"Yes," replied Bearwarden, "he is the right sort. When he gave that promise I knew his men would be there."

They soon perceived that they had reached the void of space, for, though the sun blazed with a splendour they had never before seen, the firmament was intensely black, and the stars shone as at midnight. Here they began to change their course to a curve beginning with a spiral, by charging the Callisto apergetically, and directing the current towards the moon, to act as an aid to the lunar attraction, while still allowing the earth to repel, and their motion gradually became the resultant of the two forces, the change from a straight line being so gradual, however, that for some minutes they scarcely perceived it. The coronal streamers about the sun, such as are visible on earth during a total eclipse, shone with a halo against the ultra-Cimmerian background, bursting forth to a height of twenty or thirty thousand miles above the surface in vast cyclonic storms, producing so rapid a motion that a column of incandescent gas may move ten thousand miles in less than ten minutes. Whether these great streaks were in part electrical phenomena similar to the aurora borealis, or entirely of intensely heated material thrown up by explosions within the sun's mass, they could not tell even from their point of vantage.

"I believe," said Cortlandt, pointing to the streamers, "that they are masses of gas thrown beyond the sun's atmosphere, which expand enormously when the pressure to which they are subjected in the sun is removed--for only in space freed from resistance could they move at such velocities, and that their brilliancy is increased by great electrical disturbance. If they were entirely the play of electrical forces, their change of place would be practically instantaneous, which, however rapid their movement, is not the case."

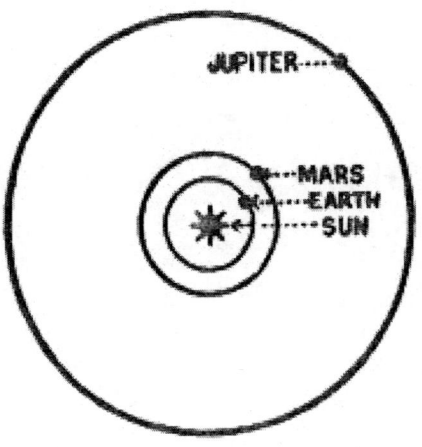

BOOK II

CHAPTER I
THE LAST OF THE EARTH

Finding that they were rapidly swinging towards their proper course, and that the earth in its journey about the sun would move out of their way, they divided their power between repelling the body they had left and increasing the attraction of the moon, and then set about getting their house in order.

Bearwarden, having the largest appetite, was elected cook, the others sagely divining that labour so largely for himself would be no trial. Their small but business-like-looking electric range was therefore soon in full blast, with Bearwarden in command. It had enough current to provide heat for cooking for four hundred hours, which was an ample margin, and it had this advantage, that, no matter how much it was used, it could not exhaust the air as any other form of heat would.

There were also a number of sixteen-candle-power incandescent lamps, so that when passing through the shadow of a planet, or at night after their arrival on Jupiter, their car would be brightly illuminated. They had also a good search-light for examining the dark side of a satellite, or exploring the spaces in Saturn's rings. Having lunched sumptuously on canned chicken soup, beef a la jardiniere, and pheasant that had been sent them by some of their admirers that morning, they put the bones and the glass can that had contained the soup into the double-doored partition or vestibule, placing a large sheet of cardboard to act as a wad between the scraps and the outside door. By pressing a button they unfastened the outside door, and the articles to be disposed of were shot off by the expansion of the air between the cardboard disk and the inside door; after which the outside door was drawn back to its place by a current sent through a magnet, but little power being required to reclose it with no resisting atmospheric pressure. As the electricity ran along a wire passing through a hermetically sealed opening in the floor, there was no way by which more air than that in the vestibule could escape; and as the somewhat flat space between the doors contained less than one cubic foot, the air-pressure inside the Callisto could not be materially lessened by a few openings.

"By filling the vestibule as full as possible," said Bearwarden, "and so displacing most of its air, we shall be able to open the outside door oftener without danger of rarefaction."

The things they had discharged flew off with considerable speed and were soon out of sight; but it was not necessary for them to move fast, provided they moved at all, for, the resistance being nil, they would be sure to go beyond the range of vision, provided enough time was allowed, even if the Callisto's speed was not being increased by apergy, in which case articles outside and not affected would be quickly left behind.

The earth, which at first had filled nearly half their sky, was rapidly growing smaller. Being almost between themselves and the sun, it looked like a crescent moon; and when it was only about twenty times the size of the moon they calculated they must have come nearly two hundred thousand miles. The moon was now on what a sailor would call the starboard bow--i. e., to the right and ahead. Being a little more than three quarters full, and only about fifty thousand miles off, it presented a splendid sight, brilliant as polished silver, and about twenty-five times as large as they had ever before seen it with the unaided eye.

It was just ten hours since they had started, and at that moment 9 A. M. in New York; but, though it was night there, the Callisto was bathed in a flood of sunlight such as never shines on earth. The only night they would have was on the side of the Callisto turned away from the sun, unless they passed through some shadow, which they intended to avoid on account of the danger of colliding with a meteor in the dark. The moon and the Callisto were moving on converging lines, the curve on which they had entered having swung them to the side nearest the earth; but they saw that their own tremendous and increasing speed would carry them in front of the moon in its nearly circular orbit. Wishing to change the direction of their flight by the moon's attraction, they shut off the power driving them from the earth, whereupon the Callisto turned its heavy base towards the moon. They were already moving at such speed that their momentum alone would carry them hundreds of thousands of miles into space, and were then almost abreast of the earth's satellite, which was but a few thousand miles away. The spectacle was magnificent. As they looked at it through their field glasses or with the unaided eye, the great cracks and craters showed with the utmost clearness, sweeping past them almost as the landscape flies past a railway train. There was something awe-inspiring in the vast antiquity of that furrowed lunar surface, by far the oldest thing that mortal eye can see, since, while observing the ceaseless political or geological changes on earth, the face of this dead satellite, on account of the absence of air and water and consequent erosion, has remained unchanged for bygone ages, as it doubtless will for many more.

They closely watched the Callisto's course. At first it did not seem to deflect from a straight line, and they stood ready to turn on the apergetic force again, when the car very slowly began to show the effect of the moon's near pull; but not till they had so far passed it that the dark side was towards them were they heading straight for Jupiter. Then they again turned on full power and got a send-off shove on the moon and earth combined, which increased their speed so rapidly that they felt they could soon shut off the current altogether and save their supply.

"We must be ready to watch the signals from the arctic circle," said Bearwarden. "At midnight, if the calculations are finished, the result will be flashed by the searchlight." It was then ten minutes to twelve, and the earth was already over four hundred thousand miles away. Focusing their glasses upon the region near the north pole, which, being turned from the sun, was towards them and in darkness, they waited.

"In this blaze of sunlight," said Cortlandt, "I am afraid we can see nothing."

Fortunately, at this moment the Callisto entered the moon's tapering shadow.

"This," said Ayrault, "is good luck. We could of course have gone into the shadow; but to change our course would have delayed us, and we might have lost part of the chance of increasing our speed."

"There will be no danger from meteors or sub-satellites here," said Bearwarden, "for anything revolving about the moon at this distance would be caught by the earth."

The sun had apparently set behind the moon, and they were eclipsed. The stars shone with the utmost splendour against the dead-black sky, and the earth appeared as a large crescent, still considerably larger than the satellite to which they were accustomed. Exactly at midnight a faint phosphorescent light, like that of a glow-worm, appeared in the region of Greenland on the planet they had left. It gradually increased its strength till it shone like a long white beam projected from a lighthouse, and in this they beheld the work of the greatest search-light ever made by man, receiving for a few moments all the electricity generated by the available dynamos at Niagara and the Bay of Fundy, the steam engines, and other sources of power in the northern hemisphere. The beam lasted with growing intensity for one minute; it then spelled out with clean-cut intervals, according to the Cable Code: "23° no' 6". The southern hemisphere pumps are now raising and storing water at full blast. We have already begun to lower the Arctic Ocean."

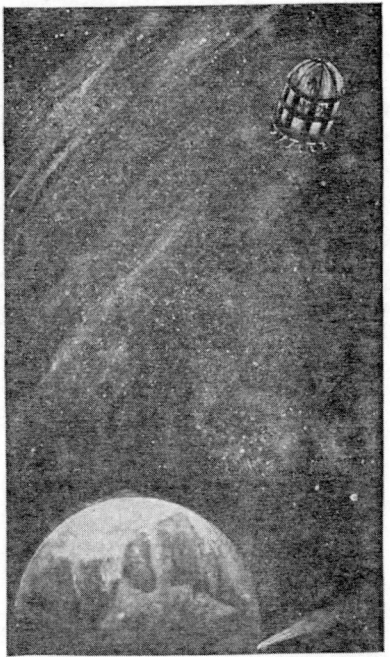

The signals from the Arctic Circle

"Victory!" shouted Bearwarden, in an ecstasy of delight. "Nearly half a degree in six months, with but one pole working. If we can add at this rate each time to the speed of straightening already acquired, we can reverse our engines in five years, and in five more the earth will be at rest and right."

"Look!" said Ayrault, "they are sending something else." The flashes came in rapid succession, reaching far into space. With their glasses fixed upon them, they made out these sentences: "Our telescopes, in whatever part of the earth was turned towards you, have followed you since you started, and did not lose sight of you till you entered the moon's shadow. On your present course you will be in darkness till 12.16, when we shall see you again."

On receiving this last earthly message, the travellers sprang to their searchlight, and, using its full power, telegraphed back the following: "Many thanks to you for good news about earth, and to Secretary Deepwaters for lending us the navy. Result of work most glorious. Remember us to everybody. Shadow's edge approaching."

This was read by the men in the great observatories, who evidently telephoned to the arctic Signal Light immediately, for it flashed back: "Got your message perfectly. Wish you greatest luck. The T. A. S. Co. has decked the Callisto's pedestal with flowers, and has ordered a tablet set up on the site to commemorate your celestial journey."

At that moment the shadow swept by, and they were in the full blaze of cloudless day. The change was so great that for a moment they were obliged to close their eyes. The polished sides of the Callisto shone so brightly that they knew they were easily seen. The power temporarily diverted in sending them the message then returned to the work of draining the Arctic Ocean, which, as the north pole was now returning to the sun, was the thing to do, and the travellers resumed their study of the heavenly bodies.

CHAPTER II
SPACE AND MARS

Never before had the travellers observed the stars and planets under such favourable conditions. No air or clouds intervened, and as the Callisto did not revolve on its axis there was no necessity for changing the direction of the glasses. After an hour of this interesting work, however, as it was already late at the longitude they had left on earth, and as they knew they had many days in space before them, they prepared to go to bed. When ready, they had only to pull down the shades; for, as apergy was not applied to them, but only to the Callisto, they still looked upon the floor as down, and closed the heavy curtains to have night or darkness. They found that the side of the Callisto turned constantly towards the sun was becoming very warm, the double-toughened glass windows making it like a greenhouse; but they consoled themselves with the thought that the sun's power on them was hourly becoming less, and they felt sure the double walls and thick upholstery would protect them almost anywhere within the solar system from the intense cold of space.

"We could easily have arranged," said Ayrault, "for night and day on alternate sides of the Callisto by having strips of metal arranged spirally on the outside as on the end of an arrow. These would have started us turning as slowly as we like, since we passed through the atmosphere at a comparatively low rate of speed."

"I am afraid," said Cortlandt, "the motion, however slow, would have made us dizzy. It would be confusing to see the heavens turning about us, and it would interfere with using the glasses."

The base and one side of the Callisto had constant sunshine, while the other side and the dome were in the blackest night. This dome, on account of its shape, sky windows, and the completeness with which it could be isolated, was an ideal observatory, and there was seldom a time during their waking hours for the rest of the journey when it was not occupied by one, two, or all the observers.

"There is something marvellous," said Cortlandt, "about the condition of space. Its absolute cold is appalling, apparently because there is nothing to absorb heat; yet we find the base of this material projectile uncomfortably warm, though, should we expose a thermometer in the shade in front, we know it would show a temperature of three hundred to four hundred degrees below zero--were the instrument capable of recording it."

Artificial darkness having been obtained, the travellers were soon asleep, Bearwarden's dreams being regaled with thoughts of his company's triumph; Ayrault's, naturally, with visions of Sylvia; while Cortlandt frequently started up, thinking he had already made some great astronomical discovery.

About 9 A. M., according to seventy-fifth meridian time, the explorers awoke feeling greatly refreshed. The tank in which the liquefied oxygen was kept automatically gave off its gas so evenly that the air remained normal, while the lime contained in cups absorbed the carbon dioxide as fast as they exhaled it. They had darkened those windows through which the sun was actually pouring, for, on account of the emptiness of the surrounding ether and consequent absence of diffusion of light, nothing but the inky blackness of space and the bright stars looked in at the rest. On raising the shades they got an idea of their speed. A small crescent, smaller than the familiar moon, accompanied by one still tinier, was all that could be seen of the earth and its satellite.

"We must," said Bearwarden, "be moving at the rate of nearly a million miles an hour, from the way we have travelled."

"We must be doing fully a million," replied Cortlandt, "for by this time we are pretty well in motion, having got a tremendous start when so near the moon, with it and the earth in line."

By steering straight for Jupiter, instead of for the place it would occupy ten days later, they knew they would swing past, for the giant planet, being in rapid motion, would advance; but they did not object to this, since it would give them a chance to examine their new world in case they wished to do so before alighting; while, if they preferred to land at once, they could easily change their course by means of the moons, the fourth, from which their car was named, being the one that they knew would be of most use. Their tremendous speed showed them they should have time for exploration on their arrival, and that they would reach their destination sooner than they had expected. The apergetic force being applied, as we have seen, only to the Callisto, just as power in starting is exerted on a carriage or railway car and only through it to the passengers, Ayrault and his companions had no unusual sensation except loss of weight, for, when they were so far from the earth, its attraction was very slight, and no other planet was near enough to take its place. After breakfast, wishing to reach the dome, and realizing that it would be unnecessary to climb, each in turn gave a slight spring and was obliged to put up his hands to avoid striking the roof. In the cool quiet of the dark dome it was difficult to believe that only twenty feet away the sun was shining with such intensity upon the metal base as to make it too hot on the inside to touch without gloves.

The first thing that attracted their attention was the size and brilliance of Mars. Although this red planet was over forty million miles from the earth when they started, they calculated that it was less than thirty million miles from them now, or five millions nearer than it had ever been to them before. This reduction in distance, and the clearness of the void through which they saw it, made it a splendid sight, its disk showing clearly. From hour to hour its size and brightness increased, till towards evening it looked like a small, full moon, the sun shining squarely upon it. They calculated that on the course they were moving they should pass about nine hundred thousand miles to the right or behind it, since it was moving towards their left. They were interested to see what effect the mass of Mars would have on the Callisto, and saw here a chance of still further increasing their speed. Notwithstanding its tremendous rate, they expected to see the Callisto swerve from its straight line and move towards Mars, whose orbital speed of nine hundred miles a minute they thought would take it out of the Callisto's way, so that no actual collision would occur even if their air-ship were left to her own devices.

Towards evening they noticed through their glasses that several apparently island peaks in the southern hemisphere, which was turned towards them, became white, from which they concluded that a snow-storm was in progress. The south polar region was also markedly glaciated, though the icecap was not as extensive as either of those at the poles of the earth.

"As the Martian winters must be fully as severe as ours," said Cortlandt, "on account of their length, the planet's distance from the sun, and the twenty-seven and a half degrees inclination of its axis, we can account for the smallness of its ice-caps only by the fact that its oceans cover but one fourth of its surface instead of three quarters, as on the earth, and there is consequently a smaller evaporation and rain and snow-fall."

They were too much interested to think of sleeping that night, and so, after dining comfortably returned to their observatory. When within four million miles of Mars the Callisto began to swerve perceptibly, its curve, as when near the moon beginning with a spiral. They swung on unconcernedly, however, knowing they could check their approach at any time. Soon Mars appeared to have a diameter ten times as great as that of the moon, and promised shortly to occupy almost one side of their sky. "We must be on the lookout for the satellites," said Cortlandt; "a collision with either would be worse than a wreck on a desert island."

They therefore turned their glasses in the direction of the satellites.

"Until Prof. Hall, at Washington, discovered the two satellites in 1877," he continued, "Mars was supposed to be without moons. The outer one, Deimos, is but six miles in diameter, and revolves about its primary in thirty hours and eighteen minutes, at a distance of fourteen thousand six hundred miles. As it takes but little longer to complete a revolution than Mars does to rotate on its axis, it remains in the Martial sky one hundred and thirty-two hours between rising and setting, passing through all the phases from new moon to full and back again four times; that is, it swings four times around Mars before going below the horizon. It is one of the smallest bodies discovered with a telescope. The inner one, Phobos, is considerably larger, having a diameter of about twenty miles. It is but twenty-seven hundred miles from Mars's surface, and completes its revolution in seven hours and thirty-eight minutes, which is shorter than any other known period, Jupiter's nearest moon being the next, with eleven hours and fifty-nine minutes. It thus revolves in less than a third of the time Mars takes to rotate, and must consequently rise in the west and set in the east, as it is continually running ahead of the surface of the planet, though the sun and all the other stars rise and set on Mars in the same way as on the earth."

When about fifteen thousand miles from Mars, they sighted Deimos directly ahead, and saw that they should pass on its left--i. e., behind--for it was moving across them. The sun poured directly upon it, making it appear full and showing all its features. There were small unevennesses on the surface, apparently seventy or a hundred feet high, which were the nearest approach to mountains, and they ran in ridges or chains. There were also unmistakable signs of volcanic action, the craters being large compared with the size of the planet, but shallow. They saw no signs of water, and the blackness of the shadows convinced them there was no air. They secured two instantaneous photographs of the little satellite as the Callisto swept by, and resumed their inspection of Mars. They noticed red and brownish patches on the peaks that had that morning turned white, from which they concluded that the snow had begun to melt under the warm spring sun. This strengthened the belief they had already formed, that on account of its twenty-seven and a half degrees inclination the changes in temperature on Mars must be great and sudden. So interested were they with this, that they did not at first see a large and bright body moving rapidly on a course that converged with theirs.

"We must be ready to repel boarders," said Bearwarden, observing it for the first time and fixing his glass upon it. "That must be Phobos."

Not ten miles off they beheld Mars's inner moon, and though their own speed caused them to overtake and rush by it like a whirlwind, the satellite's rapid motion in its orbit, in a course temporarily almost parallel with theirs, served to give them a chance the better to examine it. Here the mountain ranges were considerably more conspicuous than on Deimos, and there were boulders and loose stones upon their slopes, which looked as if there might at some time have been frost and water on its surface; but it was all dry now, neither was there any air. The evidences of volcanic action were also plainly visible, while a noticeable flattening at the poles showed that the little body had once rotated rapidly on its axis, though whether it did so still they had not time to ascertain. When abreast of it they were less than two miles distant, and they secured several instantaneous impressions, which they put aside to develop later. As the radius of Phobos's circle was far shorter than that of the parabolic curve they were making, it began to draw away, and was rapidly left behind. Applying the full apergetic force to Mars and the larger moon, they shot away like an arrow, having had their speed increased by the planet's attraction while approaching it, and subsequently by repulsion.

"Either of those," said Bearwarden, looking back at the little satellites, "would be a nice yacht for a man to explore space on. He would also, of course, need a sun to warm him, if he wished to go beyond this system, but that would not have to be a large affair--in fact, it might be smaller than the planet, and could revolve about it like a moon."

"Though a sun of that size," replied Cortlandt, "might retain its heat for the time you wished to use it, the planet part would be nothing like as comfortable as what we have here, for it would be very difficult to get enough air-pressure to breathe on so small a body, since, with its slight gravitation-pull, to secure fifteen pounds to the square inch, or anything like it, the atmosphere would have to extend thousands of miles into space, so that on a cloudy day you would be in darkness. It would be better, therefore, to have such a sun as you describe and accompany it in a yacht or private car like this, well stocked with oxygen and provisions. When passing through meteoric swarms or masses of solid matter, collision with which is the most serious risk we run, the car could follow behind its sun instead of revolving around it, and be kept from falling into it by partially reversing the attraction. As the gravitation of so small a sun would be slight, counteracting it for even a considerable time would take but little from the batteries."

"There are known to be several unclaimed masses," added Ayrault, "with diameters of a few hundred yards, revolving about the earth inside the orbit of the moon. If in some way two of these could be brought into sufficiently violent collision, they would become luminous and answer very well; the increase in bulk as a result of the consolidation, and the subsequent heat, about serving to bring them to the required size. Whenever this sun showed spots and indications of cooling, it could be made to collide with the solid head of some comet, or small asteroid, till its temperature was again right; while if, as a result of these accretions, it became unwieldy, it could be caused to rotate with sufficient rapidity on its axis to split, and we should have two suns instead of one."

"Bravo!" said Bearwarden. "There is no limit to what can be done. The idea of our present trip would have seemed more chimerical to people a hundred years ago than this new scheme appears now."

Thus they sat and talked, or studied maps and star-charts, or the stars themselves, while the hours quickly passed and they shot through space. They had now a straight stretch of over three hundred million miles, and had to cross the orbits of innumerable asteroids on the way. The apparent size of the sun had by this time considerably decreased, and the interior of the Callisto was no longer uncomfortably warm. They divided the day into twenty-four hours from force of habit, and drew the shades tightly during what they considered night, while Bearwarden distinguished himself as a cook.

CHAPTER III
HEAVENLY BODIES

The following day, while in their observatory, they saw something not many miles ahead. They watched it for hours, and in fact all day, but notwithstanding their tremendous speed they came but little nearer.

"They say a stern chase is a long one," said Bearwarden; "but that beats anything I have ever seen."

After a while, however, they found they WERE nearer, the time taken having been in part due to the deceptive distance, which was greater than they supposed.

"A comet!" exclaimed Cortlandt excitedly. "We shall really be able to examine it near."

"It's going in our direction," said Ayrault, "and at almost exactly our speed."

While the sun shone full upon it they brought their camera into play, and again succeeded in photographing a heavenly body at close range. The nucleus or head was of course turned towards the sun; while the tail, which they could see faintly, preceded it, as the comet was receding towards the cold and dark depths of space. The head was only a few miles in diameter, for it was a small comet, and was composed of grains and masses of stone and meteoric iron. Many of the grains were no larger than peas or mustard-seeds; no mass was more than four feet in diameter, and all of them had very irregular shapes. The space between the particles was never less than one hundred times their masses.

"We can move about within it," said Ayrault, as the Callisto entered the aggregation of particles, and moved slowly forward among them.

The windows in the dome, being made of toughened glass, set somewhat slantingly so as to deflect anything touching them, and having, moreover, the pressure of the inside air to sustain them, were fairly safe, while the windows in the sides and base were but little exposed. Whenever a large mass seemed dangerously near the glass, they applied an apergetic shock to it and sent it kiting among its fellows. At these times the Callisto recoiled slightly also, the resulting motion in either being in inverse ratio to its weight. There was constant and incessant movement among the individual fragments, but it was not rotary. Nothing seemed to be revolving about anything else; all were moving, apparently swinging back and forth, but no collisions took place. When the separate particles got more than a certain distance apart they reapproached one another, but when seemingly within about one hundred diameters of each other they swung off in some other direction. The motion was like that of innumerable harp-strings, which may approach but never strike one another. After a time the Callisto seemed to become endowed with the same property that the fragments possessed; for it and they repelled one another, on a near approach, after which nothing came very near.

Much of the material was like slag from a furnace, having evidently been partly fused. Whether this heat was the result of collision or of its near approach to the sun at perihelion, they could not tell, though the latter explanation seemed most simple and probable. When at about the centre of the nucleus they were in semi-darkness--not twilight, for any ray that succeeded in penetrating was dazzlingly brilliant, and the shadows, their own included, were inky black. As they approached the farther side and the sunlight decreased, they found that a diffused luminosity pervaded everything. It was sufficiently bright to enable them to see the dark side of the meteoric masses, and, on emerging from the nucleus in total darkness, they found the shadow stretching thousands of miles before them into space.

"I now understand," said Bearwarden, "why stars of the sixth and seventh magnitude can be seen through thousands of miles of a comet's tail. It is simply because there is nothing in it. The reason ANY stars are obscured is because the light in the tail, however faint, is brighter than they, and that light is all that the caudal appendage consists of, though what produces it I confess I am unable to explain. I also see why the tail always stretches away from the sun, because near by it is overwhelmed by the more powerful light; in fact, I suspect it is principally in the comet's shadow that the tail is visible. It is strange that no one ever thought of that before, or that any one feared the earth's passing through the tail of a comet. It is obvious to me now that if there were any material substance, any gas, however rarefied, in this hairlike* accompaniment, it would immediately fall to the comparatively heavy head, and surround that as a centre." * Comet means literally a hair.

"How, then," asked Cortlandt, "do you account for the spaces between those stones? However slight gravitation might be between some of the grains, if it existed at all, or was unopposed by some other force, with sufficient time--and they have eternity--every comet would come together like a planet into one solid mass. Perhaps some similar force maintains gases in the distended tail, though I know of no such, or even any analogous manifestation on earth. If the law on which we have been brought up, that 'every atom in the universe attracts every other atom,' were without exceptions or modifications, that comet could not continue to exist in its present form. Until we get some additional illustration, however, we shall be short of data with which to formulate any iconoclastic hypothesis. The source of the light, I must admit, also puzzles me greatly. There is certainly no heat to which we can attribute it."

Having gone beyond the fragments, they applied a strong repulsion charge to the comet, creating thereby a perfect whirlpool among its particles, and quickly left it. Half an hour later they again shut off the current, as the Callisto's speed was sufficient.

For some time they had been in the belt of asteroids, but as yet they had seen none near. The morning following their experience with the comet, however, they went to their observatory after breakfast as usual, and, on pointing their glasses forward, espied a comparatively large body before them, a little to their right.

"That must be Pallas," said Cortlandt, scrutinizing it closely. "It was discovered by Olbers, in 1802, and was the second asteroid found, Ceres having been the first, in 1801. It has a diameter of about three hundred miles, being one of the largest of these small planets. The most wonderful thing about it is the inclination of its orbit--thirty-five degrees--to the plane of the ecliptic; which means that at each revolution in its orbit, it swings that much above and below the imaginary plane cutting the sun at its equator, from which the earth and other larger planets vary but little. This no doubt is due to the near approach and disturbing attraction of some large comet, or else it was flung above or below the ordinary plane in the catastrophe that we think befell the large planet that doubtless formerly existed where we now find this swarm. You can see that its path makes a considerable angle to the plane of the ecliptic, and that it is now about crossing the line."

It soon presented the phase of a half moon, but the waviness of the straight line, as in the case of Venus and Mercury, showed that the size of the mountains must be tremendous compared with the mass of the body, some of them being obviously fifteen miles high. The intense blackness of the shadows, as on the moon, convinced them there was no trace of atmosphere.

"There being no air," said Cortlandt, "it is safe to assume there is no water, which helps to account for the great inequalities on the body's surface, since the mountains will seem higher when surrounded by dry ocean-bottom than they would if water came halfway up their sides. Undoubtedly, however, the main cause of their height is the slight effect of gravitation on an asteroid, and the fact that the shrinking of the interior, and consequent folding of the crust in ridges, may have continued for a time after there was no longer water on the surface to cut them down.

"The temperature and condition of a body," continued Cortlandt, "seem to depend entirely on its size. In the sun we have an incandescent, gaseous star, though its spots and the colour of its rays show that it is becoming aged, or, to be more accurate, advanced in its evolutionary development. Then comes a great jump, for Jupiter has but about one fourteen-hundredth of the mass of the sun, and we expect to find on it a firm crust, and that the planet itself is at about the fourth or fifth period of development, described by Moses as days. Saturn is doubtless somewhat more advanced. The earth we know has been habitable many hundreds of thousands or millions of years, though three fourths of its surface is still covered by water. In Mars we see a further step, three fourths of its surface being land. In Mercury, could we study it better, or in the larger satellites of Jupiter or Saturn, we might find a stepping-stone from Mars to the moon, perhaps with no water, but still having air, and being habitable in all other respects. In our own satellite we see a world that has died, though its death from an astronomical point of view is comparatively recent, while this little Pallas has been dead longer, being probably chilled through and through. From this I conclude that all bodies in the solar system had one genesis, and were part of the same nebulous mass. But this does not include the other systems and nebulae; for, compared with them, our sun, as we have seen, is itself advanced and small beside such stars as Sirius having diameters of twelve million miles."

As they left Pallas between themselves and the sun, it became a crescent and finally disappeared.

Two days later they sighted another asteroid exactly ahead. They examined it closely, and concluded it must be Hilda, put down in the astronomies as No. 153, and having almost the greatest mean distance of any of these small bodies from the sun.

When they were so near that the disk was plainly visible to the unaided eye, Hilda passed between them and Jupiter, eclipsing it. To their surprise, the light was not instantly shut off, as when the moon occults a star, but there was evident refraction.

"By George!" said Bearwarden, "here is an asteroid that HAS an atmosphere."

There was no mistaking it. They soon discovered a small ice-cap at one pole, and then made out oceans and continents, with mountains, forests, rivers, and green fields. The sight lasted but a few moments before they swept by, but they secured several photographs, and carried a vivid impression in their minds. Hilda appeared to be about two hundred miles in diameter.

"How do you account for that living world," Bearwarden asked Cortlandt, "on your theory of size and longevity?"

"There are two explanations," replied Cortlandt, "if the theory, as I still believe, is correct. Hilda has either been brought to this system from some other less matured, in the train of a comet, and been captured by the immense power of Jupiter, which might account for the eccentricity of its orbit, or some accident has happened to rejuvenate it here. A collision with another minor planet moving in an orbit that crossed its own, or with the head of a large comet, would have reconverted it into a star, perhaps after it had long been cold. A comet may first have so changed the course of one of two small bodies as to make them collide. This seems to me the most plausible theory. Over a hundred years ago the English astronomer, Chambers, wrote of having found traces of atmosphere in some of these minor planets, but it was generally thought he was mistaken. One reason we know so little about this great swarm of minor planets is, that till recently none of them showed a disk to the telescope. Inasmuch as only their light was visible, they were indistinguishable from stars, except by their slow motion. A hundred years ago only three hundred and fifty had been discovered; our photographic star-charts have since then shown the number recorded to exceed one thousand."

Comparative Size of Planet

CHAPTER IV
PREPARING TO ALIGHT

That afternoon Ayrault brought out some statistical tables he had compiled from a great number of books, and also a diagram of the comparative sizes of the planets. "I have been not a little puzzled at the discrepancies between even the best authors," he said, "scarcely any two being exactly alike, while every decade has seen accepted theories radically changed." Saying which, he spread out the result of his labours (shown on the following pages), which the three friends then studied.

Planets	Mean distance from sun in millions of miles	Semimajor axis of orbit, earth's distance as 1	Eccentricity of orbit	Inclination of orbit to eliptic	Light at perihelion	Light at aphelion	Heat, earth as 1
Mercury	36.0	0.387	0.2056	7° 0' 8"	10.58	4.59	6.67
Venus	67.2	0.723	0.0068	3° 23' 35"	1.94	1.91	1.91
The Earth	92.9	1.000	0.068	0° 0' 0"	1.03	0.997	1.00
Mars	141.5	1.524	0.0933	1° 51' 2"	0.52	0.360	1.43
Asteroids	204.4 to 325.2	2.200 to 3.5000	0.4 to 0.84	5° to 35°			
Jupiter	483.3	5.203	0.0483	1° 18' 41"	0.04	0.034	0.037
Saturn	886.0	9.539	0.0561	2° 29' 40"	0.012	0.0099	0.011
Uranus	1781.9	19.183	0.0463	0° 46' 20"	0.0027	0.0025	0.003
Neptune	2791.6	30.055	0.0090	1° 47' 2"	0.0011	0.0011	0.001

MOVEMENT IN ORBIT.

Planets	Period of revolution in years and days	Orbital velocity in miles per second.	Velocity, earth's as 1.	Mean diameter in miles.	Surface compared with earth as 1.	Volume compared with earth as 1.	Mass compared with earth as 1.
Mercury...	0.88	23 to 35	1.6	3,000	0.14	0.056	0.13
Venus.....	0.224 1/2	21.9	1.17	7,700	0.94	0.92	0.78
The Earth.	1.00	18.5	1.0	7,918	1.00	1.00	1.00
Mars......	1.88	15.0	0.81	4,230	0.28	0.139	0.124
Asteroids	3.29 to 6.56			From a few miles to 300			
Jupiter..	11.86	8.1	0.44	86,500	118.3	1309.000	316.0
Saturn...	29.46	6.0	0.32	71,000	80.4	760.0	95.0
Uranus..	84.02	4.2	0.23	31,900	16.3	65.0	14.7
Neptune.	164.78	3.4	0.18	34,800	19.3	90.0	17.1

Planets	DENSITY Compared with earth as 1	Compared with water as 1	FORCE OF GRAVITY AT SURFACE OF PLANET Compared with earth as 1	Bodies fall in one second.	Length of day.	Length of seasons	Inclination of axis.
Mercury.	1.24	7.17	0.85	13.7			
Venus...	0.92	5.21	0.83	13.4	hr mn sc 23 21 22		53+
The Earth.	1.00	5.67	1.00	16.09		Spring, 93 days Summer, 93 days Autumn, 90 days Winter, 89 days	23 1/2
Mars...	0.96	2.54	0.38	6.2		Spring, 191 days Summer, 181 days Autumn, 149 days Winter, 147 days	27 1/2
Asteroids.							
Jupiter.	0.22	1.29	2.55	40.98	9 55 28		1 1/2
Saturn..	0.13	0.63	1.15	18.53	10 29 17		27
Uranus.	0.18	1.41	0.91	14.6			102(?)
Neptune.	0.20	0.94	0.88	14.2			

"You see," Ayrault explained, "on Jupiter we shall need our apergetic outfits to enable us to make long marches, while on Saturn they will not be necessary, the increase in our weight as a result of that planet's size being considerably less than the usual load carried by the Roman soldier."

"I do not imagine," said Cortlandt, "we should long be troubled by gravitation without our apergetic outfits even on Jupiter, for, though our weight will be more than doubled, we can take off one quarter of the whole by remaining near the equator, their rapid rotation having apparently been given providentially to all the large planets. Nature will adapt herself to this change, as to all others, very readily. Although the reclamation of the vast areas of the North American Arctic Archipelago, Alaska, Siberia, and Antarctic Wilkes Land, from the death-grip of the ice in which they have been held will relieve the pressure of population for another century, at the end of that time it will surely be felt again; it is therefore a consolation to feel that the mighty planets Jupiter and Saturn, which we are coming to look upon as our heritage, will not crush the life out of any human beings by their own weight that may alight upon them."

Before going to bed that evening they decided to be up early the next day, to study Jupiter, which was already a brilliant object.

The following morning, on awakening, they went at once to their observatory, and found that Jupiter's disk was plainly visible to the naked eye, and before night it seemed as large as the full moon.

They then prepared to check the Callisto's headlong speed, which Jupiter's attraction was beginning to increase. When about two million miles from the great planet, which was considerably on their left, they espied Callisto ahead and slightly on their right, as Deepwaters had calculated it would be. Applying a mild repulsion to this--which was itself quite a world, with its diameter of over three thousand miles, though evidently as cold and dead as the earth's old moon--they retarded their forward rush, knowing that the resulting motion towards Jupiter would be helped by the giant's pull. Wishing to be in good condition for their landing, they divided the remainder of the night into watches, two going to sleep at a time, the man on duty standing by to control the course and to get photographic negatives, on which, when they were developed, they found two crescent-shaped continents, a speckled region, and a number of islands. By 7 A. M., according to Eastern standard time, they were but fifty thousand miles from Jupiter's surface, the gigantic globe filling nearly one side of the sky. In preparation for a sally, they got their guns and accoutrements ready, and then gave a parting glance at the car. Their charge of electricity for developing the repulsion seemed scarcely touched, and they had still an abundant supply of oxygen and provisions. The barometer registered twenty-nine inches, showing that they had not lost much air in the numerous openings of the vestibule. The pressure was about what would be found at an altitude of a few hundred feet, part of the rarefaction being no doubt due to the fact that they did not close the windows until at a considerable height above Van Cortlandt Park.

They saw they should alight in a longitude on which the sun had just risen, the rocky tops of the great mountains shining like helmets in its rays. Soon they felt a sharp checking of their forward motion, and saw, from the changed appearance of the stars and the sun, that they had entered the atmosphere of their new home.

Not even did Columbus, standing at the prow of the Santa Maria, with the New World before him, feel the exultation and delight experienced by these latter-day explorers of the twenty-first century. Their first adventures on landing the reader already knows.

CHAPTER V
EXPLORATION AND EXCITEMENT

When they awoke, the flowers were singing with the volume of a cathedral organ, the chant rising from all around them, and the sun was already above the horizon. Finding a deep natural spring, in which the water was at about blood-heat, they prepared for breakfast by taking a bath, and then found they had brought nothing to eat.

"It was stupid of us not to think of it," said Bearwarden, "yet it will be too much out of our way to return to the Callisto."

"We have two rifles and a gun," said Ayrault, "and have also plenty of water, and wood for a fire. All we need is game."

"The old excuse, that it has been already shot out, cannot hold here," said Cortlandt.

"Seeing that we have neither wings nor pneumatic legs, and not knowing the advantage given us by our rifles," added Bearwarden, "it should not be shy either. So far," he continued, "we have seen nothing edible, though just now we should not be too particular; but near a spring like this that kind must exist."

"The question is," said the professor, "whether the game like warm water. If we can follow this stream till it has been on the surface for some time, or till it spreads out, we shall doubtless find a huntsman's paradise."

"A bright idea," said Bearwarden. "Let's have our guns ready, and, as old Deepwaters would say, keep our weather eye open."

The stream flowed off in a southeasterly direction, so that by following it they went towards the volcanoes.

"It is hard to realize," said the professor, "that those mountains must be several hundred miles away, for the reason that they are almost entirely above the horizon. This apparent flatness and wide range of vision is of course the result of Jupiter's vast size. With sufficiently keen sight, or aided by a good glass, there is no reason why one should not see at least five hundred miles, with but a slight elevation."

"It is surprising," said Ayrault, "that in what is evidently Jupiter's Carboniferous period the atmosphere should be so clear. Our idea has been that at that time on earth the air was heavy and dense."

"So it was, and doubtless is here," replied Cortlandt; "but you must remember that both those qualities would be given it by carbonic-acid gas, which is entirely invisible and transparent. No gas that would be likely to remain in the air would interfere with sight; water vapour is the only thing that could; and though the crust of this planet, even near the surface, is still hot, the sun being so distant, the vapour would not be raised much. By avoiding low places near hot springs, we shall doubtless have very nearly as clear an atmosphere as on earth. What does surprise me is the ease with which we breathe. I can account for it only by supposing that, the Carboniferous period being already well advanced, most of the carbonic acid is already locked up in the forests or in Jupiter's coal-beds."

"How," asked Bearwarden, "do you account for the 'great red spot' that appeared here in 1878, lasted several years, and then gradually faded? It was taken as unmistakable evidence that Jupiter's atmosphere was filled with impenetrable banks of cloud. In fact, you remember many of the old books said we had probably never seen the surface."

"That has puzzled me very much," replied Cortlandt, "but I never believed the explanation then given was correct. The Carboniferous period is essentially one of great forest growth; so there would be nothing out of the way in supposing the spot, notwithstanding its length of twenty-seven thousand miles and its breadth of eight thousand miles, to have been forest. It occurred in what would correspond to the temperate region on earth. Now, though the axis of this planet is practically straight, the winds of course change their direction, and so the temperature does vary from day to day. What is more probable than that, owing perhaps to a prolonged norther or cold spell, a long strip of forest lying near the frost line was brought a few degrees below it, so that the leaves changed their colours as they do on earth? It would, it seems to me, be enough to give the surface a distinct colour; and the fact that the spot's greatest length was east and west, or along the lines of latitude, so that the whole of that region might have been exposed to the same conditions of temperature, strengthens this hypothesis. The strongest objection is, that the spot is said to have moved; but the motion--five seconds--was so slight that it might easily have been an error in observation, or the first area affected by the cold may have been enlarged on one side. It seems to me that the stability the spot DID have would make the cloud theory impossible on earth, and much more so here, with the far more rapid rotation and more violent winds. It may also have been a cloud of smoke from a volcano in eruption, such as we saw on our arrival, though it is doubtful whether in that case it would have remained nearly stationary while going through its greatest intensity and fading, which would look as though the turned leaves had fallen off and been gradually replaced by new ones; and, in addition to this, the spot since it was first noticed has never entirely disappeared, which might mean a volcanic region constantly emitting smoke, or that the surface, doubtless from some covering whose colour can change, is normally of a different shade from the surrounding region. In any case, we have as yet seen nothing that would indicate a permanently clouded atmosphere."

Though they had walked a considerable distance, the water was not much cooled; and though the stream's descent was so slight that on earth its current would have been very slow, here it rushed along like a mountain torrent, the reason, of course, being that a given amount of water on Jupiter would depress a spring balance 2.55 times as much as on the earth.

"It is strange," said Ayrault, "that, notwithstanding its great speed, the water remains so hot; you would think its motion would cool it."

"So it does," answered the professor. "It of course cools considerably more in a given period--as, for instance, one minute--than if it were moving more slowly, but on account of its speed it has been exposed to the air but a very short time since leaving the spring."

Just before them the stream now widened into a narrow lake, which they could see was straight for some distance.

"The fact is," said Bearwarden, "this water seems in such haste to reach the ocean that it turns neither to right nor to left, and does not even seem to wish to widen out."

As the huge ferns and palms grew to the water's edge, they concluded the best way to traverse the lake would be on a raft. Accordingly, choosing a large overhanging palm, Bearwarden and Ayrault fired each an explosive ball into its trunk, about eighteen inches from the ground. One round was enough to put it in the water, each explosion removing several cubic feet of wood. By repeating this process on other trees they soon had enough large timber for buoyancy, so that they had but to superimpose lighter cross-logs and bind the whole together with pliable branches and creepers to form a substantial raft. The doctor climbed on, after which Bearwarden and Ayrault cast off, having prepared long poles for navigating. With a little care they kept their bark from catching on projecting roots, and as the stream continued to widen till it was about one hundred yards across, their work became easy. Carried along at a speed of two or three miles an hour, they now saw that the water and the banks they passed were literally alive with reptiles and all sorts of amphibious creatures, while winged lizards sailed from every overhanging branch into the water as they approached. They noticed also many birds similar to storks and cranes, about the size of ostriches, standing on logs in the water, whose bills were provided with teeth.

"We might almost think we were on earth," said Ayrault, "from the looks of those storks standing on one leg, with the other drawn up, were it not for their size."

"How do you suppose they defend themselves," asked Bearwarden, "from the snakes with which the water is filled?"

"I suspect they can give a pretty good account of themselves," replied Cortlandt, "with those teeth. Besides, with only one leg exposed, there is but a very small object for a snake to strike at. For their number and size, I should say their struggle for existence was comparatively mild. Doubtless non-poisonous, or, for that matter, poisonous snakes, form a great part of their diet."

On passing the bend in the lake they noticed that the banks were slightly higher, while palms, pine-trees, and rubber plants succeeded the ferns. In the distance they now heard a tremendous crashing, which grew louder as the seconds passed. It finally sounded like an earthquake. Involuntarily they held their breath and grasped their weapons. Finally, at some distance in the woods they saw a dark mass moving rapidly and approaching the river obliquely. Palms and pine-trees went down before it like straws, while its head was continually among the upper branches. As the monster neared the lake, the water at the edges quivered, showing how its weight shook the banks at each stride, while stumps and tree-trunks on which it stepped were pressed out of sight in the ground. A general exodus of the other inhabitants from his line of march began; the moccasins slid into the water with a low splash, while the boa-constrictors and the tree-snakes moved off along the ground when they felt it tremble, and a number of night birds retreated into the denser woods with loud cries at being so rudely disturbed. The huge beast did not stop till he reached the bank, where he switched his tail, raised his proboscis, and sniffed the air uneasily, his height being fully thirty feet and his length about fifty. On seeing the raft and its occupants, he looked at them stupidly and threw back his head.

"He seems to be turning up his nose at us," said Bearwarden. "All the same, he will do well for breakfast."

As the creature moved, his chest struck a huge overhanging palm, tearing it off as though it had been a reed. Brushing it aside with his trunk, he was about to continue his march, when two rifle reports rang out together, rousing the echoes and a number of birds that screeched loudly.

CHAPTER VI
MASTODON AND WILL-O'-THE WISPS

Bearwarden's bullet struck the mammoth in the shoulder, while Ayrault's aim was farther back. As the balls exploded, a half-barrelful of flesh and hide was shot from each, leaving two gaping holes. Instantly he rushed among the trees, making his course known for some time by his roars. As he turned, Bearwarden fired again, but the ball flew over him, blowing off the top of a tree.

"Now for the chase!" said Ayrault. "There would be no excuse for losing him."

Quickly pushing their raft to shore and securing it to the bank, the three jumped off. Thanks to their rubber boots and galvanic outfits which automatically kept them charged, they were as spry as they would have been on earth. The ground all about them, and in a strip twelve feet wide where the mammoth had gone, was torn up, and the vegetation trodden down. Following this trail, they struck back into the woods, where in places the gloom cast by the thick foliage was so dense that there was a mere twilight, startling as they went numbers of birds of grey and sombre plumage, whose necks and heads, and the sounds they uttered, were so reptilian that the three terrestrials believed they must also possess poison fangs.

"The most highly developed things we have seen here," said Bearwarden, "are the flowers and fireflies, most of the birds and amphibians being simply loathsome."

As they proceeded they found tracks of blood, which were rapidly attracting swarms of the reptile birds and snakes, which, however, as a rule, fled at their approach.

"I wonder what can have caused that mammoth to move so fast, and to have seemed so ill at ease?" said the doctor. "His motive certainly was not thirst, for he did not approach the water in a direct line, neither did he drink on reaching it. One would think nothing short of an earthquake or a landslide could trouble him." "There can be no land-slide here," said Ayrault, "for the country is too flat."

"And after yesterday's eruptions," added Bearwarden, "it would seem as though the volcanoes could have scarcely enough steam left to make trouble."

The blood-tracks, continuing to become fresher, showed them they were nearing the game, when suddenly the trail took a sharp turn to the right, even returning towards the lake. A little farther it took another sharp turn, then followed a series of doublings, while still farther the ground was completely denuded of trees, its torn-up and trampled condition and the enormous amount of still warm blood showing how terrific a battle had just taken place.

While they looked about they saw what appeared to be the trunk of a tree about four feet in diameter and six feet long, with a slight crook. On coming closer, they recognized in it one of the forefeet of the mammoth, cut as cleanly as though with a knife from the leg just above the ankle, and still warm. A little farther they found the huge trunk cut to slivers, and, just beyond, the body of the unfortunate beast with three of its feet gone, and the thick hide cut and slashed like so much paper. It still breathed, and Ayrault, who had a tender heart, sent an explosive ball into its skull, which ended its suffering.

The three hunters then surveyed the scene. The largest and most powerful beast they had believed could exist lay before them dead, not from the bite of a snake or any other poison, but from mechanical injuries of which those they had inflicted formed but a very small part, and literally cut to pieces.

"I am curious to see the animal," said Cortlandt, "capable of doing this, though nothing short of dynamite bombs would protect us from him."

"As he has not stopped to eat his victim," said Bearwarden, "it is fair to suppose he is not carnivorous, and so must have had some other motive than hunger in making the attack; unless we can suppose that our approach frightened him away, which, with such power as he must possess, seems unlikely. Let us see," he continued, "parts of two legs remain unaccounted for. Perhaps, on account of their shape, he has been able the more easily to carry or roll them off, for we know that elephant foot makes a capital dish."

"From the way you talk," said Cortlandt, "one would suppose you attributed this to men. The Goliath we picture to ourselves would be a child compared to the man that could cut through these legs, though the necessity of believing him to have merely great size does not disprove his existence here. I think it probable we shall find this is the work of some animal with incisors of such power as it is difficult for us to conceive of."

"There is no indication here of teeth," said Bearwarden, "each foot being taken off with a clean cut. Besides, we are coming to believe that man existed on earth during the greater part, if not the whole, of our Carboniferous period."

"We must reserve our decision pending further evidence," said Cortlandt.

"I vote we take the heart," said Ayrault, "and cook it, since otherwise the mammoth will be devoured before our eyes."

While Bearwarden and Ayrault delved for this, Cortlandt, with some difficulty, parted the mammoth's lips and examined the teeth. "From the conical projections on the molars," said he, "this should be classed rather as a mastodon than as a mammoth."

When the huge heart was secured, Bearwarden arranged slices on sharpened sticks, while Ayrault set about starting a fire. He had to use Cortlandt's gun to clear the dry wood of snakes, which, attracted doubtless by the dead mastodon, came in such numbers that they covered the ground, while huge pterodactyls, more venomous-looking than the reptiles, hovered about the opening above.

Arranging a double line of electric wires in a circle about the mastodon and themselves, they sat down and did justice to the meal, with appetites that might have dismayed the waiting throng. Whenever a snake's head came in contact with one wire, while his tail touched the other, he gave a spasmodic leap and fell back dead. If he happened to fall across the wires, he immediately began to sizzle, a cloud of smoke arose, and he was reduced to ashes.

"Any time that we are short of mastodon or other good game," said Ayrault, "we need not hunger if we are not above grilled snake."

All laughed at this, and Bearwarden, drawing a whiskey-flask from his pocket, passed it to his friends.

"When we rig our fishing-tackle," he continued, "and have fresh fish for dinner, an entree of rattlesnake, roast mastodon for the piece de resistance, and begin the whole with turtle soup and clams, of which there must be plenty on the ocean beach, we shall want to stay here the rest of our lives."

"I suspect we shall have to," replied Ayrault "for we shall become so like Thanksgiving turkeys that the Callisto's door will be too small for us."

While they sat and talked, the flowers and plants about them softly began their song, and, as a visual accompaniment, the fire-flies they had not before noticed twinkled through the forest.

"My goodness!" exclaimed Cortlandt, "how time goes here! We started to get breakfast, and now it's growing dark."

Hastily cutting some thick but tender slices from the mastodon, and impaling them with the remains of the heart on a sharpened stake, they took up the wires, and the battery that had been supplying the current, and retraced their steps by the way they had come. Their rubber-lined cowhide boots protected them from all but the largest snakes, and as these were for the most part already enjoying their gorge, they trampled with impunity on those that remained in their path. When they had covered about half the distance to the raft, a huge boa-constrictor, which they had mistaken for a branch, fell upon Cortlandt, pinioning his arms and bearing him to the ground. Dropping their loads, Bearwarden and Ayrault threw themselves upon the monster with their hunting-knives with such vim that in a few seconds it beat a hasty retreat, leaving, as it did so, a wake of phosphorescent light.

"Are you hurt?" asked Bearwarden, helping him up.

"Not in the least," replied Cortlandt. "What surprises me is that I am not. The weight of that boa-constrictor would be very great on earth, and here I should think it would be simply crushing."

Groping their way through the rapidly growing darkness, they reached the raft without further adventure, and, once on the lake, had plenty of light. Two moons, one at three quarters and the other full, shone brightly, while the water was alive with gymnotuses and other luminous creatures. Sitting and living upon the cross-timbers, they looked up at the sky. The Great Bear and the north star had exactly the same relation to each other as when seen from the earth, while the other constellations and the Milky Way looked identically as when they had so often gazed at them before, and some idea of the immensity of space was conveyed to them. Here was no change; though they had travelled three hundred and eighty million miles, there was no more perceptible difference than if they had not moved a foot. Perhaps, they thought, to the telescopes--if there are any--among the stars, the sun was seen to be accompanied by two small, dark companions, for Jupiter and Saturn might be visible, or perhaps it seemed merely as a slightly variable star, in years when sun-spots were numerous, or as the larger planets in their revolutions occasionally intercepted a part of its light. As they floated along they noticed a number of what they took to be Will-o'-the-wisps. Several of these great globules of pale flame hovered about them in the air, near the surface of the water, and anon they rose till they hung above the trees, apparently having no forward or horizontal motion except when taken by the gentle breeze, merely sinking and rising.

"How pretty they are!" said Cortlandt, as they watched them. "For bodies consisting of marsh gas, they hold together wonderfully."

Presently one alighted on the water near them. It was considerably brighter than any glow-worm, and somewhat larger than an arc lamp, being nearly three feet in diameter; it did not emit much light, but would itself have been visible from a considerable distance. Cortlandt tried to touch it with a raft-pole, but could not reach far enough. Presently a large fish approached it, swimming near the surface of the water. When it was close to the Jack-o'-lantern, or whatever it was, there was a splash, the fish turned up its white under side, and, the breeze being away from the raft, the fire-ball and its victim slowly floated off together. There were frequently a dozen of these great globules in sight at once, rising and descending, the observers noticing one peculiarity, viz., that their brightness increased as they rose, and decreased as they sank. About two and a half hours after sunset, or midnight according to Jupiter time, they fell asleep, but about an hour later Cortlandt was awakened by a weight on his chest. Starting up, he perceived a huge white-faced bat, with its head but a few inches from his. Its outstretched wings were about eight feet across, and it fastened its sharp claws upon him. Seizing it by the throat, he struggled violently. His companions, awakened by the noise, quickly came to his rescue, grasping him just as he was in danger of being dragged off the raft, and in another moment Bearwarden's knife had entered the creature's spine.

"This evidently belongs to the blood-sucking species," said Cortlandt. "I seem to be the target for all these beasts, and henceforth shall keep my eyes open at night."

As day would break in but little over an hour, they decided to remain awake, and they pushed the dead bat overboard, where it was soon devoured by fishes. A chill had come upon the air, and the incessant noise of the forms of life about them had in a measure ceased.

Cortlandt passed around a box of quinine as a preventive against malaria, and again they lay back and looked at the stars. The most splendid sight in their sky now was Saturn. At the comparatively short distance this great planet was from them, it cast a distinct shadow, its vast rings making it appear twice its real size. With the first glimmer of dawn, the fire-balls descended to the surface of the water and disappeared within it, their lights going out. With a suddenness to which the explorers were becoming accustomed, the sun burst upon them, rising as perpendicularly as at the earth's equator, and more than twice as fast, having first tinged the sky with the most brilliant hues.

The stream had left the forest and swamp, and was now flowing through open country between high banks. Pushing the raft ashore, they stepped off on the sand, and, warming up the remains of the mastodon's heart, ate a substantial breakfast.

While washing their knives in the stream preparatory to leaving it--for they wished to return to the Callisto by completing the circle they had begun--they noticed a huge flat jelly-fish in shallow water. It was so transparent that they could see the sandy bottom through it. As it seemed to be asleep, Bearwarden stirred up the water around it and poked it with a stick. The jelly-fish first drew itself together till it touched the surface of the water, being nearly round, then it slowly left the stream and rose till it was wholly in the air, and, notwithstanding the sunlight, it emitted a faint glow.

"Ah!" exclaimed Bearwarden, "here we have one of our Jack-o'-lanterns. Let us see what it is going to do."

"It is incomprehensible to me," said Cortlandt, "how it maintains itself; for it has neither wings nor visible means of support, yet, as it was able to immerse itself in the stream, thereby displacing a volume of liquid equivalent to its bulk, it must be at least as heavy as water."

The jelly-fish remained poised in the air until directly above them, when it began to descend.

"Stand from under!" cried Bearwarden, stepping back. "I, for one, should not care to be touched."

The great soft mass came directly over the spot on which they had been standing, and stopped its descent about three feet from the ground, parallel to which it was slowly carried by the wind. A few yards off, in the direction in which it was moving, lay a long black snake asleep on the sand. When directly over its victim the jelly globule again sank till it touched the middle of the reptile's back. The serpent immediately coiled itself in a knot, but was already dead. The jellyfish did not swallow, but completely surrounded its prey, and again rose in the air, with the snake's black body clearly visible within it.

"Our Will-o'-the-wisp is prettier by night than by day," said Bearwarden. "I suggest that we investigate this further."

"How?" asked Cortlandt.

"By destroying its life," replied Bearwarden. "Give it one barrel from your gun, doctor, and see if it can then defy gravitation."

Accordingly Cortlandt took careful aim at the object, about twenty-yards away, and fired. The main portion of the jellyfish, with the snake still in its embrace, sailed away, but many pounds of jelly fell to the ground. Most of this remained where it had fallen, but a few of the larger pieces showed a faint luminosity and rose again.

"You cannot kill that which is simply a mass of protoplasm," said Cortlandt. "Doubtless each of those pieces will form a new organism. This proves that there are ramifications and developments of life which we never dreamed of."

CHAPTER VII
AN UNSEEN HUNTER

They calculated that they had come ten or twelve miles from the place at which they built the raft, while the damp salt breeze blowing from the south showed them they were near the ocean. Concluding that large bodies of water must be very much alike on all planets, they decided to make for a range of hills due north and a few miles off, and to complete the circuit of the square in returning to the Callisto. The soft wet sand was covered with huge and curious tracks, doubtless made by creatures that had come to the stream during the night to drink, and they noticed with satisfaction as they set out that the fresher ones led off in the direction in which they were going. For practice, they blew off the heads of the boa-constrictors as they hung from the trees, and of the other huge snakes that moved along the ground, with explosive bullets, in every thicket through which they passed, knowing that the game, never having been shot at, would not take fright at the noise. Sometimes they came upon great masses of snakes, intertwined and coiled like worms; in these cases Cortlandt brought his gun into play, raking them with duck-shot to his heart's content. "As the function of these reptiles," he explained, "is to form a soil on which higher life may grow, we may as well help along their metamorphosis by artificial means." They were impressed by the tremendous cannon-like reports of their firearms, which they perceived at once resulted from the great density of the Jovian atmosphere. And this was also a considerable aid to them in making muscular exertion, for it had just the reverse effect of rarefied mountain air, and they seldom had to expand their lungs fully in order to breathe.

The ground continued to be marked with very large footprints. Often the impressions were those of a biped like some huge bird, except that occasionally the creature had put down one or both forefeet, and a thick tail had evidently dragged nearly all the time it walked erect. Presently, coming to something they had taken for a large flat rock, they were surprised to see it move. It was about twelve feet wide by eighteen feet long, while its shell seemed at least a foot thick, and it was of course the largest turtle they had ever seen.

"Twenty-four people could dine at a table of this size with ease," said Bearwarden, "while it would make soup for a regiment. I wonder if it belongs to the snapping or diamond-backed species."

At this juncture the monster again moved.

"As it is heading in our direction," resumed Bearwarden, "I vote we strike for a free pass," and, taking a run, he sprang with his spiked boots upon the turtle's shell and clambered upon the flat top, which was about six feet from the ground. He was quickly followed by Ayrault, who was not much ahead of Cortlandt, for, notwithstanding his fifty years, the professor was very spry. The tortoise was almost the exact counterpart of the Glyptodon asper that formerly existed on earth, and shambled along at a jerky gait, about half as fast again as they could walk, and while it continued to go in their direction they were greatly pleased. They soon found that by dropping the butts of their rifles sharply and simultaneously on either side, just back of the head, they could direct their course, by making their steed swerve away from the stamping.

"It is strange," said Ayrault, "that, with the exception of the mastodon and this tortoise, we have seen none of the monsters that seem to appear at the close of Carboniferous periods, although the ground is covered with their tracks."

"Probably we did not reach the grounds at the right time of day," replied Bearwarden. "The large game doubtless stays in the woods and jungles till night."

"I fancy," said Cortlandt, "we shall find representatives of all the species that once lived upon the earth. In the case of the singing flowers and the Jack-o'-lantern jelly-fish, we have, in addition, seen developments the existence of which no scientist has ever before even suspected."

Occasionally the tortoise stopped, whereupon they poked it from behind with their knives. It was a vicious-looking brute, and had a huge horny beak, with which it bit off young trees that stood in its way as though they had been blades of grass. They were passing through a valley about half a mile wide, bordered on each side by woods, when Bearwarden suddenly exclaimed, "Here we have it!" and, looking forward, they unexpectedly saw a head rise and remain poised about fifteen feet from the ground. It was a dinosaur, and belonged to the scaled or armoured species. In a few moments another head appeared, and towered several feet above the first. The head was obviously reptilian, but had a beak similar to that of their tortoise. The hind legs were developed like those of a kangaroo, while the small rudimentary forepaws, which could be used as hands or for going quadruped-fashion, now hung down. The strong thick tail was evidently of great use to them when standing erect, by forming a sort of tripod.

"How I wish we could take a pair of those creatures with us when we return to the earth!" said Cortlandt.

"They would be trump cards," replied Bearwarden, "in a zoological garden or a dime museum, and would take the wind out of the sails of all the other freaks."

As they lay flat on the turtle's back, the monsters gazed at them unconcernedly, munching the palm-tree fruit so loudly that they could be heard a long distance.

The ride on the giant tortoise

"Having nothing to fear from a tortoise," resumed Cortlandt, "they may allow us to stalk them. We are in their eyes like hippocentaurs, except that we are part of a tortoise instead of part of a horse, or else they take us for a parasite or fibrous growth on the shell."

"They would not have much to fear from us as we really are," replied Bearwarden, "were it not for our explosive bullets."

"I am surprised," said Ayrault, "that graminivorous animals should be so heavily armed as these, since there can be no great struggle in obtaining their food."

"From the looks of their jaws," replied Cortlandt, "I should say they are omnivorous, and would doubtless prefer meat to what they are eating now. Something seems to have gone wrong with the animal creation hereabouts to-day."

Their war-horse clanked along like a badly rusted machine, approaching the dinosaurs obliquely. When only about fifty yards intervened, as the hunters were preparing to aim, their attention was diverted by a tremendous commotion in the woods on their left and somewhat ahead. With the crunching of dead branches and swaying of the trees, a drove of monsters made a hasty exit and sped across the open valley. Some showed only the tops of their backs above the long grass, while others shambled and leaped with their heads nearly thirty feet above the ground. The dinosaurs instantly dropped on all-fours and joined in the flight, though at about half-minute intervals they rose on their hind legs and for a few seconds ran erect. The drove passed about half a mile before the travellers, and made straight for the woods opposite; but hardly had the monsters been out of sight two minutes when they reappeared, even more precipitately than before, and fled up the valley in the same direction as the tortoise.

"The animals here," said Bearwarden, "behave as though they were going to catch a train; only our friend beneath us seems superior to haste."

"I would give a good deal to know," said Cortlandt, "what is pursuing those giants, and whether it is identical or similar to the mutilator of the mastodon. Nothing but abject terror could make them run like that."

"I have a well-formed idea," said Bearwarden, "that a hunt is going on, with no doubt two parties, one in the woods on either side, and that the hunters may be on a scale commensurate with that of their victims."

"If the excitement is caused by men," replied Cortlandt, "our exploration may turn out to be a far more difficult undertaking than we anticipated. But why, if there are men in those woods, do they not show themselves?--for they could certainly keep pace with the game more easily in the open than among the trees."

"Because," replied Bearwarden, "the men in the woods are doubtless the beaters, whose duty it is to drive the game into and up the valley, at the end of which the killing will be done."

"We may have a chance to see it," said Ayrault, "or to take a hand, for we are travelling straight in that direction, and shall be able to give a good account ourselves if our rights are challenged."

"Why," asked Cortlandt, "if the hunting parties that have been in our vicinity were only beaters, should they have mutilated the mastodon in such a way that he could not walk? And how were they able to take themselves off so quickly--for man in his natural state has never been a fast mover? I repeat, it will upset my theories if we find men."

It was obvious to them that tortoises were not much troubled by the apparently general foe, for the specimen in which they were just then interested continued his course entirely unconcerned. Soon, however, he seemed to feel fatigue, for he drew his feet and head within his shell, which he tightly closed, and after that no poking or prodding had the desired effect.

"I suspect we must depend on shank's mares for a time," said Bearwarden, cheerfully, as they scrambled down.

"We can now see," said Cortlandt, "why our friend was so unconcerned, since he has but to draw himself within himself to become invulnerable to anything short of a stroke of lightning; for no bird could have power enough to raise and drop him from a great height upon rocks, as the eagles do on earth."

"I suspect, if anxious for turtle soup," said Bearwarden, "we must attach a lightning--rod, and wait for a thunderstorm to electrocute him."

CHAPTER VIII
SPORTSMEN'S REVERIES

Feeling grateful to the huge tortoise for the good service he had rendered, they shot a number of the great snakes that were gliding about on the ground, and placed them where he would find them on awaiting. They then picked their way carefully towards stretches on which the grass was shortest. When they had gone about two miles, and had already reached higher ground, they came to a ridge of rock running at right angles to their course. This they climbed, and on looking over the edge of the crest beheld a sight that made their hearts stand still. A monster, somewhat resembling an alligator, except that the back was arched, was waddling about perhaps seventy-five yards from them. It was sixty feet long, and to the top of its scales was at least twenty-five feet high. It was constantly moving, and the travellers noticed with some dismay that its motion was far more rapid than they would have supposed it could be.

"It is also a dinosaur," said the professor, watching it sharply, "and very closely resembles the Stegosaurus ungulatus restored in the museums. The question is, What shall we do with the living specimen, now that we have it?"

"Our chairman," said Ayrault, "must find a way to kill it, so that we may examine it closely."

"The trouble is," said Bearwarden, "our bullets will explode before they penetrate the scales. In the absence of any way of making a passage for an explosive ball by means of a solid one, we must strike a vital spot. His scales being no harder than the trunk of a tree, we can wound him terribly by touching him anywhere; but there is no object in doing this unless we can kill him, especially as there is no deep stream, such as would have delayed the mastodon in reaching us, to protect us here. We must spread out so as to divert his attention from one to another."

After some consultation it was decided that Cortlandt, who had only a shot-gun, should remain where they were, while Bearwarden and Ayrault moved some distance to the right and left. At a signal from Cortlandt, who was to attract the monster's attention, the wings were to advance simultaneously. These arrangements they carried out to the letter. When Bearwarden and Ayrault had gone about twenty-five yards on either side, the doctor imitated the peculiar grunting sound of an alligator, at which the colossal monster turned and faced him, while Bearwarden and Ayrault moved to the attack. The plan of this was good, for, with his attention fixed on three objects, the dinosaur seemed confused, and though Bearwarden and Ayrault had good angles from which to shoot, there was no possibility of their hitting each other. They therefore advanced steadily with their rifles half up. Though their own danger increased with each step, in the event of their missing, the chance of their shooting wild decreased, the idea being to reach the brain through the eye. Cortlandt's part had also its risks, for, being entirely defenceless with his shot-gun against the large creature, whose attention it was his duty to attract, he staked all on the marksmanship of his friends. Not considering this, however, he stood his ground, having the thumb-piece on his Winchester magazine shoved up and ready to make a noisy diversion if necessary in behalf of either wing. Having aroused the monster's curiosity, Cortlandt sprang up, waving his arms and his gun. The dinosaur lowered his head as if to charge, thereby bringing it to a level with the rifles, either of which could have given it the fatal shot. But as their fingers pressed the triggers the reptile soared up thirty feet in the air. Ayrault pulled for his first sight, shooting through the lower jaw, and shivering that member, while Bearwarden changed his aim and sighted straight for the heart. In an instant the monster was down again, just missing Ayrault's head as he stepped back, and Bearwarden's rifle poured a stream of explosive balls against its side, rending and blowing away the heavy scales. Having drawn the dinosaur's attention to himself, he retreated, while Ayrault renewed the attack. Cortlandt, seeing that the original plan had miscarried, poured showers of small shot against the huge beast's face. Finally, one of Ayrault's balls exploded in the brain, and all was over.

"We have killed it at last," said Bearwarden "but the first attack, though artistic, had not the brilliant results we expected. These creatures' mode of fighting is doubtless somewhat similar to that of the kangaroo, which it is said puts its forepaws gently, almost lovingly, on a man's shoulders, and then disembowels him by the rapid movement of a hind leg. But we shall get used to their method, and can do better next time."

They then reloaded their weapons and, while Cortlandt examined their victim from a naturalist's point of view, Bearwarden and Ayrault secured the heart, which they thought would be the most edible part, the operation being rendered possible by the amount of armour the explosive balls had stripped off.

"To-morrow," said Bearwarden, "we must make it a point to get some well-fed birds; for I can roast, broil, or fricassee them to a turn. Life is too short to live on this meat in such a sportsman's paradise. In any case there can be no end of mastodons, mammoths, woolly rhinoceroses, moa birds, and all such shooting."

As the sun was already near the horizon, they chose a dry, sandy place, to secure as much immunity as possible from nocturnal visits, and, after procuring a supply of water from a pool, proceeded to arrange their camp for the night. They first laid out the protection-wires, setting them while the sun still shone. Next they built a fire and prepared their evening meal. While they ate it, twilight became night, and the fire-flies, twinkling in legions in the neighbouring valley, seemed like the lamps of a great city.

"Their lights," said Bearwarden, pointing to them, "are not as fine as the jelly-fish Will-o'-the wisps were last night, but they are not so dangerous. No gymnotus or electric eel that I have ever seen compared with them, and I am convinced that any one of us they might have touched would have been in kingdom come."

The balmy air soothed the travellers' brows as they reclined against mounds of sand, while the flowers in the valley sent up their dying notes. One by one the moons arose, till four--among them the Lilliputian, discovered by Prof. Barnard in 1893--were in the sky, flooding the landscape with their silvery light, and something in the surroundings touched a sympathetic cord in the men.

"Oh that I were young again," said Cortlandt, "and had life before me! I should like to remain here and grow up with this planet, in which we already perceive the next New World. The beauties of earth are barren compared with the scenes we have here."

"You remember," replied Bearwarden, "how Cicero defends old age in his De Senectute, and shows that while it has almost everything that youth has, it has also a sense of calm and many things besides."

"Yes," answered Cortlandt, "but, while plausible, it does not convince. The pleasures of age are largely negative, the old being happy when free from pain."

"Since the highest joy of life," said Ayrault, "is coming to know our Creator, I should say the old, being further advanced, would be the happier of the two. I should never regard this material life as greatly to be prized for itself. You remember the old song:

> *"'O Youth! When we come to consider*
> *The pain, the toil, and the strife,*
> *The happiest man of all is*
> *The one who has finished his life.'*

"I suspect," continued Ayrault, "that the man who reaches even the lowest plane in paradise will find far more beautiful visions than any we have here."

As they had but little rest the night before, they were all tired. The warm breeze swayed the long dry grass, causing it to give out a soft rustle; all birds except the flitting bats were asleep among the tall ferns or on the great trees that spread their branches towards heaven. There was nothing to recall a picture of the huge monsters they had seen that day, or of the still more to be dreaded terror these had borne witness to. Thus night closes the activities of the day, and in its serene grandeur the soul has time to think. While they thought, however, drowsiness overcame them, and in a little while all were asleep.

The double line of protection-wires encircled them like a silent guard, while the methodical ticking of the alarm-clock that was to wake them at the approach of danger, and register the hour of interruption, formed a curious contrast to the irregular cries of the night-hawks in the distance. Time and again some huge iguanodon or a hipsohopus would pass, shaking the ground with its tread; but so implicit was the travellers' trust in the vigilance of their mechanical and tireless watch, that they slept on as calmly and unconcernedly as though they had been in their beds at home, while the tick was as constant and regular as a sentry's march. The wires of course did not protect them from creatures having wings, and they ran some risk of a visitation from the blood-sucking bats. The far-away volcanoes occasionally sent up sheets of flame, which in the distance were like summer lightning; the torrents of lava and crashes that had sounded so thunderous when near, were now like the murmur of the ocean's ebb tide, lulling the terrestrials to deeper sleep. The pale moons were at intervals momentarily obscured by the rushing clouds in the upper air, only to reappear soon afterwards as serene as before. All Nature seemed at rest.

Shortly before dawn there was an unusually heavy step. A moment later the ever-vigilant batteries poured forth their current, and the clang of the alarm-bell made the still night ring. In an instant the three men were awake, each resting on one knee, with their backs towards the centre and their polished barrels raised. It was not long before they perceived the intruder by the moonlight. A huge monster of the Triceratops prorsus species had entered the camp. It was shaped something like an elephant, but had ten or twelve times the bulk, being over forty feet in length, not including the long, thick tail. The head carried two huge horns on the forehead and one on the nose.

"A plague on my shot-gun!" said Cortlandt. "Had I known how much of this kind of game we should see, I too should have brought a rifle."

The monster was entangled in the wires, and in another second would have stepped on the batteries that were still causing the bell to ring.

"Aim for the heart," said Bearwarden to Ayrault. "When you show me his ribs, I will follow you in the hole."

Ayrault instantly fired for a point just back of the left foreleg. The explosion had the same effect as on the mastodon, removing a half-barrel of hide, etc; and the next second Bearwarden sent a bullet less than an inch from where Ayrault's had stopped. Before the colossus could turn, each had caused several explosions in close proximity to the first. The creature was of course terribly wounded, and several ribs were cracked, but no ball had gone through. With a roar it made straight for the woods, and with surprising agility, running fully as fast as an elephant. Bearwarden and Ayrault kept up a rapid fire at the left hind leg, and soon completely disabled it. The dinosaur, however, supported itself with its huge tail, and continued to make good time. Knowing they could not give it a fatal wound at the intervening distance, in the uncertain light, they stopped firing and set out in pursuit. Cortlandt paused to stop the bell that still rang, and then put his best foot foremost in regaining his friends. For half a mile they hurried along, until, seeing by the quantity of blood on the ground that they were in no danger of losing the game, they determined to save their strength. The trail entered the woods by a narrow ravine, passed through what proved to be but a belt of timber, and then turned north to the right. Presently in the semi-darkness they saw the monster's head against the sky. He was browsing among the trees, tearing off the young branches, and the hunters succeeded in getting within seventy-five yards before being discovered. Just as he began to run, the two rifles again fired, this time at the right hind leg, which they succeeded in hamstringing. After that the Triceratops prorsus was at their mercy, and they quickly put an end to its suffering. "The sun is about to rise," said Bearwarden; "in a few minutes we shall have enough light."

They cut out a dozen thick slices of tenderloin steak, and soon were broiling and eating a substantial breakfast.

"There are not as many spectators to watch us eat here," said Cortlandt, "as in the woods. I suggest that, after returning to camp for our blankets and things, we steer for the Callisto, via this Triceratops, to see what creatures have been attracted by the body."

On finishing their meal they returned to the place at which they had passed the night. Having straightened the protection-wires, which had become twisted, and arranged their impedimenta, they set out, and were soon once more beside their latest victim.

CHAPTER IX
THE HONEY OF DEATH

At first nothing seemed to have been disturbed, when they suddenly perceived that both forelegs were missing. On further examination they found that the ponderous tail, seven feet in diameter, was cut through in two places, the thicker portion having disappeared, and that the heavy bones in this extremity of the vertebral column had been severed like straws. The cut surfaces were but little cooler than the interior of the body, showing how recently the mutilation had been effected.

"By all the gods!" exclaimed Bearwarden, "it is easy to see the method in this; the hunters have again cut off only those parts that could be easily rolled. These Jovian fellows must have weapons compared with which the old scythe chariots would be but toys, with which they amputate the legs of their victims. We must see to it that their scimitars do not come too near to us, and I venture to hope that in our bullets they will find their match. What say you, doctor?"

"I see no depression such as such heavy bodies would necessarily have made had they been rolled along the ground, neither does it seem to me that these curious tracks in the sand are those of men."

The loose earth looked as if the cross-ties of some railroad had been removed, the space formerly occupied having been but partly filled, and these depressions were across the probable direction of motion.

"Whatever was capable of chasing mastodons and carrying such weights," said Ayrault, "will, I suspect, have little to fear from us. Probably nothing short of light artillery would leave much effect."

"I dare say," replied Bearwarden, "we had better give the unknown quantity a wide berth, though I would give a year's salary to see what it is like. The absence of other tracks shows that his confreres leave 'Scissor-jaw' alone."

Keeping a sharp lookout in all directions, they resumed their march along the third side of the square which was to bring them back to the Callisto. Their course was parallel to the stream, and on comparatively high ground. Cortlandt's gun did good service, bringing down between fifty and sixty birds that usually allowed them to get as near as they pleased, and often seemed unwilling to leave their branches. By the time they were ready for luncheon they saw it would be dark in an hour. As the rapidity of the planet's rotation did not give them a chance to become tired, they concluded not to pitch their camp, but to resume the march by moonlight, which would be easy in the high, open country they were traversing.

While in quest of fire-wood, they came upon great heaps of bones, mostly those of birds, and were attracted by the tall, bell-shaped flowers growing luxuriantly in their midst. These exhaled a most delicious perfume, and at the centre of each flower was a viscous liquid, the colour of honey.

"If this tastes as well as it looks," said Bearwarden, "it will come in well for dessert"; saying which he thrust his finger into the recesses of the flower, intending to taste the essence. Quietly, but like a flash, the flower closed, his hand being nearly caught and badly scratched by the long, sharp thorns that now appeared at the edges.

"Ha!" he exclaimed, "a sensitive and you may almost say a man-eating plant. This doubtless has been the fate of these birds, whose bones now lie bleaching at its feet after they have nourished its lips with their lives. No doubt the plant has use for them still, since their skeletons may serve to fertilize its roots."

Wishing to investigate further, Bearwarden placed one of the birds they had shot within the bell of another flower, which immediately contracted with such force that they saw drops of blood squeezed out. After some minutes the flower opened, as beautiful as ever, and discharged an oblong ball compressed to about the size of a hen's egg, though the bird that was placed within it had been as large as a small duck. Towards evening these flowers sent up their most beautiful song, to hear which flocks of birds came from far and near, alighting on the trees, and many were lured to death by the siren strains and the honey.

Before resuming their journey, the travellers paid a parting visit to the bell-shaped lilies on their pyramids of bones. The flowers were closed for the night, and the travellers saw by the moonlight that the white mounds were simply alive with diamond-headed snakes. These coiled themselves, flattened their heads, and set up such a hissing on the explorers' approach that they were glad to retire, and leave this curious contrast of hideousness and beauty to the fire-flies and the moons. Marching along in Indian file, the better to avoid treading on the writhing serpents that strewed the ground, they kept on for about two hours. They frequently passed huge heaps or mounds of bones, evidently the remains of bears or other large animals.

The carnivorous plants growing at their centre were often like hollow trees, and might easily have received the three travellers in one embrace. But as before, the mounds were alive with serpents that evidently made them their homes, and raised an angry hiss whenever the men approached.

"The wonder to me," said Bearwarden, "is, that these snakes do not protect the game, by keeping it from the life-devouring plants. It may be that they do not show themselves by day or when the victims are near, or that the quadrupeds on which these plants live take a pleasure, like deer, in killing them by jumping with all four feet upon their backs or in some other way, and after that are entrapped by the flowers."

Shortly after midnight they rested for a half hour, but the dawn found them trudging along steadily, though somewhat wearily, and having about completed the third side of their square. Accordingly, they soon made a right-angle turn to the left, and had been picking their way over the rough ground for nearly two hours, with the sun already high in the sky, when they noticed a diminution of light. Glancing up, they saw that one of the moons was passing across the sun, and that they were on the eve of a total eclipse.

"Since all but the fifth moon," said Cortlandt, "revolve exactly in the plane of Jupiter's equator, any inhabitants that settle there will become accustomed to eclipses, for there must be one of the sun, and also of the moons, at each revolution, or about forty-five hundred in every Jovian year. The reason we have seen none before is, because we are not exactly on the equator."

They had a glimpse of the coronal streamers as the last portion of the sun was covered, and all the other phenomena that attend an eclipse on earth. For a few minutes there was a total return to night. The twinkling stars and other moons shone tranquilly in the sky, and even the noise of the insects ceased. Presently the edge of the sun that had been first obscured reappeared, and then Nature went through the phenomenon of an accelerated dawn. Without awaiting a full return of light, the travellers proceeded on their way, and had gone something over a hundred yards when Ayrault, who was marching second, suddenly grasped Bearwarden, who was in front, and pointed to a jet-black mass straight ahead, and about thirty yards from a pool of warm water, from which a cloud of vapour arose. The top of the head was about seven feet high, and the length of the body exceeded thirty feet. The six legs looked as strong as steel cables, and were about a foot through, while a huge, bony proboscis nine feet in length preceded the body. This was carried horizontally between two and three feet from the ground. Presently a large ground sloth came to the pool to drink, lapping up the water at the sides that had partly cooled. In an instant the black armored monster rushed down the slope with the speed of a nineteenth-century locomotive, and seemed about as formidable. The sloth turned in the direction of the sound, and for a moment seemed paralyzed with fear; it then started to run, but it was too late, for the next second the enormously exaggerated ant--for such it was--overtook it. The huge mandible shears that when closed had formed the proboscis, snapped viciously, taking off the sloth's legs and then cutting its body to slivers. The execution was finished in a few seconds, and the ponderous insect carried back about half the sloth to its hiding-place, where it leisurely devoured it.

"This reminds me," said Bearwarden, "of the old lady who never completed her preparations for turning in without searching for burglars under the bed. Finally she found one, and exclaimed in delight, 'I've been looking for you fifty years, and at last you are here!' The question is, now that we have found our burglar, what shall we do with him?"

"I constantly regret not having a rifle," replied Cortlandt, "though it is doubtful if even that would help us here."

A battle royal on Jupiter

"Let us sit down and wait," said Ayrault; "there may be an opening soon."

Anon a woolly rhinoceros, resembling the Rhinoceros tichorhinus that existed contemporaneously on earth with the mammoth, came to drink the water that had partly cooled. It was itself a formidable-looking beast, but in an instant the monster again rushed from concealment with the same tremendous speed. The rhinoceros turned in the direction of the sound, and, lowering its head, faced the foe. The ant's shears, however, passed beneath the horn, and, fastening upon the left foreleg, cut it off with a loud snap.

"Now is our chance," exclaimed Cortlandt; "we may kill the brute before he is through with the rhinoceros."

"Stop a bit, doctor," said Bearwarden. "We have a good record so far; let us keep up our reputation for being sports. Wait till he can attend to us."

The encounter was over in less than a minute, three of the rhinoceros's legs being taken off, and the head almost severed from the body. Taking up the legs in its mandibles, the murderous creature was returning to its lair, when, with the cry of "Now for the fray!" Bearwarden aimed beneath the body and blew off one of the farther armoured legs, from the inside. "Shoot off the legs on the same side," he counselled Ayrault, while he himself kept up a rapid fire. Cortlandt tried to disconcert the enemy by raining duck-shot on its scale-protected eyes, while the two rifles tore off great masses of the horn that covered the enormously powerful legs. The men separated as they retreated, knowing that one slash of the great shears would cut their three bodies in halves if they were caught together. The monster had dropped the remains of the rhinoceros when attacked, and made for the hunters at its top speed, which was somewhat reduced by the loss of one leg. Before it came within cutting distance, however, another on the same side was gone, Ayrault having landed a bullet on a spot already stripped of armour. After this the men had no difficulty in keeping out of its way, though it still moved with some speed, snipping off young trees in its path like grass. Finally, having blown the scales from one eye, the travellers sent in a bullet that exploded in the brain and ended its career.

"This has been by all odds the most exciting hunt we have had," said Ayrault, "both on account of the determined nature and great speed of the attack, and the almost impossibility of finding a vulnerable spot."

"Anything short of explosive bullets," added Bearwarden, "would have been powerless against this beast, for the armour in many places is nearly a foot thick."

"This is also the most extraordinary as well as most dangerous creature with which we have had to deal," said Cortlandt, "because it is an enormously enlarged insect, with all the inherent ferocity and strength. It is almost the exact counterpart of an African soldier-ant magnified many hundred thousand times. I wonder," he continued thoughtfully, "if our latter-day insects may not be the deteriorated (in point of size) descendants of the monsters of mythology and geology, for nothing could be a more terrible or ferocious antagonist than many of our well-known insects, if sufficiently enlarged. No animal now alive has more than a small fraction of the strength, in proportion to its size, of the minutest spider or flea. It may be that through lack of food, difficulties imposed by changing climate, and the necessity of burrowing in winter, or through some other conditions changed from what they were accustomed to, their size has been reduced, and that the fire-flies, huge as they seemed, are a step in advance of this specimen in the march of deterioration or involution, which will end by making them as insignificant as those on earth. These ants have probably come into the woods to lay their eggs, for, from the behaviour of the animals we watched from the turtle, there must have been several; or perhaps a war is in progress between those of a different colour, as on earth, in which case the woods may be full of them. Doubtless the reason the turtle seemed so unconcerned at the general uneasiness of the animals was because he knew he could make himself invulnerable to the marauder by simply closing his shell, and we were unmolested because it did not occur to the ant that any soft-shelled creatures could be on the turtle's back."

"I think," said Bearwarden, "it will be the part of wisdom to return to the Callisto, and do the rest of our exploring on Jupiter from a safe height; for, though we succeeded in disabling this beauty, it was largely through luck, and had we not done so we should probably have provided a bon bouche for our deceased friend, instead of standing at his grave."

Accordingly they proceeded, and were delighted, a few minutes later, to see the sunlight reflected from the projectile's polished roof.

CHAPTER X
CHANGING LANDSCAPES

On reaching the Callisto, Ayrault worked the lock he had had placed on the lower door, which, to avoid carrying a key, was opened by a combination. The car's interior was exactly as they had left it, and they were glad to be in it again.

"Now," said Bearwarden, "we can have a sound and undisturbed sleep, which is what I want more than anything else. No prowlers can trouble us here, and we shall not need the protection-wires."

They then opened a window in each side--for the large glass plates, admitting the sun when closed, made the Callisto rather warm--and placed a stout wire netting within them to keep out birds and bats, and then, though it was but little past noon, got into their comfortable beds and slept nine hours at a stretch. Their strong metal house was securely at rest, receiving the sunlight and shedding the rain and dew as it might have done on earth. No winds or storms, lightnings or floods, could trouble it, while the multiformed monsters of antiquity and mythology restored in life, with which the terrestrials had been thrown into such close contact, roamed about its polished walls. Not even the fiercest could affect them, and they would but see themselves reflected in any vain assaults. The domed symmetrical cylinder stood there as a monument to human ingenuity and skill, and the travellers' last thought as they fell asleep was, "Man is really lord of creation."

The following day at about noon they awoke, and had a bath in the warm pool. They saw the armoured mass of the great ant evidently undisturbed, while the bodies of its victims were already shining skeletons, and raised a small cairn of stones in memory of the struggle they had had there.

"We should name this place Kentucky," said Bearwarden, "for it is indeed a dark and bloody ground," and, seeing the aptness of the appellation, they entered it so on their charts. While Ayrault got the batteries in shape for resuming work, Bearwarden prepared a substantial breakfast. This consisted of oatmeal and cream kept hermetically sealed in glass, a dish of roast grouse, coffee, pilot bread, a bottle of Sauterne, and another of Rhine wine.

"This is the last meal we shall take hereabouts," said their cook, as they plied their knives and forks beneath the trees, "so here is a toast to our adventures, and to all the game we have killed." They drained their glasses in drinking this, after which Bearwarden regaled them with the latest concert-hall song which he had at his tongue's end.

About an hour before dark they re-entered their projectile, and, as a mark of respect to their little ship, named the great branch of the continent on which they had alighted Callisto Point. They then got under way. The batteries had to develop almost their maximum power to overcome Jupiter's attraction; but they were equal to the task, and the Callisto was soon in the air. Directing their apergy to the mountains towards the interior of the continent, and applying repulsion to any ridge or hill over which they passed, thereby easing the work of the batteries engaged in supporting the Callisto, they were soon sweeping along at seventy-five to one hundred miles an hour. By keeping the projectile just strongly enough charged to neutralize gravitation, they remained for the most part within two hundred feet of the ground, seldom rising to an altitude of more than a mile, and were therefore able to keep the windows at the sides open and so obtain an unobstructed view. If, however, at any time they felt oppressed by Jupiter's high barometric pressure, and preferred the terrestrial conditions, they had but to rise till the barometer fell to thirty. Then, if an object of interest recalled them to sea-level, they could keep the Callisto's inside pressure at what they found on the Jovian mountains, by screwing up the windows. On account of the distance of sixty-four thousand miles from Jupiter's equator to the pole, they calculated that going at the speed of a hundred miles an hour, night and day, it would take them twenty-five terrestrial days to reach the pole even from latitude two degrees at which they started. But they knew that, if pressed for time, they could rise above the limits of the atmosphere, and move with planetary speed; while, if they wished a still easier method of pursuing their observation, they had but to remain poised between the sun and Jupiter, beyond the latter's upper air, and photograph or map it as it revolved before them.

By sunset they had gone a hundred miles. Wishing to push along, they closed the windows, rose higher to avoid any mountain-tops that might be invisible in the moonlight, and increased their speed. The air made a gentle humming sound as they shot through it, and towards morning they saw several bright points of light in which they recognized, by the aid of their glasses, sheets of flame and torrents of molten glowing lava, bursting at intervals or pouring steadily from several volcanoes. From this they concluded they were again near an ocean, since volcanoes need the presence of a large body of water to provide steam for their eruptions.

With the rising sun they found the scene of the day before entirely changed. They were over the shore of a vast ocean that extended to the left as far as they could see, for the range of vision often exceeded the power of sight. The coast-line ran almost due north and south, while the volcanoes that dotted it, and that had been luminous during the night, now revealed their nature only by lines of smoke and vapours. They were struck by the boldness and abruptness of the scenery. The mountains and cliffs had been but little cut down by water and frost action, and seemed in the full vigour of their youth, which was what the travellers had a right to expect on a globe that was still cooling and shrinking, and consequently throwing up ridges in the shape of mountains far more rapidly than a planet as matured and quiescent as the earth. The absence of lakes also showed them that there had been no Glacial period, in the latitudes they were crossing, for a very long time.

"We can account for the absence of ice-action and scratches," said Cortlandt, "in one of two ways. Either the proximity of the internal heat to the surface prevents water from freezing in all latitudes, or Jupiter's axis has always been very nearly perpendicular to its orbit, and consequently the thermometer has never been much below thirty-two degrees Fahrenheit; for, at the considerable distance we are now from the sun, it is easy to conceive that, with the axis much inclined, there might be cold weather, during the Northern hemisphere's winter, that would last for about six of our years, even as near the equator as this. The substantiation of an ice-cap at the pole will disprove the first hypothesis; for what we took for ice before alighting may have been but banks of cloud, since, having been in the plane of the planet's equator at the time, we had naturally but a very oblique view of the poles; while the absence of glacial scratches shows, I take it, that though the axis may have been a good deal more inclined than at present, it has not, at all events since Jupiter's Palaeozoic period, been as much so as that of Uranus or Venus. The land on Jupiter, corresponding to the Laurentian Hills on earth, must even here have appeared at so remote a period that the first surface it showed must long since have been worn away, and therefore any impressions it received have also been erased. "Comparing this land with the photographs we took from space, I should say it is the eastern of the two crescent-shaped continents we found apparently facing each other. Their present form I take to be only the skeleton outline of what they will be at the next period of Jupiter's development. They will, I predict, become more like half moons than crescents, though the profile may be much indented by gulfs and bays, their superficial area being greatly increased, and the intervening ocean correspondingly narrowed. We know that North America had a very different shape during the Cretaceous or even the Middle Tertiary period from what it has now, and that the Gulf of Mexico extended up the valley of the Mississippi as far as the Ohio, by the presence of a great coral reef in the Ohio River near Cincinnati. We know also that Florida and the Southeastern Atlantic States are a very recent addition to the continent, while the pampas of the Argentine Republic have, in a geological sense, but just been upheaved from the sea, by the fact that the rivers are all on the surface, not having had time to cut down their channels below the surrounding country. By similar reasoning, we know that the cañon of the Colorado is a very old region, though the precipitateness of its banks is due to the absence of rain, for a local water-supply would cut back the banks, having most effect where they were steepest, since at those points it would move with the greatest speed. Thus the majestic cañon owes its existence to two things: the length of time the river has been at work, and the fact that the water flowing through it comes from another region where, of course, there is rain, and that it is merely in transit, and so affects only the bed on which it moves. Granting that this is the eastern of the two continents we observed, it evidently corresponds more in shape to the Eastern hemisphere on earth than to the New World, both of which are set facing one another, since both drain towards the Atlantic Ocean. But the analogy here holds also, for the past outlines of the Eastern hemisphere differed radically from what they are now. The Mediterranean Sea was formerly of far greater extent than we see it to-day, and covered nearly the whole of northern Africa and the old upheaved sea-bottom that we see in the Desert of Sahara. Much of this great desert, as we know, has a considerable elevation, though part of it is still below the level of the Mediterranean.

"Perhaps a more striking proof of this than are the remains of fishes and marine life that are found there, is the dearth of natural harbours and indentations in Africa's northern coast, while just opposite, in southern Europe, there are any number; which shows that not enough time has elapsed since Africa's upheaval for liquid or congealed water to produce them. Many of Europe's best harbours, and Boston's, in our country, have been dug out by slow ice-action in the oft-recurring Glacial periods. The Black and Caspian Seas were larger than we now find them; while the Adriatic extended much farther into the continent, covering most of the country now in the valley of the Po. In Europe the land has, of course, risen also, but so slowly that the rivers have been able to keep their channels cut down; proof of their ability to perform which feat we see when an ancient river passes through a ridge of hills or mountains. The river had doubtless been there long before the mountains began to rise, but their elevation was so gradual that the rate of the river's cutting down equalled or exceeded their coming up; proof of which we have in the patent fact that the ancient river's course remains unchanged, and is at right angles to the mountain chain. From all of which we see that the Eastern hemisphere's crescent hollow--of which, I take it, the Mediterranean, Black, and Caspian Sea depressions are the remains--has been gradually filled in, by the elevation of the sea's bottom, and the extension of deltas from the detrital matter brought from the high interior of the continents by the rivers, or by the combined action of the two. Now, since the Gulf of Mexico has been constantly growing smaller, and the Mediterranean is being invaded by the land, I reason that similar causes will produce like effects here, and give to each continent an area far greater than our entire globe. The stormy ocean we behold in the west, which corresponds to our Atlantic, though it is far more of a mare clausum in the geographical sense, is also destined to become a calm and placid inland sea. There are, of course, modifications of and checks to the laws tending to increase the land area. England was formerly joined to the continent, the land connecting the two having been rather washed away by the waves and great tides than by any sinking of the English Channel's bottom, the whole of which is comparatively shallow. Another case of this kind is seen in Cape Cod and the islands of Martha's Vineyard and Nantucket, all of which are washing away so rapidly that they would probably disappear before the next Glacial period, were we not engaged in preventing its recurrence. These detached islands and sand-bars once formed one large island, which at a still earlier time undoubtedly was joined to the mainland. The sands forming the detached masses are in a great processional march towards the equator, but it is the result simply of winds and waves, there being no indication of subsidence. Along the coast of New Jersey we see denudation and sinking going on together, the well-known *sunken forest* being an instance of the latter. The border of the continent proper also extends many miles under the ocean before reaching the edge of the Atlantic basin. Volcanic eruptions sometimes demolish parts of headlands and islands, though these recompense us in the amount of material brought to the surface, and in the increased distance they enable water to penetrate by relieving the interior of part of its heat, for any land they may destroy."

CHAPTER XI
A JOVIAN NIAGARA

Four days later, after crossing a ridge of mountains that the pressure on the aneroid barometer showed to be about thirty-two thousand feet high, and a stretch of flat country a few miles in width, they came to a great arm of the sea. It was about thirty miles wide at its mouth, which was narrowed like the neck of a bottle, and farther inland was over one hundred miles across, and though their glasses, the clear air, and the planet's size enabled them to see nearly five hundred miles, they could not find its end. In the shallow water along its shores, and on the islands rising but a few feet above the waves, they saw all kinds of amphibians and sea-monsters. Many of these were almost the exact reproduction in life of the giant plesiosaurs, dinosaurs, and elasmosaurs, whose remains are preserved in the museums on earth. The reptilian bodies of the elasmosaurs, seventy-five feet in length, with the forked tongues, distended jaws and fangs of a snake, were easily taken for the often described but probably mythical sea-serpent, as partially coiled they occasionally raised their heads twelve or fifteen feet.

"Man in his natural state," said Cortlandt, "would have but small chance of surviving long among such neighbours. Buckland, I think, once indulged in the jeu d'esprit of supposing an ichthyosaur lecturing on the human skull. 'You will at once perceive,' said the lecturer, 'that the skull before us belonged to one of the lower order of animals. The teeth are very insignificant, the power of the jaws trifling, and altogether it seems wonderful how the creature could have procured food.' Armed with modern weapons, and in this machine, we are, of course, superior to the most powerful monster; but it is not likely that, had man been so surrounded during the whole of his evolution, he could have reached his present plane." Notwithstanding the striking similarity of these creatures to their terrestrial counterparts that existed on earth during its corresponding period, there were some interesting modifications. The organs of locomotion in the amphibians were more developed, while the eyes of all were larger, the former being of course necessitated by the power of gravity, and the latter by the greater distance from the sun.

"The adaptability and economy of Nature," said Cortlandt, "have always amazed me. In the total blackness of the Kentucky Mammoth Cave, where eyes would be of no use to the fishes, our common mother has given them none; while if there is any light, though not as much as we are accustomed to, she may be depended upon to rise to the occasion by increasing the size of the pupil and the power of the eye. In the development of the ambulatory muscles we again see her handiwork, probably brought about through the 'survival of the fittest.' The fishes and those wholly immersed need no increase in power, for, though they weigh more than they would on earth, the weight of the water they displace is increased at the same rate also, and their buoyancy remains unchanged. If the development of life here so closely follows its lines on earth, with the exception of comparatively slight modifications, which are exactly what, had we stopped to think, we should have expected to find, may we not reasonably ask whether she will not continue on these lines, and in time produce beings like ourselves, but with more powerful muscles and eyes capable of seeing clearly with less light? Reasoning by analogy, we can come to no other conclusion, unless their advent is anticipated by the arrival of ready-made colonists from the more advanced earth, like ourselves. In that case man, by pursuing the same destructive methods that he has pursued in regard to many other species, may exterminate the intervening links, and so arrest evolution."

Before leaving Deepwaters Bay they secured a pail of its water, which they found, on examination, contained a far larger percentage of salt and solid material than the oceans on earth, while a thermometer that they immediately immersed in it soon registered eighty-five degrees Fahrenheit; both of which discoveries confirmed them in what they already knew, namely, that Jupiter had advanced comparatively little from the condition in which the water on the surface is hot, in which state the earth once was.

They were soon beyond the estuary at which they had stopped to study the forms of life and to make this test, and kept on due north for several days, occasionally rising above the air. As their familiarity with their surroundings increased, they made notes of several things. The mountains covered far more territory at their bases than the terrestrial mountains, and they were in places very rugged and showed vast yawning chasms. They were also wooded farther up their sides, and bore but little snow; but so far the travellers had not found them much higher than those on earth, the greatest altitude being the thirty-two thousand feet south of Deepwaters Bay, and one other ridge that was forty thousand; so that, compared with the size of the planet and its continents, they seemed quite small, and the continents themselves were comparatively level. They also noted that spray was blown in vast sheets, till the ocean for miles was white as milk. The wind often attained tornado strength, and the whole surface of the water, about what seemed to be the storm centre, frequently moved with rapidity in the form of foam. Yet, notwithstanding this, the waves were never as large as those to which they were accustomed on earth. This they accounted for very easily by the fact that, while water weighed 2.55 times as much as on earth, the pressure of air was but little more than half as much again, and consequently its effect on all but the very surface of the heavy liquid was comparatively slight.

"Gravity is a useful factor here," observed Cortlandt, as they made a note of this; "for, in addition to giving immunity from waves, it is most effective in checking the elevation of high mountains or table-lands in the high latitudes, which we shall doubtless find sufficiently cool, or even cold, while in tropical regions, which might otherwise be too hot, it interferes with them least, on account of being partly neutralized by the rapid rotation with which all four of the major planets are blessed."

At sunrise the following morning they saw they were approaching another great arm of the sea. It was over a thousand miles wide at its mouth, and, had not the photographs showed the contrary, they would have thought the Callisto had reached the northern end of the continent. It extended into the land fifteen thousand miles, and, on account of the shape of its mouth, they called it Funnel Bay. Rising to a height, they flew across, and came to a great table-land peninsula, with a chain of mountains on either side. The southern range was something over, and the northern something less than, five thousand feet in height, while the table-land between sloped almost imperceptibly towards the middle, in which, as they expected, they found a river compared to which the Mississippi or the Amazon would be but a brook. In honour of the President of the Terrestrial Axis Straightening Company, they called this great projection, which averaged about four thousand miles across by twelve thousand miles long, Bearwarden Peninsula. They already noticed a change in climate; the ferns and palms became fewer, and were succeeded by pines, while the air was also a good deal cooler, which was easily accounted for by their altitude--though even at that height it was considerably denser than at sea-level on earth--and by the fact that they were already near latitude thirty.

The exposed points on the plateau, as also the summits of the first mountains they had seen before alighting, were devoid of vegetation, scarcely so much as a blade of grass being visible. Since they could not account for this by cold, they concluded that the most probable explanation lay in the tremendous hurricanes that, produced by the planet's rapid rotation, frequently swept along its surface, like the earth's trade-winds, but with far more violence. On reaching the northern coast of the peninsula they increased their elevation and changed their course to northeast, not caring to remain long over the great body of water, which they named Cortlandt Bay. The thousands of miles of foam fast flew beneath them, the first thing attracting their attention being a change in the ocean's colour. In the eastern shore of Cortlandt Bay they soon observed the mouth of a river, ten miles across, from which this tinted water issued in a flood. On account of its colour, which reminded them of a stream they knew so well, they christened it the Harlem.

Believing that an expedition up its valley might reveal something of interest, they began the ascent, remaining at an elevation of a few hundred feet. For about three hundred miles they followed this river, which had but few bends, while its sides became more and more precipitous, till it flowed through a cañon four and a half miles across. Though they knew from the wide discoloration of Cortlandt Bay that the volume of water discharged was tremendous, the stream seldom moved at a rate of more than five miles an hour, and for a time was free from rocks and rapids, from which they concluded that it must be very deep. Half an hour later they saw a cloud of steam or mist, which expanded, and almost obscured the sky as they approached. Next they heard a sound like distant thunder, which they took for the prolonged eruption of some giant crater, though they had not expected to find one so far towards the interior of the continent. Presently it became one continuous roar, the echo in the cañon, whose walls were at this place over six hundred feet high, being simply deafening, so that the near discharge of the heaviest artillery would have been completely drowned. "One would think the end of the world was approaching!" shouted Cortlandt through his hands.

"Look!" Bearwarden roared back, "the wind is scattering the mist."

As he spoke, the vapoury curtain was drawn aside, revealing a waterfall of such vast proportions as to dwarf completely anything they had ever seen or even imagined. A somewhat open horseshoe lip, three and a half miles straight across and over four miles following the line of the curve, discharged a sheet of water forty feet thick at the edge into an abyss six hundred feet below. Two islands on the brink divided this sheet of liquid into three nearly equal parts, while myriads of rainbows hovered in the clouds of spray. Two things especially struck the observers: the water made but little curve or sweep on passing over the edge, and then rushed down to the abyss at almost lightning speed, shivering itself to infinitesimal particles on striking any rock or projection at the side. Its behaviour was, of course, due to its weight, and to the fact that on Jupiter bodies fall 40.98 feet the first second, instead of sixteen feet, as on earth, and at correspondingly increasing speed.

Finding that they were being rapidly dazed and stunned by the noise, the travellers caused the Callisto to rise rapidly, and were soon surveying the superb sight from a considerable elevation. Their minds could grasp but slowly the full meaning and titanic power of what they saw, and not even the vast falls in their nearness could make their significance clear. Here was a sheet of water three and a half miles wide, averaging forty feet in depth, moving at a rapid rate towards a sheer fall of six hundred feet. They felt, as they gazed at it, that the power of that waterfall would turn backward every engine and dynamo on the earth, and it seemed as if it might almost put out the fires of the sun. Yet it was but an illustration of the action of the solar orb exerted on a vast area of ocean, the vapour in the form of rain being afterwards turned into these comparatively narrow limits by the topography of the continent. Compared with this, Niagara, with its descent of less than two hundred feet, and its relatively small flow of water, would be but a rivulet, or at best a rapid stream. Reluctantly leaving the fascinating spectacle, they pursued their exploration along the river above the falls. For the first few miles the surface of the water was near that of the land; there were occasional rapids, but few rocks, and the foaming torrent moved at great speed, the red sandstone banks of the river being as polished as though they had been waxed. After a while the obstructions disappeared, but the water continued to rush and surge along at a speed of ten or twelve miles an hour, so that it would be easily navigable only for logs or objects moving in one direction. The surface of the river was soon on an average fifty feet below the edge of the banks, this depression being one result of the water's rapid motion and weight, which facilitated the carving of its channel.

When they had followed up the river about sixty miles towards its source they came upon what at first had the appearance of an ocean. They knew, however, from its elevation, and the flood coming from it, that the water must be fresh, as they soon found it was. This lake was about three hundred miles wide, and stretched from northeast to southwest. There was rolling land with hills about its shores, and the foliage on the banks was a beautiful shade of bluish purple instead of the terrestrial ubiquitous green.

When near the great lake's upper end, they passed the mouth of a river on their left side, which, from its volume, they concluded must be the principal source, and therefore they determined to trace it. They found it to be a most beautiful stream, averaging two and a half miles in width, evidently very deep, and with a full, steady current. After proceeding for several hours, they found that the general placidity grew less, the smooth surface occasionally became ruffled by projecting rocks and rapids, and the banks rose till the voyagers again found themselves in a ravine or cañon.

During their sojourn on Jupiter they had had but little experience with the tremendous winds that they knew, from reason and observation, must rage in its atmosphere. They now heard them whistling over their heads, and, notwithstanding the protection afforded by the sides of the cañon, occasionally received a gust that made the Callisto swerve. They kept on steadily, however, till sunset, at which time it became very dark on account of the high banks, which rose as steeply as the Palisades on the Hudson to a height of nearly a thousand feet. Finding a small island near the eastern bank, they were glad to secure the Callisto there for the night, below the reach of the winds, which they still heard singing loudly but with a musical note in what seemed to them like the sky.

"It is incomprehensible to me." said Ayrault, as they sat at dinner, "how the sun, at a distance of four hundred and eighty-three million miles, can raise the amount of water we have here passing us, and compared with which the discharge of the greatest river on earth would be insignificant, to say nothing of the stream we ascended before reaching this."

"We must remember," replied Cortlandt, "that many of the conditions are different here from those that exist on earth. We know that some of the streams are warm, and even hot, and that the temperature of Deepwaters Bay, and doubtless that of the ocean also, is considerably higher than ours. This would facilitate evaporation. The density of the atmosphere and the tremendous winds, of which I suspect we may see more later, must also help the sun very much in its work of raising vapour. But the most potent factor is undoubtedly the vast size of the basin that these rivers drain."

"The great speed at which the atmospheric currents move," said Bearwarden, "coupled with the comparative lowness of the mountain chains and the slight obstruction they offer to their passage, must distribute the rain very thoroughly, notwithstanding the great unbroken area of the continents. There can be no such state of things here as exists in the western part of South America, where the Andes are so high that any east-bound clouds, in crossing them, are shoved up so far into a cold region that all moisture they may have brought from the Pacific is condensed into rain, with which parts of the western slope are deluged, while clouds from the Atlantic have come so far they have already dispersed their moisture, in consequence of which the region just east of the Andes gets little if any rain. It is bad for a continent to have its high mountains near the ocean from which it should get its rain, and good for it to have them set well back."

"I should not be surprised," said Cortlandt, "if we saw another waterfall to-morrow, though not in the shape of rain. In the hour before we stopped we began to see rapids and protruding rocks. That means that we are coming to a part of the channel that is comparatively new, since the older parts have had time to wear smooth. I take it, then, that we are near the foot of a retreating cascade, which we may hope soon to see. That is exactly the order in which we found smooth water and rapids in river No. 1, which we have named the Harlem."

After this, not being tired, they used the remaining dark hours for recording their recent adventures.

CHAPTER XII
HILLS AND VALLEYS

With the first light they resumed their journey, and an hour after setting out they sighted, as Cortlandt had predicted, another cloud of vapour. The fall--for such it proved to be--was more beautiful than the other, for, though the volume of water was not so great, it fell at one leap, without a break, and at the same tremendous speed, a distance of more than a thousand feet. The cañon rang with the echoes, while the spray flew in sheets against the smooth, glistening, sandstone walls. Instead of coming from a river, as the first fall had, this poured at once from the rocky lip, about two miles across, of a lake that was eleven hundred feet above the surging mass in the vale below.

"It is a thousand pities," said Bearwarden, "that this cataract has got so near its source; for, at the rate these streams must cut, this one in a few hundred years, unless something is done to prevent it, will have worn back to the lake, and then good-bye to the falls, which will become a series of rapids. Perhaps the first effect will be merely to reduce by a few feet the height of the falls, in which case they will remain in practically the same place."

About the shores of this lake they saw rhinoceroses with long thick wool, and herds of creatures that much resembled buffaloes.

"I do not see," said Bearwarden, "why the identical species should not exist here that till recently, in a geological sense, inhabited the earth. The climate and all other conditions are practically the same on both planets, except a trifling difference in weight, to which terrestrials would soon adapt themselves. We know by spectroscopic analysis that hydrogen, iron, magnesium, and all our best-known substances exist in the sun, and even the stars, while the earth contains everything we have found in meteorites. Then why make an exception of life, instead of supposing that at corresponding periods of development the same living forms inhabit all? It would be assuming the eternal sterilization of the functions of Nature to suppose that our earth is the only body that can produce them."

"The world of organic life is so much more complex," replied Cortlandt, "than that of the crystal, that it requires great continuity. So far we certainly have seen no men, or anything like them, not even so much as a monkey, though I suppose, according to your reasoning, Jupiter has not advanced far enough to produce even that."

"Exactly," replied Bearwarden, "for it will require vast periods; and, according to my belief, at least half the earth's time of habitability had passed before man appeared. But we see Jupiter is admirably suited for those who have been developed somewhere else, and it would be an awful shame if we allowed it to lie unimproved till it produces appreciative inhabitants of its own, for we find more to admire in one half-hour than its entire present population during its lifetime. Yet, how magnificent this world is, and how superior in its natural state to ours! The mountainous horns of these crescent-shaped continents protect them and the ocean they enclose from the cold polar marine currents, and in a measure from the icy winds; while the elevated country on the horns near the equator might be a Garden of Eden, or ideal resort. To be sure, the continents might support a larger population, if more broken up, notwithstanding the advantage resulting from the comparatively low mountains along the coasts, and the useful winds. A greater subdivision of land and water, more great islands connected by isthmuses, and more mediterraneans joined by straits, would be a further advantage to commerce; but with the sources of power at hand, the resistless winds and water-power, much increased in effectiveness by their weight, the great tides when several moons are on the same side, or opposite the sun, internal heat near the surface, and abundant coal-supply doubtless already formed and also near the surface, such small alterations could be made very easily, and would serve merely to prevent our becoming rusty.

"As Jupiter's distance from the sun varies from 506,563,000 miles at aphelion to only 460,013,000 at perihelion, this difference, in connection with even the slight inclination of the axis, must make a slight change in seasons, but as the inclination is practically nothing, almost the entire change results from the difference in distance. This means that the rise or fall in temperature is general on every degree of latitude, all being warmed simultaneously, more or less, as the planet approaches or departs from the sun. It means also that about the same conditions that Secretary Deepwaters suggested as desirable for the earth, prevail here, and that Jupiter represents, therefore, about the acme of climate naturally provided. On account of its rapid rotation and vast size, the winds have a tornado's strength, but they are nothing at this distance from the sun to what they would be if a planet with its present rate of rotation and size were where Venus or even the earth is. In either of these positions no land life with which we are acquainted could live on the surface; for the slope of the atmospheric isobars--i. e., the lines of equal barometric pressure that produce wind by becoming tilted through unequal expansion, after which the air, as it were, flows downhill--would be too great. The ascending currents about the equator would also, of course, be vastly strengthened; so that we see a wise dispensation of Providence in placing the large planets, which also rotate so rapidly, at a great distance from the sun, which is the father of all winds, rotation alone, however rapid, being unable to produce them."

They found this lake was about six times the size of Lake Superior, and that several large and small streams ran into its upper end. These had their sources in smaller lakes that were at slightly higher elevations. Though the air was cool, the sun shone brightly, while the ground was covered with flowers resembling those of the northern climes on earth, of all shapes and lines. Twice a day these sent up their song, and trees were covered with buds, and the birds twittered gaily. The streams murmured and bubbled, and all things reminded the travellers of early morning in spring.

"If anything could reconcile me," said Bearwarden, "to exchange my active utilitarian life for a rustic poetical existence, it would be this place, for it is far more beautiful than anything I have seen on earth. It needs but a Maud Muller and a few cows to complete the picture, since Nature gives us a vision of eternal peace and repose."

Somehow the mention of Maud Muller, and the delicate and refined flowers, whose perfume he inhaled, brought up thoughts that were never far below the surface in Ayrault's mind. "The place is heavenly enough," said he, "to make one wish to live and remain here forever, but to me it would be Hamlet with Hamlet left out."

"Ah! poor chap," said Cortlandt, "you are in love, but you are not to be pitied, for though the thrusts at the heart are sharp, they may be the sweetest that mortals know."

The following morning they reluctantly left the picturesque shores of Lake Serenity, with their beautiful tints and foliage, and resumed the journey, to explore a number of islands in the ocean in the west, which were recorded on their negatives. Ascending to rarefied air, they saw great chains of mountains, which they imagined ran parallel to the coast, rising to considerable altitudes in the east. The tops of all glistened with a mantle of snow in the sunlight, while between the ridges they saw darker and evidently fertile valleys. They passed, moving northwest, over large and small lakes, all evidently part of the same great system, and continued to sweep along for several days with a beautiful panorama, as varying as a kaleidoscope, spread beneath their eyes. They observed that the character of the country gradually changed. The symmetrically rounded mountains and hills began to show angles, while great slabs of rock were split from the faces. The sides also became less vertical, and there was an accumulation of detrital fragments about their bases. These heaps of fractured stone had in some cases begun to disintegrate and form soil, on which there was a scant growth of vegetation; but the sides and summits, whose jaggedness increased with their height, were absolutely bare.

"Here," said Cortlandt, "we have unmistakable evidence of frost and ice action. The next interesting question is, How recently has denudation occurred? The absence of plant life at the exposed places," he continued, as if lecturing to a class, "can be accounted for here, as nearer the equator, by the violence of the wind; but I greatly doubt whether water will now freeze in this latitude at any season of the year, for, even should the Northern hemisphere's very insignificant winter coincide with the planet's aphelion, the necessary drop from the present temperature would be too great to be at all probable. If, then, it is granted that ice does not form here now, notwithstanding the fact that it has done so, the most plausible conclusion is that the inclination of Jupiter's axis is automatically changing, as we know the earth's has often done. There being nothing incompatible in this view with the evidence at hand, we can safely assume it correct for the time being at least. When farther south, you remember, we found no trace of ice action, notwithstanding the comparative slowness with which we decided that the ridges in the crust had been upheaved on account of the resisting power of gravity, and, as I see now, also on account of Jupiter's great mass, which must prevent its losing its heat anything like as fast as the earth has, in which I think also we have the explanation of the comparatively low elevation of the mountains that we found we could not account for by the power of gravitation alone.* From the fact that the exposed surface farther south must be old, on account of the slow upheaval and the slight wear to which it is exposed, about the only wearing agent being the wind, which would be powerless to erase ice-scratches, especially since, on account of gravity's power, it cannot, like our desert winds, carry much sand--which, as we know, has cut away the base of the Sphinx--I think it is logical to conclude that, though Jupiter's axis is changing naturally as the earth's has been, it has never varied as much as twenty-three and a half degrees, and certainly to nothing like the extent to which we see Venus and Uranus tilted to-day."

* It is well known that mountain chains are but ridges or foldings in the crust upheaved as the interior cools and shrinks. This is proved by reason and by experiments with viscous clay or other material placed upon a sheet

of stretched rubber, which is afterwards allowed to contract, whereupon the analogues of mountain ridges are thrown up.

"I follow you," said Bearwarden, "and do not see how we could arrive at anything else. From Jupiter's low specific gravity, weighing but little more than an equal bulk of water, I should say the interior must be very hot, or else is composed of light material, for the crust's surface, or the part we see, is evidently about as dense as what we have on earth. These things have puzzled me a good deal, and I have been wondering if Jupiter may not have been formed before the earth and the smaller planets."

"The discrepancies between even the best authorities," replied Cortlandt, "show that as yet but little has been discovered from the earth concerning Jupiter's real condition. The two theories that try to account for its genesis are the ring theory and the nebulous. We know that the sun is constantly emitting vast volumes of heat and light, and that, with the exception of the heat resulting from the impact of falling meteors, it receives none from outside, the principal source being the tremendous friction and pressure between the cooling and shrinking strata within the great mass of the sun itself. A seeming paradox therefore comes in here, which must be considered: If the sun were composed entirely of gas, it would for a time continue to grow hotter; but the sun is incessantly radiating light and heat, and consequently becoming smaller. Therefore the farther back we go the hotter we find the sun, and also the larger, till, instead of having a diameter of eight hundred and eighty thousand miles, it filled the space now occupied by the entire solar system. Here is where the two theories start. According to the first, the revolving nebulous mass threw off a ring that became the planet Neptune, afterwards another that contained the material for Uranus, and so on, the lightest substance in the sun being thrown off first, by which they accounted for the lightness of the four great planets, and finally Mars, the earth, and the small dense planets near the sun. The advocates of this theory pointed to Saturn's rings as an illustration of the birth of a planet, or, rather, in that case a satellite. According to this, the major planets have had a far longer separate existence than the minor, which would account for their being so advanced notwithstanding their size. This theory may again come into general acceptance, but for the present it has been discredited by the nebulous. According to this second theory, at the time the sun filled all the space inside of Neptune's, orbit, or extended even farther, several centres of condensation were formed within the nebulous, gaseous mass. The greatest centre became the sun, and the others, large and small, the planets, which--as a result of the spiral motion of the whole, such as is now going on before our eyes in the great nebulæ of fifty-one M. Canuin venaticorum, and many others--began to revolve about the greatest central body of gas.

As the separate masses cooled, they shrank, and their surfaces or extreme edges, which at first were contiguous, began to recede, which recession is still going on with some rapidity on the part of the sun, for we may be sure its diameter diminishes as its density increases. According to either theory, as I see it, the major planets, on account of their distance from the central mass, have had longer separate existences than the minor, and are therefore more advanced than they would be had all been formed at the same time.

"This theory explains the practical uniformity in the chemical composition of all members of this system by assuming that they were all once a part of the same body, and you may say brothers and sisters of the sun, instead of its offspring. It also makes size the only factor determining temperature and density, but of course modified by age, since otherwise Jupiter would have a far less developed crust than that with which we find it. I have always considered the period from the molten condition to that with a crust as comparatively short, which stands to reason, for radiation has then no check; and the period from the formation of the crust, which acts as a blanket, to the death of a planet, as very long. I have not found this view clearly set forth in any of the books I have read, but it seems to me the simplest and most natural explanation. Now, granted that the solar system was once a nebula, on which I think every one will agree--the same forces that changed it into a system of sun and planets must be at work on fifty-one M. Canum venaticorum, Andromeda, and ninety-nine M. Virginis, and must inevitably change them to suns, each with doubtless a system of planets.

"If, then, the condition of a nebula or star depends simply on its size, it is reasonable to suppose that Andromeda, Sirius, and all the vast bodies we see, were created at the same time as our system, which involves the necessity of one general and simultaneous creation day. But as Sirius, with its diameter of twelve million miles, must be larger than some of the nebulae will be when equally condensed, we must suppose rather that nebulae are forming and coming into the condition of bright and dead stars, much as apples or pears on a fruit tree are constantly growing and developing, so that the Mosaic description of the creation would probably apply in point of time only to our system, or perhaps to our globe, though the rest will doubtless pass through precisely the same stages. This, I think, I will publish, on our return, as the Cortlandt astronomical doctrine, as the most rational I have seen devised, and one that I think we may safely believe, until, perhaps, through increased knowledge, it can be disproved."

After they crossed a line of hills that ran at right angles to their course they found the country more rolling. All streams and water-courses flowed in their direction, while their aneroid showed them that they were gradually descending. When they were moving along near the surface of the ground, a delicious and refined perfume exhaled by the blue and white flowers, that had been growing smaller as they journeyed northward, frequently reached their nostrils. To Cortlandt and Bearwarden it was merely the scent of a flower, but to Ayrault it recalled mental pictures of Sylvia wearing violets and lilies that he had given her. He knew that the greatest telescopes on earth could not reveal the Callisto moving about in Jupiter's sunshine, as even a point of light, at that distance, and, notwithstanding Cortlandt's learning and Bearwarden's joviality, he felt at times extremely lonely.

They swept along steadily for fifty hours, having bright sunny days and beautifully moonlit nights. They passed over finely rounded hills and valleys and well-watered plains. As they approached the ocean and its level the temperature rose, and there was more moisture in the air. The plants and flowers also increased in size, again resembling somewhat the large species they had seen near the equator.

"This would be the place to live," said Bearwarden, looking at iron mountains, silver, copper, and lead formations, primeval forests, rich prairies, and regions evidently underlaid with coal and petroleum, not to mention huge beds of aluminum clay, and other natural resources, that made his materialistic mouth water. "It would be joy and delight to develop industries here, with no snow avalanches to clog your railroads, or icy blizzards to paralyze work, nor weather that blights you with sun-strokes and fevers. On our return to the earth we must organize a company to run regular interplanetary lines. We could start on this globe all that is best on our own. Think what boundless possibilities may be before the human race on this planet, which on account of its vast size will be in its prime when our insignificant earth is cold and dead and no longer capable of supporting life! Think also of the indescribable blessing to the congested communities of Europe and America, to find an unlimited outlet here! Mars is already past its prime, and Venus scarcely habitable, but in Jupiter we have a new promised land, compared with which our earth is a pygmy, or but little more than microscopic."

"I see," said Ayrault, "that the possibilities here have no limit; but I do not see how you can compare it to the promised land, since, till we undertook this journey, no one had even thought of Jupiter as a habitable place." "I trace the Divine promise," replied Bearwarden, "in what you described to us on earth as man's innate longing and desire to rise, and in the fact that the Almighty has given the race unbounded expansiveness in very limited space. This would look to me as the return of man to the garden of Eden through intellectual development, for here every man can sit under his own vine and fig-tree."

"It seems to me," said Cortlandt, "that no paradise or heaven described in anything but the Bible compares with this. According to Virgil's description, the joys on the banks of his river Lethe must have been most sad and dreary, the general idleness and monotony apparently being broken only by wrestling matches between the children, while the rest strolled about with laurel wreaths or rested in the shade. The pilot Palinurus, who had been drowned by falling overboard while asleep, but who before that had presumably done his duty, did not seem especially happy; while the harsh, resentful disposition evidently remained unsoftened, for Dido became like a cliff of Marpesian marble when Æneas asked to be forgiven, though he had doubtless considered himself in duty bound to leave her, having been twice commanded to do so by Mercury, the messenger of Jove. She, like the rest, seems to have had no occupation, while the consciences of few appear to have been sufficiently clear to enable them to enjoy unbroken rest."

"The idleness in the spirit-land of all profane writers," added Bearwarden, "has often surprised me too. Though I have always recommended a certain amount of recreation for my staff--in fact, more than I have generally had myself--an excess of it becomes a bore. I think that all real progress comes through thorough work. Why should we assume that progress ceases at death? I believe in the verse that says, 'We learn here on earth those things the knowledge of which is perfected in heaven.'"

"According to that," said Cortlandt, "you will some day be setting the axis of heaven right, for in order to do work there must be work to be done--a necessary corollary to which is that heaven is still imperfect."

"No," said Bearwarden, bristling up at the way Cortlandt sometimes received his speeches, "it means simply that its development, though perfect so far as it goes, may not be finished, and that we may be the means, as on earth, of helping it along."

"The conditions constituting heaven," said Ayrault, "may be as fixed as the laws of Nature, though the products of those conditions might, it seems to me, still be forming and subject to modification thereby. The reductio ad absurdu would of course apply if we supposed the work of creation absolutely finished."

CHAPTER XIII
NORTH-POLAR DISCOVERIES

Two days later, on the western horizon, they beheld the ocean. Many of the streams whose sources they had seen when they crossed the divide from the lake basin, and whose courses they had followed, were now rivers a mile wide, with the tide ebbing and rising within them many hundreds of miles from their mouths. When they reached the shore line they found the waves breaking, as on earth, upon the sands, but with this difference: they had before noted the smallness of the undulations compared with the strength of the wind, the result of the water's weight. These waves now reminded them of the behaviour of mercury, or of melted lead when stirred on earth, by the rapidity with which the crests dropped. Though the wind was blowing an on-shore gale, there was but little combing, and when there was any it lasted but a second. The one effort of the crests and waves seemed to be to remain at rest, or, if stirred in spite of themselves, to subside.

When over the surface of the ocean, the voyagers rose to a height of thirty thousand metres, and after twenty-four hours' travelling saw, at a distance of about two hundred miles, what looked like another continent, but which they knew must be an island. On finding themselves above it, they rose still higher to obtain a view of its outlines and compare its shape with that of the islands in the photographs they had had time to develop. The length ran from southeast to northwest. Though crossed by latitude forty, and notwithstanding Jupiter's distance from the sun, the southern side had a very luxuriant vegetation that was almost semi-tropical. This they accounted for by its total immunity from cold, the density of the air at sea-level, and the warm moist breezes it received from the tepid ocean. The climate was about the same as that of the Riviera or of Florida in winter, and there was, of course, no parching summer.

"This shows me," said Bearwarden, "that a country's climate depends less on the amount of heat it receives from the sun than on the amount it retains; proof of which we have in the tops of the Himalayas perpetually covered with snow, and snow-capped mountains on the very equator, where they get the most direct rays, and where those rays have but little air to penetrate. It shows that the presence of a substantial atmosphere is as necessary a part of the calculation in practice as the sun itself. I am inclined to think that, with the constant effect of the internal heat on its oceans and atmosphere, Jupiter could get along with a good deal less solar heat than it receives, in proof of which I expect to find the poles themselves quite comfortable. The reason the internal heat is so little taken into account on earth is because, from the thickness of the crust, it cannot make itself felt; for if the earth were as chilled through as ice, the people on the surface would not feel the difference." A Jovian week's explorations disclosed the fact that though the island's general outlines were fairly regular, it had deep-water harbours, great rivers, and land-locked gulfs and bays, some of which penetrated many hundred miles into the interior. It also showed that the island's length was about six thousand miles, and its breadth about three thousand, and that it had therefore about the superficial area of Asia. They found no trace of the great monsters that had been so numerous on the mainland, though there were plenty of smaller and gentle-looking creatures, among them animals whose build was much like that of the prehistoric horse, with undeveloped toes on each side of the hoof, which in the modern terrestrial horse have disappeared, the hoof being in reality but a rounded-off middle finger. "It is wonderful," said Bearwarden, "how comparatively narrow a body of water can keep different species entirely separate. The island of Sumatra, for instance, is inhabited by marsupials belonging to the distinct Australian type, in which the female, as in the kangaroo, carries the slightly developed young in a pouch; while the Malay peninsula, joined to the mainland, has all the highly developed animals of Asia and the connected land of the Eastern hemisphere, the narrow Malacca Strait being all that has kept marsupials and mammals apart, though the separating power has been increased by the rapid current setting through. This has decreased the chance of creatures carried to sea on drift-wood or uprooted trees getting safely over to such a degree that apparently none have survived; for, had they done so, we may be certain that the mammals, with the advantage their young have over the marsupials, would soon have run them out, the marsupials being the older and the less perfect form of life of the two."

Before leaving the beautiful sea-girt region beneath them, Cortlandt proposed that it be named after their host, which Bearwarden seconded, whereupon they entered it as Ayrault Island on the charts. After this they rose to a great height, and flew swiftly over three thousand miles of ocean till they came to another island not quite as large as the first. It was four thousand five hundred miles long by something less than three thousand wide, and was therefore about the size of Africa. It had several high ranges of mountains and a number of great rivers and fine harbours, while murmuring, bubbling brooks flowed through its forest glades. There were active volcanoes along the northern coast, and the blue, crimson, and purple lines in the luxuriant foliage were the most beautiful they had ever seen.

"I propose," said Bearwarden, "that we christen this Sylvialand." This Cortlandt immediately seconded, and it was so entered on the charts.

"These two islands," said Bearwarden, "may become the centres of civilization. With flying machines and cables to carry passengers and information, and ships of great displacement for the interchange of commodities, there is no limit to their possible development. The absence of large waves will also be very favourable to sea-spiders, which will be able to run at tremendous speeds. The constancy in the eruptions of the volcanoes will offer a great field to Jovian inventors, who will unquestionably be able to utilize their heat for the production of steam or electricity, to say nothing of an inexhaustible supply of valuable chemicals. They may contain the means of producing some force entirely different from apergy, and as superior to electricity as that is to steam. Our earthly volcanoes have been put to slight account because of the long intervals between eruptions."

After leaving Sylvialand they went westward to the eastern of the two crescent continents. It was separated from the island by about six thousand miles of ocean, and had less width than the western, having about the proportions of a three-day crescent, while the western had the shape of the moon when four or five days old. They found the height of the mountains and plateaus somewhat less than on the eastern continent, but no great difference in other respects, except that, as they went towards the pole, the vegetation became more like that of Scotland or a north temperate region than any they had seen. On reaching latitude fifty they again came out over the ocean to investigate the speckled condition they had observed there. They found a vast archipelago covering as great an area as the whole Pacific Ocean. The islands varied from the size of Borneo and Madagascar to that of Sicily and Corsica, while some contained but a few square miles. The surface of the archipelago was about equally divided between land and water.

"It would take good navigation or an elaborate system of light-houses," said Bearwarden, "for a captain to find the shortest course through these groups."

The islands were covered with shade trees much resembling those on earth, and the leaves on many were turning yellow and red, for this hemisphere's autumn had already begun.

"The Jovian trees," said Cortlandt, "can never cease to bear, though the change of seasons is evidently able to turn their colour, perhaps by merely ripening them. When a ripe leaf falls off, its place is doubtless soon taken by a bud, for germination and fructification go on side by side."

Before leaving, they decided to name this Twentieth Century Archipelago, since so much of the knowledge appertaining to it had been acquired in their own day. At latitude sixty the northern arms of the two continents came within fifteen hundred miles of each other. The eastern extension was split like the tail of a fish, the great bay formed thereby being filled with islands, which also extended about half of the distance across. The western extremity shelved very gradually, the sand-bars running out for miles just below the surface of the water.

After this the travellers flew northward at great speed in the upper regions of the air, for they were anxious to hasten their journey. They found nothing but unbroken sea, and not till they reached latitude eighty-seven was there a sign of ice. They then saw some small bergs and field ice, but in no great quantities. As their outside thermometer, when just above the placid water--for there were no waves here--registered twenty-one degrees Fahrenheit, they accounted for this scarcity of ice by the absence of land on which fresh water could freeze, and by the fact that it was not cold enough to congeal the very salt sea-water.

Finally they reached another archipelago a few hundred miles in extent, the larger islands of which were covered with a sheet of ice, at the edges of which small icebergs were being formed by breaking off and slowly floating. Finding a small island on which the coating was thin, they grounded the Callisto, and stepped out for the first time in several days. The air was so still that a small piece of paper released at a height of six feet sank slowly and went as straight as the string of a plumb-line. The sun was bisected by the line of the horizon, and appeared to be moving about them in a circle, with only its upper half visible. As Jupiter's northern hemisphere was passing through its autumnal equinox, they concluded they had landed exactly at the pole. "Now to work on our experiment," said Cortlandt. "I wonder how we may best get below the frozen surface?" "We can explode a small quantity of dynamite," replied Bearwarden, "after which the digging will be comparatively easy."

While Cortlandt and Bearwarden prepared the mine, Ayrault brought out a pickaxe, two shovels, and the battery and wires with which to ignite the explosive. They made their preparations within one hundred feet of the Callisto, or much nearer than an equivalent amount of gunpowder could have been discharged.

"This recalls an old laboratory experiment, or rather lecture," said Cortlandt, as they completed the arrangements, "for the illustration is not as a rule carried out. Explode two pounds of powder on an iron safe in a room with the windows closed, and the windows will be blown out, while the safe remains uninjured. Explode an equivalent amount of dynamite on top of the safe, and it will be destroyed, while the glass panes are not even cracked. This illustrates the difference in rapidity with which the explosions take place. To the intensely rapid action of dynamite the air affords as much resistance as a solid substance, while the explosion of the powder is so slow that the air has time to move away; hence the destruction of the windows in the first case, and the safe in the second." When they had moved beyond the danger line, Bearwarden, as the party's practising engineer, pressed the button, and the explosion did the rest. They found that the ground was frozen to a depth of but little more than a foot, below which it became perceptibly warm. Plying their shovels vigorously, they had soon dug the hole so deep that its edges were above their heads. When the floor was ten feet below the surrounding level the thermometer registered sixty.

"This is scarcely a fair test," said Cortlandt, "since the heat rises and is lost as fast as given off. Let us therefore close the opening and see in what time it will melt a number of cubic feet of ice."

Accordingly they climbed out, threw in about a cart-load of ice, and covered the opening with two of the Callisto's thick rugs. In half an hour all the ice had melted, and in another half hour the water was hot.

"No arctic expedition need freeze to death here," said Bearwarden, "since all a man would have to do would be to burrow a few feet to be as warm as toast."

As the island on which they had landed was at one side of the archipelago, but was itself at the exact pole, it followed that the centre of the archipelago was not the part farthest north. This in a measure accounted for the slight thickness of ice and snow, for the isobaric lines would slope, and consequently what wind there was would flow towards the interior of the archipelago, whose surface was colder than the surrounding ocean. The moist air, however, coming almost entirely from the south, would lose most of its moisture by condensation in passing over the ice-laden land, and so, like the clouds over the region east of the Andes, would have but little left to let fall on this extreme northern part. The blanketing effect of a great thickness of snow would also cause, the lower strata of ice to melt, by keeping in the heat constantly given off by the warm planet. "I think there can be no question," said Cortlandt, "that, as a result of Jupiter's great flattening at the poles and the drawing of the crust, which moves faster in Jupiter's rotation than any other part, towards the equator, the crust must be particularly thin here; for, were it as thin all over, there would be no space for the coal-beds, which, judging from the purity of the atmosphere, must be very extensive. Further, we can recall that the water in the hot spring near which we alighted, which evidently came from a far greater depth than we have here, was not as hot as this. The conclusion is clear that elsewhere the internal heat is not as near the surface as here." "The more I see of Jupiter," exclaimed Bearwarden enthusiastically, "the more charmed I become. It almost exactly supplies what I have been conjuring up as my idea of a perfect planet. Its compensations of high land near the equator, and low with effective internal heat at the poles, are ideal. The gradual slope of its continental elevations, on account of their extent, will ease the work of operating railways, and the atmosphere's density will be just the thing for our flying machines, while Nature has supplied all sources of power so lavishly that no undertaking will be too great. Though land as yet, to judge by our photographs, occupies only about one eighth of the surface, we know, from the experience of the other planets, that this is bound to increase; so that, if the human race can perpetuate itself on Jupiter long enough, it will undoubtedly have one fourth or a larger proportion for occupation, though the land already upheaved comprises fully forty times the area of our entire globe, which, as we know, is still three-fourths water." "Since we have reached what we might call the end of Jupiter, and still have time," continued Ayrault, "let us proceed to Saturn, where we may find even stranger things than here. I hoped we could investigate the great red spot, but am convinced we have seen the beginning of one in Twentieth Century Archipelago, and what, under favourable conditions, will be recognized as such on earth."

It was just six terrestrial weeks since they had set out, and therefore February 2d on earth.

"It would be best, in any case, to start from Jupiter's equator," said Cortlandt, "for the straight line we should make from the surface here would be at right angles to Saturn. We shall probably, in spite of ourselves, swing a few degrees beyond the line, and so can get a bird's-eye view of some portion of the southern hemisphere."

"All aboard for Saturn!" cried Bearwarden enthusiastically, in his jovial way. "This will be a journey."

CHAPTER XIV
THE SCENE SHIFTS

Having returned the rugs to the Callisto, they applied the maximum power of the batteries to rising, closed all openings when the barometer registered thirty, and moved off into space. When Several thousand miles above the pole, they diverted part of the power to attracting the nearest moon that was in the plane of Jupiter's equator, and by the time their upward motion had ceased were moving well in its direction. Their rapid motion aided the work of resisting gravity, since their car had in fact become a small moon, revolving, like those of Uranus or that of Neptune, in an orbit varying greatly from the plane of the ecliptic. As they flew south at a height ranging from two thousand to three thousand miles, the planet revolved before them, and they had a chance of obtaining a thorough view. There were but a few scattered islands on the side of the Northern hemisphere opposite to that over which they had reached the pole, and in the varying colours of the water, which they attributed to temperature or to some substance in solution, they recognized what they had always heard described on earth as the bands of Jupiter, encircling the planet with great belts, the colour varying with the latitude. At about latitude forty-five these bands were purple, farther south light olive green, and at the equator a brown orange. Shortly after they swung across the equator the ocean again became purple, and at the same time a well-defined and very brilliant white spot came into view. Its brightness showed slight variations in intensity, though its general shape remained unchanged. It had another peculiarity, in that it possessed a fairly rapid motion of its own, as it moved eastward across the surface of the ocean. It exhibited all the phenomena of the storm they had watched in crossing Secretary Deepwaters Bay, but covered a larger area, and was far more violent. Their glasses showed them vast sheets of spray driven along at tremendous speed, while the surface was milky white.

"This," said Bearwarden, picking up a book, "solves to my mind the mystery of the white spot described by the English writer Chambers, in 1889, as follows:

"'During the last few years a brilliant white spot has been visible on the equatorial border of the great southern belt. A curious fact in connection with this spot is, that it moves with a velocity of some two hundred and sixty miles per hour greater than the red spot. Denning obtained one hundred and sixty-nine observations of this bright marking during the years 1880-1883, and determined the period as nine hours, fifty minutes, eight and seven tenths seconds (five and a half minutes less than that of the red spot). Although the latter is now somewhat faint, the white spot gives promise of remaining visible for many years. During the year 1886 a large number of observations of Jupiter were made at the Dearborn Observatory, Chicago, U. S., by Prof. G. W. Hough, using the eighteen-and-a-half-inch refractor of the observatory. Inasmuch as these observations are not only of high intrinsic interest, but are in conflict, to some extent, with previous records, a somewhat full abstract of them will be useful: The object of general interest was the great red spot. The outline, shape, and size of this remarkable object has remained without material change from the year 1879, when it was first observed here, until the present time. According to our observations, during the whole of this period it has shown a sharp and well-defined outline, and at no time has it coalesced or been joined to any belt in its proximity, as has been alleged by some observers. During the year 1885 the middle of the spot was very much paler in colour than the margins, causing it to appear as an elliptical ring. The ring form has continued up to the present time. While the outline of the spot has remained very constant, the colour has changed materially from year to year. During the past three years (1884-'86) it has at times been very faint, so as barely to be visible. The persistence of this object for so many years leads me to infer that the formerly accepted theory, that the phenomena seen on the surface of the planet are atmospheric, is no longer tenable. The statement so often made in text-books, that in the course of a few days or months the whole aspect of the planet may be changed, is obviously erroneous. The oval white spots on the southern hemisphere of the planet, nine degrees south of the equator, have been systematically observed at every opposition during the past eight years. They are generally found in groups of three or more, but are rather difficult to observe. The rotation period deduced from them is nearly the same as from the great red spot. These spots usually have a slow drift in longitude of about five seconds daily in the direction of the planet's rotation, when referred to the great red spot; corresponding to a rotation period of twenty seconds less than the latter.'

"This shows," continued Bearwarden, "that as long ago as towards the close of the nineteenth century the old idea that we saw nothing but the clouds in Jupiter's atmosphere was beginning to change; and also how closely the two English writers and Prof. Hough were studying the subject, though their views did not entirely agree. A white spot is merely a storm-centre passing round and round the planet, the wind running a little ahead of the surface, which accounts for its rapid rotation compared with the red spot, which is a fixture. A critic may say we have no such winds on earth; to which I reply, that winds on a planet of Jupiter's size, with its rate of rotation--though it is 480,000,000 miles from the sun and the internal heat is so near the surface--and with land and water arranged as they are, may and indeed must be very different from those prevailing on earth, the conditions producing and affecting them being so changed. Though the storm-centre moves two hundred and sixty miles an hour, the wind need not blow at that rate."

Later they saw several smaller spots drifting eastward, but concluded that any seaworthy ship might pass safely through them, for, though they were hurricanes of great violence, the waves were small.

"There would be less danger," said Bearwarden, "of shipping seas here than there is on earth; the principal risk to travellers would be that of being blown from the deck. On account of the air's weight in connection with its velocity, this would necessitate some precaution."

The next object of interest was the great red spot. It proved, as Cortlandt had predicted, to be a continent, with at that time no special colour, though they easily recognized it by comparing its outlines with those of the spot in the map. Its length, as they already knew, was twenty-seven thousand miles, and its breadth about eight thousand miles, so that it contained more square miles than the entire surface of the earth, land and water included.

"It is clear," said Cortlandt, "that at some season of Jupiter's long year a change takes place that affects the colour of the leaves--some drought or prolonged norther; for it is obvious that that is the simplest explanation. In like manner we may expect that at some times more white spots will move across the ocean than at others."

"On account of the size of these continents and oceans," said Bearwarden, "it is easy to believe that many climatic conditions may prevail here that can scarcely exist on earth. But what a magnificent world to develop, with its great rivers, lakes, and mountains showing at even this distance, and what natural resources must be lying there dormant, awaiting our call! This constantly recurs to my mind. The subjugation and thorough opening up of this red spot continent will probably supply more interesting problems than straightening the axis of the earth."

"At our next visit," replied Ayrault, "when we have established regular interplanetary lines of travel, we may have an opportunity to examine it more closely." Then they again attracted the nearest moon beyond which they had swung, increased the repulsion on Jupiter, and soared away towards Saturn.

"We have a striking illustration of Jupiter's enormous mass," said Cortlandt, as the apparent diameter of the mighty planet rapidly decreased, "in the fact that notwithstanding its numerous moons, it still rotates so rapidly. We know that the earth's days were formerly but half or a quarter as long as now, having lasted but six or eight hours. The explanation of the elongation is simple: the earth rotates in about twenty-four hours, while the moon encircles it but once in nearly twenty-eight days, so that our satellite is continually drawing the oceans backward against its motion. These tidal brakes acting through the friction of the water on the bottom, its unequal pressure, and the impact of the waves on the shore, are continually retarding its rotation, so that the day is a fraction of a second longer now than it was in the time of Caesar. This same action is of course taking place in Jupiter and the great planets, in this case there being five moons at work. Our moon, we know, rotates on its axis but once while it revolves about the earth, this being no doubt due to its own comparative smallness and the great attraction of the earth, which must have produced tremendous tides before the lunar oceans disappeared from its surface."

In crossing the orbits of the satellites, they passed near Ganymede, Jupiter's largest moon.

"This," said Cortlandt, "was discovered by Galileo in 1610. It is three thousand four hundred and eighty miles in diameter, while our moon is but two thousand one hundred and sixty, revolves at a distance of six hundred and seventy-eight thousand three hundred miles from Jupiter, completes its revolution in seven days and four hours, and has a specific gravity of 1.87."

In passing, they observed that Ganymede possessed an atmosphere, and continents and oceans of large area. "Here," said Bearwarden, "we have a body with a diameter about five hundred miles greater than the planet Mercury. Its size, light specific gravity, atmosphere, and oceans seem to indicate that it is less advanced than that planet, yet you think Jupiter has had a longer separate existence than the planets nearer the sun?"

"Undoubtedly," said Cortlandt. "Jupiter was condensed while in the solar-system nebula, and began its individual existence and its evolutionary career long before Mercury was formed. The matter now in Ganymede, however, doubtless remained part of the Jupiter-system nebula till after Mercury's creation, and, being part of so great a mass, did not cool very rapidly. I should say that this satellite has about the same relation to Jupiter that Jupiter has to the sun, and is therefore younger in point of time as well as of development than the most distant Callisto, and older, at all events in years, than Europa and Io, both of which are nearer. This supposition is corroborated by the fact that Europa, the smallest of these four, is also the densest, having a specific gravity of 2.14, its smallness having enabled it to overtake Ganymede in development, notwithstanding the latter's start. In the face of the evidence before us we must believe this, or else that, perhaps, as in the case of the asteroid Hilda, something like a collision has rejuvenated it. This might account for its size, and for the Nautical Almanac's statement that there is a 'small and variable' inclination to its orbit, while Io and Europa revolve exactly in the plane of Jupiter's equator."

They had about as long a journey before them as they had already made in going from the earth to Jupiter. The great planet soon appeared as a huge crescent, since it was between them and the sun; its moons became as fifth- and sixth-magnitude stars, and in the evening of the next day Jupiter's disk became invisible to the unaided eye. Since there were no way stations, in the shape of planets or asteroids, between Jupiter and Saturn, they kept the maximum repulsion on Jupiter as long as possible, and moved at tremendous speed. Saturn was somewhat in advance of Jupiter in its orbit, so that their course from the earth had been along two sides of a triangle with an obtuse angle between. During the next four terrestrial days they sighted several small comets, but spent most of their time writing out their Jovian experiences. During the sixth day Saturn's rings, although not as much tilted as they would be later in the planet's season, presented a most superb sight, while they spun in the sun's rays. Soon after this the eight moons became visible, and, while slightly reducing the Callisto's speed, they crossed the orbits of Iapetus, Hyperion, and Titan, when they knew they were but seven hundred and fifty thousand miles from Saturn.

"I am anxious to ascertain," said Cortlandt, "whether the composition of yonder rings is similar to that of the comet through which we passed. I am sure they shine with more than reflected light."

"We have been in the habit," said Ayrault, "of associating heat with light, but it is obvious there is something far more subtle about cometary light and that of Saturn's rings, both of which seem to have their birth in the intense cold of interplanetary space."

Passing close to Mimas, Saturn's nearest moon, they supplemented its attraction, after swinging by, by their own strong pull, bringing their speed down to dead slow as they entered the outside ring. At distances often of half a mile they found meteoric masses, sometimes lumps the size of a house, often no larger than apples, while small particles like grains of sand moved between them. There were two motions. The ring revolved about

Saturn, and the particles vibrated among themselves, evidently kept apart by a mutual repulsion, which seemed both to increase and decrease faster than gravitation; for on approaching one another they were more strongly repelled than attracted, but when they separated the repulsion decreased faster than the attraction, so that after a time divergence ceased, and they remained at fixed distances.

The Callisto soon became imbued with motion also, but nothing ever struck it. When any large mass came unusually near, both it and their car emitted light, and they rapidly separated. The sunlight was not as strong here as it had been when they entered the comet, and as they penetrated farther they were better able to observe the omnipresent luminosity. They were somewhat puzzled by the approach of certain light-centres, which seemed to contain nothing but this concentrated brightness. Occasionally one of these centres would glow very brightly near them, and simultaneously recede. At such times the Callisto also glowed, and itself recoiled slightly. At first the travellers could not account for this, but finally they concluded that the centres must be meteoric masses consisting entirely of gases, possessing weight though invisible.

"We have again to face," said Cortlandt, "that singular law that till recently we did not suppose existed on earth. All kinds of suppositions have been advanced in explanation of these rings. Some writers have their thickness, looked at from the thin edge, as four hundred miles, some one hundred, and some but forty. One astronomer of the nineteenth century, a man of considerable eminence, was convinced that they consisted of sheets of liquid. Now, it should be obvious that no liquid could maintain itself here for a minute, for it would either fall upon the planet as a crushing hail, or, if dependent for its shape on its own tenacity, it would break if formed of the toughest steel, on account of the tremendous weight. Any number of theories have been advanced by any number of men, but in weight we have the rub. No one has ever shown how these innumerable fragments maintain themselves at a height of but a few thousand miles above Saturn, withstanding the giant's gravitation-pull. Their rate of revolution, though rapid, does not seem fast enough to sustain them. Neither have I ever seen it explained why the small fragments do not fall upon the large ones, though many astronomers have pictured the composition of these rings as we find they exist. Nor do we know why the molecules of a gas are driven farther apart by heat, while their activity is also increased, though if this activity were revolution about one another to develop the centrifugal, it would not need to be as strong then as when they are cold and nearer together. There may be explanations, but I have found none in any of the literature I have read. It seems to me that all this leads to but one conclusion, viz.: apergy is the constant and visible companion of gravitation, on these great planets Jupiter and Saturn, perhaps on account of some peculiar influence they possess, and also in comets, in the case of large masses, while on earth it appears naturally only among molecules--those of gases and every other substance."

"I should go a step further," said Bearwarden, "and say our earth has the peculiarity, since it does not possess the influence necessary to generate naturally a great or even considerable development of apergy. The electricity of thunderstorms, northern lights, and other forces seems to be produced freely, but as regards apergy our planet's natural productiveness appears to be small."

The omnipresent luminosity continued, but the glow was scarcely bright enough to be perceived from the earth.

"I believe, however," said Bearwarden, referring to this, "that whenever a satellite passes near these fragments, preferably when it enters the planet's shadow, since that will remove its own light, it will create such activity among them as to make the luminosity visible to the large telescopes or gelatine plates on earth."

"Now," said Ayrault, "that we have evolved enough theories to keep astronomers busy for some time, if they attempt to discuss them, I suggest that we alight and leave the abstract for the concrete."

Whereupon they passed through the inner ring and rapidly sank to the ground.

BOOK III

CHAPTER I
SATURN

Landing on a place about ten degrees north of the equator, so that they might obtain a good view of the great rings--since ON the line only the thin edge would be visible--they opened a port-hole with the same caution they had exercised on Jupiter. Again there was a rush of air, showing that the pressure without was greater than that within; but on this occasion the barometer stopped at thirty-eight, from which they calculated that the pressure was nineteen pounds to the square inch on their bodies, instead of fifteen as at sea-level on earth. This difference was so slight that they scarcely felt it. They also discarded the apergetic outfits that had been so useful on Jupiter, as unnecessary here. The air was an icy blast, and though they quickly closed the opening, the interior of the Callisto was considerably chilled.

"We shall want our winter clothes," said Bearwarden; "it might be more comfortable for us exactly on the equator, though the scene at night will be far finer here, if we can stand the climate. Doubtless it will also be warmer soon, for the sun has but just risen."

"I suspect this is merely one of the cold waves that rush towards the equator at this season, which corresponds to about the 10th of our September," replied Cortlandt. "The poles of Saturn must be intensely cold during its long winter of fourteen and three quarter years, for, the axis being inclined twenty-seven degrees from the perpendicular of its orbit, the pole turned from the sun is more shut off from its heat than ours, and in addition to this the mean distance--more than eight hundred and eighty million miles--is very great. Since the chemical composition of the air we have inhaled has not troubled our lungs, it is fair to suppose we shall have no difficulty in breathing."

Having dressed themselves more warmly, and seen by a thermometer they had placed outside that the temperature was thirty-eight degrees

Fahrenheit, which had seemed very cold compared with the warmth inside the Callisto, they again opened the port-hole, this time leaving it open longer. What they had felt before was evidently merely a sudden gust, for the air was now comparatively calm.

Finding that the doctor's prediction as to the suitability of the air to their lungs was correct, they ventured out, closing the door as they went.

Expecting, as on Jupiter, to find principally vertebrates of the reptile and bird order, they carried guns and cartridges loaded with buckshot and No. 1, trusting for solid-ball projectiles to their revolvers, which they shoved into their belts. They also took test-tubes for experiments on the Saturnian bacilli. Hanging a bucket under the pipe leading from the roof, to catch any rain that might fall--for they remembered the scarcity of drinking-water on Jupiter--they set out in a southwesterly direction.

Walking along, they noticed on all sides tall lilies immaculately pure in their whiteness, and mushrooms and toadstools nearly a foot high, the former having a delicious flavour and extreme freshness, as though only an hour old. They had seen no animal life, or even sign of it, and were wondering at its dearth, when suddenly two large white birds rose directly in front of them. Like thought, Bearwarden and Ayrault had their guns up, snapping the thumb-pieces over "safe" and pulling the triggers almost simultaneously. Bearwarden, having double buckshot, killed his bird at the first fire; but Ayrault, having only No. 1, had to give his the second barrel, almost all damage in both cases being in the head. On coming close to their victims they found them to measure twelve feet from tip to tip, and to have a tremendous thickness of feathers and down.

"From the looks of these beauties," said Bearwarden, "I should say they probably inhabited a pretty cold place."

"They are doubtless northern birds," said Cortlandt, "that have just come south. It is easy to believe that the depth to which the temperature may fall in the upper air of this planet must be something startling."

As they turned from the cranes, to which species the birds seemed to belong, they became mute with astonishment. Every mushroom had disappeared, but the toadstools still remained.

"Is it possible we did not see them?" gasped Ayrault.

"We must inadvertently have walked some distance since we saw them," said Cortlandt.

"They were what I looked forward to for lunch," exclaimed Bearwarden.

They were greatly perplexed. The mushrooms were all about them when they shot the birds, which still lay where they had fallen.

"We must be very absent-minded," said the doctor, "or perchance our brains are affected by the air. We must analyze it to see if it contains our own proportion of oxygen and nitrogen. There was a good deal of carbonic-acid gas on Jupiter, but that would hardly confuse our senses. The strange thing is, that we all seem to have been impressed the same way."

Concluding that they must have been mistaken, they continued on their journey. All about they heard a curious humming, as that of bees, or like the murmuring of prayers in a resonant cathedral. Thinking it was the wind in the great trees that grew singly around them, they paid no attention to it until, emerging on an open plain and finding that the sound continued, they stopped.

"Now," said Bearwarden, "this is more curious than anything we found on Jupiter. Here we have an incessant and rather pleasant sound, with no visible cause."

"It may possibly be some peculiarity of the grass," replied Cortlandt, "though, should it continue when we reach sandy or bare soil, I shall believe we need a dose of quinine."

"I FEEL perfectly well," said Ayrault; "how is it with you?"

Each finding that he was in a normal state, they proceeded, determined, if possible, to discover the source from which the sounds came. Suddenly Bearwarden raised his gun to bring down a long-beaked hawk; but the bird flew off, and he did not shoot. "Plague the luck!" said he; "I went blind just as I was about to pull. A haze seemed to cover both barrels, and completely screened the bird."

"The Callisto will soon be hidden by those trees," said Cortlandt. "I think we had better take our bearings, for, if our crack shot is going to miss like that, we may want canned provisions."

Accordingly, he got out his sextant, took the altitude of the sun, got cross-bearings and a few angles, and began to make a rough calculation. For several minutes he worked industriously, used the rubber at the end of his pencil, tried again, and then scratched out. "That humming confuses me so that I cannot work correctly," said he, "while the most irrelevant things enter my mind in spite of me, and mix up my figures."

"I found the same thing," said Bearwarden, "but said nothing, for fear I should not be believed. In addition to going blind, for a moment I almost forgot what I was trying to do."

Changing their course slightly, they went towards a range of hills, in the hope of finding rocky or sandy soil, in order to test the sounds, and ascertain if they would cease or vary.

Having ascended a few hundred feet, they sat down near some trees to rest, the musical hum continuing meanwhile unchanged. The ground was strewn with large coloured crystals, apparently rubies, sapphires, and emeralds, about the size of hens' eggs, and also large sheets of isinglass. Picking up one of the latter, Ayrault examined it. Points of light and shade kept forming on its surface, from which rings radiated like the circles spreading in all directions from a place in still water at which a pebble is thrown. He called his companions, and the three examined it. The isinglass was about ten inches long by eight across, and contained but few impurities. In addition to the spreading rings, curious forms were continually taking shape and dissolving.

"This is more interesting," said Bearwarden, "than sounding shells at the sea-shore. We must make a note of it as another thing to study."

They then spread their handkerchiefs on a mound of earth, so as to make a table, and began examining the gems.

"Does it not seem to you," asked Ayrault, a few minutes later, addressing his companions, "as though we were not alone? I have thought many times there was some one--or perhaps several persons--here besides ourselves." "The same idea has occurred to me," replied Cortlandt. "I was convinced, a moment ago, that a shadow crossed the page on which I was taking notes. Can it be there are objects about us we cannot see? We know there are vibrations of both light and sound that do not affect our senses. I wish we had brought the magnetic eye; perchance that might tell us."

"Anything sufficiently dense to cast a shadow," said Ayrault, "should be seen, since it would also be able to make an image on our retinas. I believe any impressions we are receiving are produced through our minds, as if some one were thinking very intently about us, and that neither the magnetic eye nor a sensitive plate could reveal anything."

They then returned to the study of the isinglass, which they were able to split into extremely thin sheets. Suddenly a cloud passed over the table, and almost immediately disappeared, and then a sharpened pencil with which Ayrault had been writing began to trace on a sheet of paper, in an even hand, and with a slight frictional sound.

"Stop!" said Bearwarden; "let us each for himself describe in writing what he has seen."

In a moment they had done this, and then compared notes. In each case the vision was the same. Then they looked at the writing made by the invisible hand. "Absorpta est mors in Victoria," it ran.

"Gentlemen," began Bearwarden, as if addressing a meeting, "this cannot be coincidence; we are undoubtedly and unquestionably in the presence of a spirit or of several spirits. That they understand Latin, we see; and, from what they say, they may have known death. Time may show whether they have been terrestrials like ourselves. Though the conditions of life here might make us delirious, it is scarcely possible that different temperaments like ours should be affected in so precisely the same way; besides, in this writing we have tangible proof."

"It is perfectly reasonable," said Ayrault, "to conclude it was a spirit, if we may assume that spirits have the power to move the pencil, which is a material object. Nobody doubts nowadays that after death we live again; that being the case, we must admit that we live somewhere. Space, as I take it, can be no obstacle to a spirit; therefore, why suppose they remain on earth?"

"This is a wonderful place," said Cortlandt. "We have already seen enough to convince us of the existence of many unknown laws. I wish the spirit would reveal itself in some other way."

As he finished speaking, the rays of the distant and cold-looking sun were split, and the colours of the spectrum danced upon the linen cloth, as if obtained by a prism. In astonishment, they rose and looked closely at the table, when suddenly a shadow that no one recognized as his own appeared upon the cover. Tracing it to its source, their eyes met those of an old man with a white robe and beard and a look of great intelligence on his calm face. They knew he had not been in the little grove thirty seconds before, and as this was surrounded by open country there was no place from which he could have come.

CHAPTER II
THE SPIRIT'S FIRST VISIT

"Greetings and congratulations," he said. "Man has steadfastly striven to rise, and we see the results in you."

"I have always believed in the existence of spirits," said Cortlandt, "but never expected to see one with my natural eyes."

"And you never will, in its spiritual state," replied the shade, "unless you supplement sight with reason. A spirit has merely existence, entity, and will, and is entirely invisible to your eyes."

"How is it, then, that we see and hear you?" asked Cortlandt. "Are you a man, or a spectre that is able to affect our senses?"

"I WAS a man," replied the spirit, "and I have given myself visible and tangible form to warn you of danger. My colleagues and I watched you when you left the cylinder and when you shot the birds, and, seeing your doom in the air, have been trying to communicate with you."

"What were the strange shadows and prismatic colours that kept passing across our table?" asked Bearwarden.

"They were the obstructions and refractions of light caused by spirits trying to take shape," replied the shade.

"Do you mind our asking you questions?" said Cortlandt.

"No," replied their visitor. "If I can, I will answer them."

"Then," said Cortlandt, "how is it that, of the several spirits that tried to become embodied, we see but one, namely, you?"

"That," said the shade, "is because no natural law is broken. On earth one man can learn a handicraft better in a few days than another in a month, while some can solve with ease a mathematical problem that others could never grasp. So it is here. Perhaps I was in a favourable frame of mind on dying, for the so-called supernatural always interested me on earth, or I had a natural aptitude for these things; for soon after death I was able to affect the senses of the friends I had left."

"Are we to understand, then," asked Cortlandt, "that the reason more of our departed do not reappear to us is because they cannot?" "Precisely," replied the shade. "But though the percentage of those that can return and reappear on earth is small, their number is fairly large. History has many cases. We know that the prophet Samuel raised the witch of Endor at the behest of Saul; that Moses and Elias became visible in the transfiguration; and that after his crucifixion and burial Christ returned to his disciples, and was seen and heard by many others."

"How," asked Bearwarden deferentially, "do you occupy your time?"

"Time," replied the spirit, "has not the same significance to us that it has to you. You know that while the earth rotates in twenty-four hours, this planet takes but about ten; and the sun turns on its own axis but once in a terrestrial month; while the years of the planets vary from less than three months for Mercury to Neptune's one hundred and sixty-four years. Being insensible to heat and cold, darkness and light, we have no more changing seasons, neither is there any night. When a man dies," he continued with solemnity, "he comes at once into the enjoyment of senses vastly keener than any he possessed before. Our eyes--if such they can be called--are both microscopes and telescopes, the change in focus being effected as instantaneously as thought, enabling us to perceive the smallest microbe or disease-germ, and to see the planets that revolve about the stars. The step of a fly is to us as audible as the tramp of a regiment, while we hear the mechanical and chemical action of a snake's poison on the blood of any poor creature bitten, as plainly as the waves on the shore. We also have a chemical and electrical sense, showing us what effect different substances will have on one another, and what changes to expect in the weather. The most complex and subtle of our senses, however, is a sort of second sight that we call intuition or prescience, which we are still studying to perfect and understand. With our eyes closed it reveals to us approaching astronomical and other bodies, or what is happening on the other side of the planet, and enables us to view the future as you do the past. The eyes of all but the highest angels require some light, and can be dazzled by an excess; but this attribute of divinity nothing can obscure, and it is the sense that will first enable us to know God. By means of these new and sharpened faculties, which, like children, we are continually learning to use to better advantage, we constantly increase our knowledge, and this is next to our greatest happiness."

"Is there any limit," asked Bearwarden, "to human progress on the earth?"

"Practically none," replied the spirit. "Progress depends largely on your command of the forces of Nature. At present your principal sources of power are food, fuel, electricity, the heat of the interior of the earth, wind, and tide. From the first two you cannot expect much more than now, but from the internal heat everywhere available, tradewinds, and falling water, as at Niagara, and from tides, you can obtain power almost without limit. Were this all, however, your progress would be slow; but the Eternal, realizing the shortness of your lives, has given you power with which to rend the globe. You have the action of all uncombined chemicals, atmospheric electricity, the excess or froth of which you now see in thunderstorms, and the electricity and magnetism of your own bodies. There is also molecular and sympathetic vibration, by which Joshua not understandingly levelled the walls of Jericho; and the power of your minds over matter, but little more developed now than when I moved in the flesh upon the earth. By lowering large quantities of high-powered explosives to the deepest parts of the ocean bed, and exploding them there, you can produce chasms through which some water will be forced towards the heated interior by the enormous pressure of its own weight. At a comparatively slight depth it will be converted into steam and produce an earthquake. This will so enlarge your chasm, that a great volume of water will rush into the red-hot interior, which will cause a series of such terrific eruptions that large islands will be upheaved. By the reduction of the heat of that part of the interior there will also be a shrinkage, which, in connection with the explosions, will cause the earth's solid crust to be thrown up in folds till whole continents appear. Some of the water displaced by the new land will also, as a result of the cooling, be able permanently to penetrate farther, thereby decreasing by that much the amount of water in the oceans, so that the tide-level in your existing seaports will be but slightly changed. By persevering in this work, you will become so skilled that it will be possible to evoke land of whatever kind you wish, at any place; and by having high table-land at the equator, sloping off into low plains towards north and south, and maintaining volcanoes in eruption at the poles to throw out heat and start warm ocean currents, it will be possible, in connection with the change you are now making in the axis, to render the conditions of life so easy that the earth will support a far larger number of souls.

"With the powers at your disposal you can also alter and improve existing continents, and thereby still further increase the number of the children of men. Perhaps with mild climate, fertile soil, and decreased struggle for existence, man will develop his spiritual side.

"Finally, you have apergy, one of the highest forces, for it puts you almost on a plane with angels, and with it you have already visited Jupiter and Saturn. It was impossible that man should remain chained to the earth during the entire life of his race, like an inferior animal or a mineral, lower even in freedom of body than birds. Heretofore you have, as I have said, seen but one side in many workings of Nature, as if you had discovered either negative or positive electricity, but not both; for gravitation and apergy are as inseparably combined in the rest of the universe as those two, separated temporarily on earth that the discovery of the utilization of one with the other might serve as an incentive to your minds. You saw it in Nature on Jupiter in the case of several creatures, suspecting it in the boa-constrictor and Will-o'-the-wisp and jelly-fish, and have standing illustrations of it in all tailed comets--luminosity in the case of large bodies being one manifestation--in the rings of this planet, and in the molecular motion and porosity of all gases, liquids, and solids on earth; since what else is it that keeps the molecules apart, heat serving merely to increase its power? God made man in his own image; does it not stand to reason that he will allow him to continue to become more and more like himself? Would he begrudge him the power to move mountains through the intelligent application of Nature's laws, when he himself said they might be moved by faith? So far you have been content to use the mechanical power of water, its momentum or dead weight merely; to attain a much higher civilization, you must break it up chemically and use its constituent gases."

"How," asked Bearwarden, "can this be done?"

"Force superheated steam," replied the spirit, "through an intensely heated substance, as you now do in making water-gas--preferably platinum heated by electricity--apply an apergetic shock, and the oxygen and hydrogen will separate like oil and water, the oxygen being so much the heavier. Lead them in different directions as fast as the water is decomposed--since otherwise they would reunite--and your supply of power will be inexhaustible."

"Will you not stay and dine with us?" asked Ayrault. "While in the flesh you must be subject to its laws, and must need food to maintain your strength, like ourselves."

"It will give me great pleasure," replied the spirit, "to tarry with you, and once more to taste earthly food, but most of all to have the blessed joy of being of service to you. Here, all being immaterial spirits, no physical injury can befall any of us; and since no one wants anything that any one else can give, we have no opportunity of doing anything for each other. You see we neither eat nor sleep, neither can any of us again know physical pain or death, nor can we comfort one another, for every one knows the truth about himself and every one else, and we read one another's thoughts as an open book."

"Do you," asked Bearwarden, "not eat at all?"

"We absorb vitality in a sense," replied the spirit. "As the sun combines certain substances into food for mortals, it also produces molecular vibration and charges the air with magnetism and electricity, which we absorb without effort. In fact, there is a faint pleasure in the absorption of this strength, when, in magnetic disturbances, there is an unusual amount of immortal food. Should we try to resist it, there would eventually be a greater pressure without than within, and we should assimilate involuntarily. We are part of the intangible universe, and can feel no hunger that is not instantly appeased, neither can we ever more know thirst."

"Why," asked Cortlandt reverently, "did the angel with the sword of flame drive Adam from the Tree of Life, since with his soul he had received that which could never die?"

"That was part of the mercy of God," the shade replied; "for immortality could be enjoyed but meagrely on earth, where natural limitations are so abrupt. And know this, ye who are something of chemists, that had Adam eaten of that substance called fruit, he would have lived in the flesh to this day, and would have been of all men the most unhappy."

"Will the Fountain of Youth ever be discovered?" asked Cortlandt.

"That substances exist," replied the spirit, "that render it impossible for the germs of old age and decay to lodge in the body, I know; in fact, it would be a break in the continuity and balance of Nature did they not; but I believe their discovery will be coincident with Christ's second visible advent on earth. You are, however, only on the shore of the ocean of knowledge, and, by continuing to advance in geometric ratio, will soon be able to retain your mortal bodies till the average longevity exceeds Methuselah's; but, except for more opportunities of doing good, or setting a longer example to your fellows by your lives, where would be the gain?

"I now see how what appeared to me while I lived on earth insignificant incidents, were the acts of God, and that what I thought injustice or misfortune was but evidence of his wisdom and love; for we know that not a sparrow falleth without God, and that the hairs of our heads are numbered. Every act of kindness or unselfishness on my part, also, stands out like a golden letter or a white stone, and gives me unspeakable comfort. At the last judgment, and in eternity following, we shall have very different but just as real bodies as those that we possessed in the flesh. The dead at the last trump will rise clothed in them, and at that time the souls in paradise will receive them also."

"I wonder," thought Ayrault, "on which hand we shall be placed in that last day."

"The classification is now going on," said the spirit, answering his thought, "and I know that in the final judgment each individual will range himself automatically on his proper side."

"Do tell me," said Ayrault, "how you were able to answer my thought."

"I see the vibrations of the grey matter of your brain as plainly as the movements of your lips; in fact, I see the thoughts in the embryonic state taking shape."

When their meal was ready they sat down, Ayrault placing the spirit on his right, with Cortlandt on his left, and having Bearwarden opposite. On this occasion their chief had given them a particularly good dinner, but the spirit took only a slice of meat and a glass of claret.

"Won't you tell us the story of your life," said Ayrault to the spirit, "and your experiences since your death? They would be of tremendous interest to us."

"I was a bishop in one of the Atlantic States," replied the spirit gravely, "and died shortly before the civil war. People came from other cities to hear my sermons, and the biographical writers have honoured my memory by saying that I was a great man. I was contemporaneous with Daniel Webster and Henry Clay. Shortly after I reached threescore and ten, according to earthly years, I caught what I considered only a slight cold, for I had always had good health, but it became pneumonia. My friends, children, and grandchildren came to see me, and all seemed going well, when, without warning, my physician told me I had but a few hours to live. I could scarcely believe my ears; and though, as a Churchman, I had ministered to others and had always tried to lead a good life, I was greatly shocked. I suddenly remembered all the things I had left undone and all the things I intended to do, and the old saying, 'Hell is paved with good intentions,' crossed my mind very forcibly. In less than an hour I saw the physician was right; I grew weaker and my pulse fluttered, but my mind remained clear. I prayed to my Creator with all my soul, 'O spare me a little, that I may recover my strength, before I go hence, and be no more seen.' As if for an answer, the thought crossed my brain, 'Set thine house in order, for thou shalt not live, but die.' I then called my children and made disposition of such of my property and personal effects as were not covered by my will. I also gave to each the advice that my experience had shown me he or she needed. Then came another wave of remorse and regret, and again an intense longing to pray; but along with the thought of sins and neglected duties came also the memory of the honest efforts I had made to obey my conscience, and these were like rifts of sunshine during a storm. These thoughts, and the blessed promises of religion I had so often preached in the churches of my diocese, were an indescribable comfort, and saved me from the depths of blank despair. Finally my breathing became laboured, I had sharp spasms of pain, and my pulse almost stopped. I felt that I was dying, and my sight grew dim. The crisis and climax of life were at hand. 'Oh!' I thought, with the philosophers and sages, 'is it to this end I lived? The flower appears, briefly blooms amid troublous toil, and is gone; my body returns to its primordial dust, and my works are buried in oblivion. The paths of life and glory lead but to the grave.' My soul was filled with conflicting thoughts, and for a moment even my faith seemed at a low ebb. I could hear my children's stifled sobs, and my darling wife shed silent tears. The thought of parting from them gave me the bitterest wrench. With my fleeting breath I gasped these words, 'That mercy I showed others, that show thou me.' The darkened room grew darker, and after that I died. In my sleep I seemed to dream. All about were refined and heavenly flowers, while the most delightful sounds and perfumes filled the air. Gradually the vision became more distinct, and I experienced an indescribable feeling of peace and repose. I passed through fields and scenes I had never seen before, while every place was filled with an all-pervading light. Sometimes I seemed to be miles in air; countless suns and their planets shone, and dazzled my eyes, while no bird-of-paradise was as happy or free as I. Gradually it came to me that I was awake, and that it was no dream. Then I remembered my last moments, and perceived that I had died. Death had brought freedom, my work in the flesh was ended, I was indeed alive.

"'O Death, where is thy sting? O Grave, where is thy victory?' In my dying moments I had forgotten what I had so often preached--'Thou fool, that which thou sowest is not quickened except it die.' In a moment my life lay before me like a valley or an open page. All along its paths and waysides I saw the little seeds of word and deed that I had sown extending and bearing fruit forever for good or evil. I then saw things as they were, and realized the faultiness of my former conclusions, based as they had been on the incomplete knowledge obtained through embryonic senses. I also saw the Divine purpose in life as the design in a piece of tapestry, whereas before I had seen but the wrong side. It is not till we have lost the life in the flesh that we realize its dignity and value, for every hour gives us opportunities of helping or elevating some human being--it may be ourselves--of doing something in His service.

"Now that time is past, the books are closed, and we can do nothing further ourselves to alter our status for eternity, however much we may wish to. It is on this account, and not merely to save you from death, which in itself is nothing, that I now tell you to run to the Callisto, seal the doors hermetically, and come not forth till a sudden rush of air that you will see on the trees has passed. A gust in which even birds drop dead, if they are unable to escape, will be here when you reach safety. Do not delay to take this food, and eat none of it when you return, for it will be filled with poisonous germs." "How can we find you?" asked Ayrault, grasping his hand. "You must not leave us till we know how we can see you again." "Think hard and steadfastly of me, you three," replied the spirit, "if you want me, and I shall feel your thought"; saying which, he vanished before their eyes, and the three friends ran to the Callisto.

CHAPTER III
DOUBTS AND PHILOSOPHY

On reaching it, they climbed the ladder leading to the second-story opening, and entering through this, they closed the door, screwing it tightly in place.

"Now," said Cortlandt, "we can see what changes, if any, this wonderful gust will effect."

"He made no strictures on our senses, such as they are," said Bearwarden, "but implied that evolution would be carried much further in us, from which I suppose we may infer that it has not yet gone far. I wish we had recorked those brandy peaches, for now they will be filled with poisonous germs. I wonder if our shady friend could not tell us of an antiseptic with which they might be treated?"

"Those fellows," thought Ayrault, who had climbed to the dome, from which he had an extended view, "would jeer at an angel, while the deference they showed the spirit seems, as usual, to have been merely superficial."

"Let us note," said Cortlandt, "that the spirit thermometer outside has fallen several degrees since we entered, though, from the time taken, I should not say that the sudden change would be one of temperature."

Just then they saw a number of birds, which had been resting in a clump of trees, take flight suddenly; but they fell to the ground before they had risen far, and were dashed to pieces. In another moment the trees began to bend and sway before the storm; and as they gazed, the colour of the leaves turned from green and purple to orange and red. The wind blew off many of these, and they were carried along by the gusts, or fluttered to the ground, which was soon strewed with them. It was a typical autumnal scene. Presently the wind shifted, and this was followed by a cold shower of rain.

"I think the worst is over," said Bearwarden. "The Sailor's Guide says:

'When the rain's before the wind,
Halliards, sheets, and braces mind;
When the wind's before the rain,
Soon you can make sail again.'

Doubtless that will hold good here."

This proved to be correct; and, after a repetition of the precautions they had taken on their arrival on the planet in regard to the inhalability of the air, they again sallied forth. They left their magazine shot-guns, taking instead the double-barrelled kind, on account of the rapidity with which this enabled them to fire the second barrel after the first, and threw away the water that had collected in the bucket, out of respect to the spirit's warning. They noticed a pungent odour, and decided to remain on high ground, since they had observed that the birds, in their effort to escape, had flown almost vertically into the air. On reaching the grove in which they had seen the storm, they found their table and everything on it exactly as they had left it. Bearwarden threw out the brandy peaches on the ground, exclaiming that it was a shame to lose such good preserves, and they proceeded on their walk. They passed hundreds of dead birds, and on reaching the edge of the toadstool valley were not a little surprised to find that every toadstool had disappeared.

"I wonder," said the doctor, "if there can be any connection between the phenomenon of the disappearance of those toadstools and the death of the birds? We could easily discover it if they had eaten them, or if in any other way the plants could have entered their bodies; but I see no way in which that can have happened." Resolving to investigate carefully any other fungi they might see, they resumed their march. The cold, distant-looking sun, apparently about the size of an orange, was near the horizon. Saturn's rotation on its axis occupying only ten hours and fourteen minutes, being but a few minutes longer than Jupiter's, they knew it would soon be night. Finding a place on a range of hills sheltered by rocks and a clump of trees of the evergreen species, they arranged themselves as comfortably as possible, ate some of the sandwiches they had brought, lighted their pipes, and watched the dying day. Here were no fire-flies to light the darkening minutes, nor singing flowers to lull them to sleep with their song but six of the eight moons, each at a different phase, and with varied brightness, bathed the landscape in their pale, cold rays; while far above them, like a huge rainbow, stretched the great rings in effulgent sheets, reaching thousands of miles into space, and flooded everything with their silvery light.

"How poor a place compared with this," they thought to themselves, "is our world!" and Ayrault wished that his soul was already free; while the dead leaves rustling in the gentle breeze, and the nightwinds, sighing among the trees, seemed to echo his thought. Far above their heads, and in the vastness of space, the well-known stars and constellations, notwithstanding the enormous distance they had now come, looked absolutely unchanged, and seemed to them emblematic of tranquillity and eternal repose. The days were changed by their shortness, and by the apparent loss of power in the sun; and the nights, as if in compensation, were magnificently illuminated by the numerous moons and splendid rings, though neither rings nor satellites shone with as strong a light as the terrestrial moon. But in nothing outside of the solar system was there any change; and could Æneas's Palinurus, or one of Philip of Macedon's shepherds, be brought to life here, he would see exactly the same stars in the same positions; and, did he not know of his own death or of the lapse of time, he might suppose, so far as the heavens were affected, that he had but fallen asleep, or had just closed his eyes.

"I have always regretted," said Cortlandt, "that I was not born a thousand years later."

"Were it not," added Ayrault, "that our earth is the vestibule to space, and for the opportunities it opens, I should rather never have lived, for life in itself is unsatisfying."

"You fellows are too indefinite and abstract for me," said Bearwarden. "I like something tangible and concrete. The utilitarianism of the twentieth century, by which I live, paradoxical though it may seem, would be out of place in space, unless we can colonize the other planets, and improve their arrangements and axes."

Mixed with Ayrault's philosophical and metaphysical thoughts were the memories of his sweetheart at Vassar, and he longed, more than his companions, for the spirit's return, that he might ask him if perchance he could tell him aught of her, and whether her thoughts were then of him.

Finally, worn out by the fatigue and excitement of the day, they set the protection-wires, more from force of habit than because they feared molestation and, rolling themselves in their blankets--for the night was cold--were soon fast asleep; Ayrault's last thought having been of his fiancee, Cortlandt's of the question he wished to ask the spirit, and Bearwarden's of the progress of his Company in the work of straightening the terrestrial axis. Thus they slept seven hundred and ninety million miles beyond their earth's orbit, and more than eight hundred million from the place where the earth was then. While they lay unconscious, the clouds above them froze, and before morning there was a fall of snow that covered the ground and them as they lay upon it. Soon three white mounds were all that marked their presence, and the cranes and eagles, rising from their roosts in response to the coming day, looked unconcernedly at all that was human that they had ever seen. Finally, wakened by the resounding cries of these birds, Bearwarden and Cortlandt arose, and meeting Ayrault, who had already risen, mistook the snowy form before them for the spirit, and thinking the dead bishop had revisited them, they were preparing to welcome him, and to propound the questions they had formulated, when Ayrault's familiar voice showed them their mistake.

"Seeing your white figures," said he, "rise apparently in response to those loud calls, reminded me of what the spirit told us of the last day, and of the awakening and resurrection of the dead."

The scene was indeed weird. The east, already streaked with the rays of the rising far-away sun, and the pale moons nearing the horizon in the west, seemed connected by the huge bow of light. The snow on the dark evergreens produced a contrast of colour, while the other trees raised their almost bare and whitened branches against the sky, as though in supplication to the mysterious rings, which cast their light upon them and on the ground. As they gazed, however, the rings became grey, the moons disappeared, and another day began. Feeling sure the snow must have cleared the air of any deleterious substances it contained the day before, they descended into the neighbouring valley, which, having a southerly exposure, was warm in comparison with the hills. As they walked they disturbed a number of small rodents, which quickly ran away and disappeared in their holes.

"Though we have seen none of the huge creatures here," said Cortlandt, "that were so plentiful on Jupiter, these burrowers belong to a distinctly higher scale than those we found there, from which I take it we may infer that the evolution of the animal kingdom has advanced further on this planet than on Jupiter, which is just what we have a right to expect; for Saturn, in addition to being the smaller and therefore more matured of the two, has doubtless had a longer individual existence, being the farther from the sun."

Notwithstanding the cold of the night, the flowers, especially the lilies, were as beautiful as ever, which surprised them not a little, until, on examining them closely, they found that the stems and veins in the leaves were fluted, and therefore elastic, so that, should the sap freeze, it could expand without bursting the cells, thereby enabling the flowers to withstand a short frost. They noticed that many of the curiously shaped birds they saw at a distance from time to time were able to move with great rapidity along the ground, and had about concluded that they must have four legs, being similar to winged squirrels, when a long, low quadruped, about twenty-five feet from nostrils to tail, which they were endeavouring to stalk, suddenly spread two pairs of wings, flapping the four at once, and then soared off at great speed.

"I hope we can get one of those, or at least his photograph," said Cortlandt.

"If they go in pairs," said Bearwarden, "we may find the companion near."

At that moment another great winged lizard, considerably larger than the first, rose with a snort, not twenty yards on their left. Cortlandt, who was a good shot with a gun at short range, immediately raised his twelve-bore and fired both barrels at the monster; but the double-B shots had no more disabling effect than if they had been number eights. They, however, excited the creature's ire; for, sweeping around quickly, it made straight for Cortlandt, breathing at him when near, and almost overpowering the three men with the malodorous, poisonous cloud it exhaled. Instantly Bearwarden fired several revolver bullets down its throat, while Ayrault pulled both barrels almost simultaneously, with the muzzles but a few inches from its side. In this case the initial velocity of the heavy buckshot was so great, and they were still so close together, that they penetrated the leathery hide, tearing a large hole. With a roar the wounded monster beat a retreat, first almost prostrating them with another blast of its awful breath.

"It would take a stronger light than we get here," said Bearwarden, "to impress a negative through that haze. I think," he continued, "I know a trick that will do the business, if we see any more of these dragons." Saying which, he withdrew the cartridges from his gun, and with his hunting-knife cut the tough paper shell nearly through between the wads separating the powder from the shot, drawing his knife entirely around.

"Now," said he, "when I fire those, the entire forward end of the cartridge will go out, keeping the fifteen buckshot together like a slug, and with such penetration that it will go through a two-inch plank. It is a trick I learned from hunters, and, unless your guns are choke-bore, in which case it might burst the barrel, I advise you to follow suit."

Finding they had brought straight-bored guns, they arranged their cartridges similarly, and set out in the direction in which the winged lizards or dragons had gone.

CHAPTER IV
A PROVIDENTIAL INTERVENTION

The valley narrowed as they advanced, the banks rising gently on both sides. Both dragons had flown straight to a grove of tall, spreading trees. On coming near to this, they noticed a faint smell like that of the dragon, and also like the trace they found in the air on leaving the Callisto the day before, after they had sought safety within it. Soon it almost knocked them down.

"We must get to windward," said Cortlandt. "I already feel faint, and believe those dragons could kill a man by breathing on him."

Accordingly, they skirted around the grove, and having made a quarter circle--for they did not wish the dragons to wind them--again drew nearer. Tree after tree was passed, and finally they saw an open space twelve or fifteen acres in area at the centre of the grove, when they were arrested by a curious sound of munching. Peering among the trunks of the huge trees, they advanced cautiously, but stopped aghast. In the opening were at least a hundred dragons devouring the toadstools with which the ground was covered. Many of them were thirty to forty feet long, with huge and terribly long, sharp claws, and jaws armed with gleaming batteries of teeth. Though they had evidently lungs, and the claws and mouth of an animal, they reminded the observers in many respects of insects enormously exaggerated, for their wings, composed of a sort of transparent scale, were small, and moved, as they had already seen, at far greater speed than those of a bird. Their projecting eyes were also set rigidly in their heads instead of turning, and consisted of a number of flat surfaces or facets, like a fly's eye, so that they could see backward and all around, each facet seeing anything the rays from which came at right angles to its surface. This beautiful grove was doubtless their feeding-ground, and, as such, was likely to be visited by many more. Concluding it would be wise to let their wounded game escape, the three men were about to retreat, having found it difficult to breathe the air even at that distance from the monsters, when the wounded dragon that they had observed moving about in a very restless manner, and evidently suffering a good deal from the effect of its wounds, espied them, and, with a roar that made the echoes ring, started towards them slowly along the ground, followed by the entire herd, the nearer of which now also saw them. Seeing that their lives were in danger, the hunters quickly regained the open, and then stretched their legs against the wind. The dragons came through the trees on the ground, and then, raising themselves by their wings, the whole swarm, snorting, and darkening the air with their deadly breath, made straight for the men, who by comparison looked like Lilliputians. With the slug from his right barrel Bearwarden ended the wounded dragon's career by shooting him through the head, and with his left laid low the one following. Ayrault also killed two huge monsters, and Cortlandt killed one and wounded another. Their supply of prepared cartridges was then exhausted, and they fell back on their revolvers and ineffective spreading shot. Resolved to sell their lives dearly, they retreated, keeping their backs to the wind, with the poisonous dragons in front. But the breeze was very slight, and they were being rapidly blinded and asphyxiated by the loathsome fumes, and deafened by the hideous roaring and snapping of the dragons' jaws. Realizing that they could not much longer reply to the diabolical host with lead, they believed their last hour had come, when the ground on which they were making their last stand shook, there was a rending of rocks and a rush of imprisoned steam that drowned even the dragons' roar, and they were separated from them by a long fissure and a wall of smoke and vapour. Struggling back from the edge of the chasm, they fell upon the ground, and then for the first time fully realized that the earthquake had saved them, for the dragons could not come across the opening, and would not venture to fly through the smoke and steam. When they recovered somewhat from the shock, they cut a number of cartridges in the same way that they had prepared those that had done them such good service, and kept one barrel of each gun loaded with that kind.

'The combat with the dragons

"We may thank Providence," said Bearwarden, "for that escape. I hope we shall have no more such close calls."

With a parting glance at the chasm that had saved their lives, and from which a cloud still arose, they turned slightly to the right of their former course and climbed the gently rising bank. When near the top, being tired of their exciting experiences, they sat down to rest. The ground all about them was covered with mushrooms, white on top and pink underneath.

"This is a wonderful place for fungi," said Ayrault. "Here, doubtless, we shall be safe from the dragons, for they seemed to prefer the toadstools." As he lay on the ground he watched one particular mushroom that seemed to grow before his eyes. Suddenly, as he looked, it vanished. Dumfounded at this unmistakable manifestation of the phenomenon they thought they had seen on landing, he called his companions, and, choosing another mushroom, the three watched it closely. Presently, without the least noise or commotion, that also disappeared, leaving no trace, and the same fate befell a number of others. At a certain point of their development they vanished as completely as a bubble of air coming to the surface of water, except that they caused no ripple, leaving merely a small depression where they had stood.

"Well," said Bearwarden, "in all my travels I never have seen anything like this. If I were at a sleight-of-hand performance, and the prestidigitateur, after doing that, asked for my theory, I should say, 'I give it up.' How is it with you, doctor?" he asked, addressing Cortlandt.

"There must be an explanation," replied Cortlandt, "only we do not know the natural law to which the phenomenon is subject, having had no experience with it on earth. We know that all substances can be converted into gases, and that all gases can be reduced to liquids, and even solids, by the application of pressure and cold. If there is any way by which the visible substance of these fungi can be converted into its invisible gases, as water into oxygen and hydrogen, what we have seen can be logically explained. Perhaps, favoured by some affinity of the atmosphere, its constituent parts are broken up and become gases at this barometric pressure and temperature. We must ask the spirit, if he visits us again."

"I wish he would," said Ayrault; "there are lots of things I should like to ask him."

"Presidents of corporations and other chairmen," said Bearwarden, "are not usually superstitious, and I, of course, take no stock in the supernatural; but somehow I have a well-formed idea that our friend the bishop, with the great power of his mind over matter, had a hand in that earthquake. He seems to have an exalted idea of our importance, and may be exerting himself to make things pleasant."

At this point the sun sank below the horizon, and they found themselves confronted with night.

"Dear, dear!" said Bearwarden, "and we haven't a crumb to eat. I'll stand the drinks and the pipes," he continued, passing around his ubiquitous flask and tobacco-pouch.

"If I played such pranks with my interior on earth," said Cortlandt, helping himself to both, "as I do on this planet, it would give me no end of trouble, but here I seem to have the digestion of an ostrich."

So they sat and smoked for an hour, till the stars twinkled and the rings shone in their glory. "Well," said Ayrault, finally, "since we have nothing but motions to lay on the table, I move we adjourn."

"The only motion I shall make," said Cortlandt, who was already undressed, "will be that of getting into bed," saying which, he rolled himself in his blanket and soon was fast asleep.

Having decided that, on account of the proximity of the dragons, a man must in any event be on the watch, they did not set the protection-wires. From the shortness of the nights, they divided them into only two watches of from two hours to two and a half each, so that, even when constant watch duty was necessary, each man had one full night's sleep in three. On this occasion Ayrault and Cortlandt were the watchers, Cortlandt having the morning and Ayrault the evening watch. Many curious quadruped birds, about the size of large bears, and similar in shape, having bear-shaped heads, and several creatures that looked like the dragons, flew about them in the moonlight; but neither watcher fired a shot, as the creatures showed no desire to make an attack. All these species seemed to belong to the owl or bat tribe, for they roamed abroad at night.

CHAPTER V
AYRAULT'S VISION

When Ayrault's watch was ended, he roused Cortlandt, who took his place, and feeling a desire for solitude and for a last long look at the earth, he crossed the top of the ridge on the slope of which they had camped, and lay down on the farther side. The South wind in the upper air rushed along in the mighty whirl, occasionally carrying filmy clouds across the faces of the moons; but about Ayrault all was still, and he felt a quiet and serene repose. He had every intention of remaining awake, and was pondering on the steadfastness of the human heart and the constancy of love, when his meditations began to wander, and, with his last thoughts on Sylvia, he fell asleep. Not a branch moved, nor did a leaf fall, yet before Ayrault's sleeping eyes a strange scene was enacted. A figure in white came near and stood before him, and he recognized in it one Violet Slade, a very attractive girl to whom he had been attentive in his college days. She was at that time just eighteen, and people believed that she loved him, but for some reason, he knew not why, he had not proposed.

"I thought you had died," he said, as she gazed at him, "but you are now looking better than ever."

"From the world's point of view I AM dead," she replied. "I died and was buried. It is therefore permissible that I should show you the truth. You never believed I loved you. I have wished earnestly to see you, and to have you know that I did."

"I did you an injustice," Ayrault answered, perceiving all that was in her heart. "Could mortals but see as spirits do, there would be no misunderstandings."

"I am so glad to see you," she continued, "and to know you are well. Had you not come here, we could probably not have met until after your death; for I shall not be sufficiently advanced to return to earth for a long time, though my greatest solace while there was my religion, which is all that brought me here. We, however, know that as our capacity for true happiness increases we shall be happier, and that after the resurrection there will be no more tears. Farewell," she whispered, while her eyes were filled with love.

Ayrault's sleep was then undisturbed for some time, when suddenly an angel, wreathed in light, appeared before him and spoke these words: "He that walked with Adam and talked with Moses has sent me to guard you while you sleep. No plague or fever, wild beast or earthquake, can molest you, for you are equally protected from the most powerful monster and the most insidious disease-germ. 'Blessed is the man whose offences are covered and whose sins are forgiven.' Sleep on, therefore, and be refreshed, for the body must have rest."

"A man may rest indeed," replied Ayrault, "when he has a guardian angel. I had the most unbounded faith in your existence before I saw you, and believe and know that you or others have often shielded me from danger and saved my life. Why am I worthy of so much care?"

"'Whoso dwelleth under the defence of the Most High shall abide under the shadow of the Almighty,'" answered the angel, and thereupon he became invisible, a diffused light taking his place. Shortly afterwards this paled and completely vanished.

"Not only am I in paradise," thought Ayrault; "I believe I am also in the seventh heaven. Would I might hear such words again!"

A group of lilies then appeared before the sleeper's eyes. In the midst was one lily far larger than the rest, and of a dazzling white. This spoke in a gentle voice, but with the tones of a trombone:

"Thy thoughts and acts are a pleasure to me. Thou hast raised no idols within thy heart, and thy faith is as incense before me. Thy name is now in the Book of Life. Continue as thou hast begun, and thou shalt live and reign forever."

Hereupon the earth shook, and Ayrault was awakened. Great boulders were rolling and crashing down the slope about him, while the dawn was already in the east.

Ayrault's Vision

"My mortal eyes and senses are keener here while I sleep than when I wake," he thought, as he looked about him, "for spirits, unable to affect me while waking, have made themselves felt in my more sensitive state while I was asleep. Nevertheless, this is none other but the house of God, and this is the gate of heaven.

"The boulders were still in motion when I opened my eyes," he mused; "can it be that there is hereabouts such a flower as in my dreams I seemed to see?" and looking beyond where his head had lain, he beheld the identical lily surrounded by the group that his closed eyes had already seen. Thereupon he uncovered his head and departed quickly. Crossing the divide, he descended to camp, where he found Cortlandt in deep thought.

"I cannot get over the dreams," said the doctor, "I had in the first part of the night. Notwithstanding yesterday's excitement and fatigue, my sleep was most disturbed, and I was visited by visions of my wife, who died long ago. She warned me against skepticism, and seemed much distressed at my present spiritual state."

"I," said Bearwarden, who had been out early, and had succeeded in bringing in half a dozen birds, "was so disturbed I could not sleep. It seemed to me as though half the men I have ever known came and warned me against agnosticism and my materialistic tendencies. They kept repeating, 'You are losing the reality for the shadow.'"

"I am convinced," said Ayrault, "that they were not altogether dreams, or, if dreams indeed, that they were superinduced by a higher will. We know that angels have often appeared to men in the past. May it not be that, as our appreciativeness increases, these communications will recur?" Thereupon he related his own experiences.

"The thing that surprised me," said Cortlandt, as they finished breakfast, "was the extraordinary realism of the scene. We must see if our visions return on anything but an empty stomach."

CHAPTER VI
A GREAT VOID AND A GREAT LONGING

Resuming their march, the travellers proceeded along the circumference of a circle having a radius of about three miles, with the Callisto in the centre. In crossing soft places they observed foot-prints forming in the earth all around them. The impressions were of all sizes, and ceased when they reached rising or hard ground, only to reappear in the swamps, regulating their speed by that of the travellers. The three men were greatly surprised at this.

"You may observe," said Cortlandt, "that the surface of the impression is depressed as you watch it, as though by a weight, and you can see, and even hear, the water being squeezed out, though whatever is doing it is entirely invisible. They must be made by spirits sufficiently advanced to have weight, but not advanced enough to make themselves visible."

Moved by a species of vandalism, Bearwarden raised his twelve-bore, and fired an ordinary cartridge that he had not prepared for the dragons, at the space directly over the nearest forming prints. There was a brilliant display of prismatic colours, as in a rainbow, and though the impressions already made remained, no new ones were formed.

"Now you have done it!" said Cortlandt. "I hoped to be able to investigate this further."

"We shall doubtless see other and perhaps more wonderful things," replied Bearwarden. "I must say this gives me an uncanny feeling." When they had completed a little over half their circle, they came upon another of the groves with which Saturn seemed to abound, at the edge of which, in a side-hill, was a cave, the entrance of which was composed of rocky masses that had apparently fallen together, the floor being but little higher than the surface outside. The arched roof of the vestibule was rendered watertight by the soil that had formed upon it, which again was overgrown by vines and bushes.

"This," said Bearwarden, "will be a good place to camp, for the cave will protect us from dragons, unless they should take a notion to breathe at us from the outside, and it will keep us dry in case of rain. To-morrow we can start with this as a centre, and make another circuit."

"We can explore Saturn on foot," said Cortlandt, "and far more thoroughly than Jupiter, on account of its comparative freedom from monsters. Not even the dragons can trouble us, unless we meet them in large numbers."

Thereupon they set about getting fuel for their fire. Besides collecting some of the dead wood that was lying all about, they split up a number of resinous pine and fir trees with explosive bullets from their revolvers, so that soon they not only had a roaring fire, but filled the back part of the cave with logs to dry, in case they should camp there again at some later day. Neither Cortlandt nor Bearwarden felt much like sleeping, and so, after finishing the birds the president had brought down that morning, they persuaded Ayrault to sit up and smoke with them. Wrapping themselves in their blankets--for there was a chill in the air--they sat about the camp-fire they had built in the mouth of the cave. Two moons that were at the full rose rapidly in the clear, cold sky. On account of their distance from the sun, they were less bright than the terrestrial moon, but they shone with a marvellously pure pale light. The larger contained the exact features of a man. There was the somewhat aquiline nose, a clear-cut and expressive mouth, and large, handsome eyes, which were shaded by well-marked eyebrows. The whole face was very striking, but was a personification of the most intense grief. The expression was indeed sadder than that of any face they had ever seen. The other contained the profile of a surpassingly beautiful young woman. The handsome eyes, shaded by lashes, looked straight ahead. The nose was perfect, and the ear small, while the hair was artistically arranged at the top and back of the head. This moon also reflected a pure white ray. The former appeared about once and a quarter, the latter but three quarters, the size of the terrestrial moon, and the travellers immediately recognized them by their sizes and relative positions as Tethys and Dione, discovered by J. D. Cassini in March, 1684. The sad face was turned slightly towards that of its companion, and it looked as if some tale of the human heart, some romance, had been engraved and preserved for all time on the features of these dead bodies, as they silently swung in their orbits forever and anon were side by side.

"In all the ages," said Cortlandt, "that these moons have wandered with Saturn about the sun, and with the solar system in its journey through space, they can never have gazed upon the scene they now behold, for we may be convinced that no mortal man has been here before."

"We may say," said Ayrault, "that they see in our bodies a type of the source from which come all the spiritual beings that are here."

"If, as the writers of mythology supposed," replied Cortlandt, "inanimate objects were endowed with senses, these moons would doubtless be unable to perceive the spiritual beings here; for the satellites, being material, should, to be consistent, have only those senses possessed by ourselves, so that to them this planet would ordinarily appear deserted."

"I shall be glad," said Bearwarden, gloomily, "when those moons wane and are succeeded by their fellows, for one would give me an attack of the blues, while the other would subject me to the inconvenience of falling in love."

As he spoke, the upper branches of the trees in the grove began to sway as a cold gust from the north sighed among them. "Lose no more opportunities," it seemed to cry, "for life is short and uncertain. Soon you will all be colder than I, and your future, still as easily moulded as clay, will be set as Marpesian marble, more fixed than the hardest rock."

"Paradise," said Cortlandt, "contains sights and sounds that might, I should think, arouse sad reminiscences without the aid of the waters of Lethe, unless the joy of its souls in their new resources and the sense of forgiveness outweigh all else."

With a parting look at the refined, silvery moon, and its sorrow-laden companion, they retired to the sheltering cave, piled up the fire, and talked on for an hour.

"I do not see how it is," said Bearwarden, "that these moons, considering their distance from the sun, and the consequently small amount of light they receive, are so bright."

"A body's brightness in reflecting light," replied Cortlandt, "depends as much on the colour and composition of its own surface as on the amount it receives. It is conceivable that these moons, if placed at the earth's distance from the sun, would be far brighter than our moon, and that our familiar satellite, if removed to Saturn, would seem very dim. We know how much more brilliant a mountain in the sunlight is when clad in snow than when its sides are bare. These moons evidently reflect a large proportion of the light they receive."

When they came out shortly after midnight the girl's-face moon had already set, leaving a dark and dreary void in the part of the sky it had so ideally filled. The inexpressibly sad satellite (on account of its shorter distance and more rapid rate of revolution) was still above the horizon, and, being slightly tilted, had a more melancholy, heart-broken look than before. While they gazed sadly at the emptiness left by Dione, Cortlandt saw Ayrault's expression change, and, not clearly perceiving its cause, said, wishing to cheer him: "Never mind, Dick; to-morrow night we shall see it again."

"Ah, prosaic reasoner," retorted Bearwarden, who saw that this, like so many other things, had reminded Ayrault of Sylvia, "that is but small consolation for having lost it now, though I suppose our lot is not so hard as if we were never to see it again. In that moon's face I find the realization of my fancied ideal woman; while that sad one yonder seems as though some celestial lover, in search of his fate, had become enamoured of her, and tried in vain to win her, and the grief in his mind had impressed itself on the then molten face of a satellite to be the monument throughout eternity of love and a broken heart. If the spirits and souls of the departed have any command of matter, why may not their intensest thoughts engrave themselves on a moon that, when dead and frozen, may reflect and shine as they did, while immersed in the depths of space? At first Dione bored me; now I should greatly like to see her again."

"History repeats itself," replied Cortlandt, "and the same phases of life recur. It is we that are in a changed receptive mood. The change that seems to be in them is in reality in us. Remain as you are now, and Dione will give you the same pleasure tomorrow that she gave to-day."

To Ayrault this meant more than the mere setting to rise again of a heavenly body. The perfume of a flower, the sighing of the wind, suggesting some harmony or song, a full or crescent moon, recalled thoughts and associations of Sylvia. Everything seemed to bring out memory, and he realized the utter inability of absence to cure the heart of love. "If Sylvia should pass from my life as that moon has left my vision," his thoughts continued, "existence would be but sadness and memory would be its cause, for the most beautiful sounds entail sorrow; the most beautiful sights, intense pain. Ah," he went on with a trace of bitterness, while his friends fell asleep in the cave, "I might better have remained in love with science; for whose studies Nature, which is but a form of God, in the right spirit, is not dependent for his joy or despair on the whims of a girl. She, of course, sees many others, and, being only twenty, may forget me. Must I content myself with philosophical rules and mathematical formulæ, when she, whose changefulness I may find greater than the winds that sigh over me, now loves me no longer? O love, which makes us miserable when we feel it, and more miserable still when it is gone!"

He strung a number of copper wires at different degrees of tension between two trees, and listened to the wind as it ranged up and down on this improvised Æolian harp. It gradually ran into a regular refrain, which became more and more like words. Ayrault was puzzled, and then amazed. There could be no doubt about it. "You should be happy," it kept repeating--"you should be happy," in soft musical tones.

"I know I should," replied Ayrault, finally recognizing the voice of Violet Slade in the song of the wind, "and I cannot understand why I am not. Tell me, is this paradise, Violet, or is it not rather purgatory?"

The notes ranged up and down again, and he perceived that she was causing the wind to blow as she desired--in other words, she was making it play upon his harp.

"That depends on the individual," she replied. "It is rather sheol, the place of departed spirits. Those whose consciences made them happy on earth are in paradise here; while those good enough to reach heaven at last, but in whom some dross remains, are further refined in spirit, and to them it is purgatory. Those who are in love can be happy in but one way while their love lasts. What IS happiness, anyway?"

"It is the state in which desires are satisfied, my fair Violet," answered Ayrault.

"Say, rather, the state in which desire coincides with duty," replied the song. "Self-sacrifice for others gives the truest joy; being with the object of one's love, the next. You never believed that I loved you. I dissembled well; but you will see for yourself some day, as clearly as I see your love for another now."

"Yes," replied Ayrault, sadly, "I am in love. I have no reason to believe there is cause for my unrest, and, considering every thing, I should be happy as man can be; yet, mirabile dictu, I am in--hades, in the very depths!"

"Your beloved is beyond my vision; your heart is all I can see. Yet I am convinced she will not forget you. I am sure she loves you still."

"I have always believed in homoeopathy to the extent of the *similia similibus curantur*, Violet, and it is certain that where nothing else will cure a man of love for one woman, his love for another will. You can see how I love Sylvia, but you have never seemed so sweet to me as to-day."

"It is a sacrilege, my friend, to speak so to me now. You are done with me forever. I am but a disembodied spirit, and escaped hades by the grace of the Omnipotent, rather than by virtue of any good I did on earth. So far as any elasticity is left in my opportunities, I am dead as yon moon. You have still the gift that but one can give. Within your animal body you hold an immortal soul. It is pliable as wax; you can mould it by your will. As you shape that soul, so will your future be. It is the ark that can traverse the flood. Raise it, and it will raise you. It is all there is in yourself. Preserve that gift, and when you die you will, I hope, start on a plane many thousands of years in advance of me. There should be no more comparison between us than between a person with all his senses and one that is deaf and blind. Though you are a layman, you should, with your faith and frame of mind, soon be but little behind our spiritual bishop."

"I supposed after death a man had rest. Is he, then, a bishop still?"

"The progress, as he told you, is largely on the old lines. As he stirred men's hearts on earth, he will stir their souls in heaven; and this is no irksome or unwelcome work."

"You say he WILL do this in heaven. Is he, then, not there yet?"

"He was not far from heaven on earth, yet technically none of us can be in heaven till after the general resurrection. Then, as we knew on earth, we shall receive bodies, though, as yet, concerning their exact nature we know but little more than then. We are all in sheol--the just in purgatory and paradise, the unjust in hell."

"Since you are still in purgatory, are you unhappy?"

"No, our state is very happy. All physical pain is past, and can never be felt again. We know that our evil desires are overcome, and that their imprints are being gradually erased. I occasionally shed an intangible tear, yet for most of those who strove to obey their consciences, purgatory, when essential, though occasionally giving us a bitter twinge, is a joy-producing state. Not all the glories imaginable or unimaginable could make us happy, were our consciences ill at ease. I have advanced slowly, yet some things are given us at once. After I realized I had irrevocably lost your love, though for a time I had hoped to regain it, I became very restless; earth seemed a prison, and I looked forward to death as my deliverer. I bore you no malice; you had never especially tried to win me; the infatuation--that of a girl of eighteen--had been all on my side. I lived five sad and lonely years, although, as you know, I had much attention. People thought me cold and heartless. How could I have a heart, having failed to win yours, and mine being broken? Having lost the only man I loved, I knew no one else could replace him, and I was not the kind to marry for pique. People thought me handsome, but I felt myself aged when you ceased to call. Perhaps when you and she who holds all your love come to sheol, she may spare you to me a little, for as a spirit my every thought is known; or perhaps after the resurrection, when I, too, can leave this planet, we shall all soar through space together, and we can study the stars as of old."

"Your voice is a symphony, sweetest Violet, and I love to hear your words. Ah, would you could once more return to earth, or that I were an ethereal spirit, that we might commune face to face! I would follow you from one end of Shadowland to the other. Of what use is life to me, with distractions that draw my thoughts to earth as gravitation drew my body? I wish I were a shade."

"You are talking for effect, Dick--which is useless here, for I see how utterly you are in love."

"I AM in love, Violet; and though, as I said, I have no reason to doubt Sylvia's steadfastness and constancy, I am very unhappy. I have always heard that time is a balsam that cures all ills, yet I become more wretched every day."

"Do all you can to preserve that love, and it will bring you joy all your life. Your happiness is my happiness. What distresses you, distresses me."

The tones here grew fainter and seemed about to cease.

"Before you leave me," cried Ayrault, "tell me how and when I may see or hear you again."

"While you remain on this planet, I shall be near; but beyond Saturn I cannot go."

"Yet tell me, Violet, how I may see you? My love unattained, you perceive, makes me wretched, while you always gave me calm and peace. If I may not kiss the hand I almost asked might be mine, let me have but a glance from your sweet eyes, which will comfort me so much now."

"If you break the ice in the pool behind you, you shall see me till the frame melts."

After this the silence was broken only by the sighing of the wind in the trees. The pool had suddenly become covered with ice several inches thick. Taking an axe, Ayrault hewed out a parallelogram about three feet by four and set it on end against the bank. The cold grey of morning was already colouring the east, and in the growing light Ayrault beheld a vision of Violet within the ice. The face was at about three fourths, and had a contemplative air. The hair was arranged as he had formerly seen it, and the thoughtful look was strongest in the beautiful grey eyes, which were more serious than of yore. Ayrault stood riveted to the spot and gazed. "I could have been happy with her," he mused, "and to think she is no more!"

As drops fell from the ice, tears rose to his eyes.

"What a pretty girl!" said Bearwarden to Cortlandt, as they came upon it later in the day. "The face seems etched or imprinted by some peculiar form of freezing far within the ice."

The next morning they again set out, and so tramped, hunted, and investigated with varying success for ten Saturnian days. They found that in the animal and plant forms of life Nature had often, by some seeming accident, struck out in a course very different from any on the earth. Many of the animals were bipeds and tripeds, the latter arranged in tandem, the last leg being evidently an enormously developed tail, by which the creature propelled itself as with a spring. The quadrupeds had also sometimes wings, and their bones were hollow, like those of birds. Whether this great motive and lifting power was the result of the planet's size and the power of gravitation, or whether some creatures had in addition the power of developing a degree of apergetic repulsion to offset it, as they suspected in the case of the boa-constrictor that fell upon Cortlandt on Jupiter, they could not absolutely ascertain. Life was far less prolific on Saturn than on Jupiter, doubtless as a result of its greater distance from the sun, and of its extremes of climate, almost all organic life being driven to the latitudes near the equator. There were, as on Jupiter, many variations from the forms of life to which they were accustomed, and adaptations to the conditions in which they found themselves; but, with the exception of the strange manifestations of spirit life, they found the workings of the fundamental laws the same. Often when they woke at night the air was luminous, and they were convinced that if they remained there long enough it would be easy to devise some telegraphic code of light-flashes by which they could communicate with the spirit world, and so get ideas from the host of spirits that had already solved the problem of life and death, but who were not as yet sufficiently developed to be able to return to the earth. One day they stopped to investigate what they had supposed to be an optical illusion. They observed that leaves and other light substances floated several inches above the surface of the water in the pools. On coming to the edge and making tests, they found a light liquid, as invisible as air, superimposed upon the water, with sufficient buoyancy to sustain dry wood and also some forms of life. They also observed that insects coming close to the surface and apparently inhaling it, rapidly increased in size and weight, from which they concluded it must throw off nitrogen, carbon, or some other nourishment in the form of gas. The depth upon the water was unaffected by rain, which passed through it, but depended rather on the condition of the atmosphere, from which it was evidently condensed. There seemed also to be a relation between the amount of this liquid and the activity of the spirits. Finally, when their ammunition showed signs of running low, they decided to return to the Callisto, go in it to the other side of the planet, and resume their investigations there. Accordingly, they set out to retrace their steps, returning by a course a few miles to one side of the way they had come, and making the cave their objective point. Arriving there one evening about sunset, they pitched their camp. The cave was sheltered and comfortable, and they made preparation for passing the night.

"I shall be sorry," said Ayrault, as they sat near their fire, "to leave this place without again seeing the bishop. He said we could impress him anywhere, but it may be more difficult to do that at the antipodes than here." "It does seem," said Bearwarden, "as though we should be missing it in not seeing him again, if that is possible. Nothing but a poison-storm brought him the first time, and it is not certain that even in such an emergency would he come again uncalled." "I think," said Ayrault, "as none of the spirits here are malevolent, they would warn us of danger if they could. The bishop's spirit seems to have been the only one with sufficiently developed power to reappear as a man. I therefore suggest that to-morrow we try to make him feel our thought and bring him to us."

CHAPTER VII
THE SPIRIT'S SECOND VISIT

Accordingly, the next morning they concentrated their minds simultaneously on the spirit, wishing with all their strength that he should reappear.

"Whether he be far or near," said Ayrault, "he must feel that, for we are using the entire force of our minds."

Shadows began to form, and dancing prismatic colours appeared, but as yet there was no sign of the deceased bishop, when suddenly he took shape among them, his appearance and disappearance being much like that of stereopticon views on the sheet before a lantern. He held himself erect, and his thoughtful, dignified face had the same calm expression it had worn before.

"We attracted your attention," said Ayrault, "in the way you said we might, because we longed so to see you."

"Yes," added Bearwarden and Cortlandt, "we felt we *MUST* see you again."

"I am always at your service," replied the spirit, "and will answer your questions. With regard to my visibility and invisibility"--he continued, with a smile, "for I will not wait for you to ask the explanation of what is in your minds--it is very simple. A man's soul can never die; a manifestation of the soul is the spirit; this has entity, consciousness, and will, and these also live forever. As in the natural or material life, as I shall call it, will affects the material first. Thus, a child has power to move its hand or a material object, as a toy, before it can become the medium in a psychological seance. So it is here. Before becoming visible to your eyes, I, by my will, draw certain material substances in the form of gases from the ground, water, or air around me. These take any shape I wish--not necessarily that of man, though it is more natural to appear as we did on earth--and may absorb a portion of light, and so be able to cast a shadow or break up the white rays into prismatic colours, or they may be wholly invisible. By an effort of the will, then, I combine and condense these gases--which consist principally of oxygen, hydrogen, nitrogen, and carbon--into flesh, blood, water, or anything else. You have already learned on earth that, by the application of heat, every solid and every liquid substance, which is solid or liquid simply because of the temperature at which you find it, can be expanded into gas or gases; and that by cold and pressure every gas can be reduced to a liquid or a solid. On earth the state of a substance, whether solid, liquid, or gaseous, depends simply upon those two conditions. Here neither thermal nor barometric changes are required, for, by mastering the new natural laws that at death become patent to our senses, we have all the necessary control. It requires but an effort of my will to be almost instantly clothed in human form, and but another effort to rearrange the molecules in such a way as to make the envelope visible. Some who have been dead longer, or had a greater natural aptitude than I, have advanced further, and all are learning; but the difference in the rate at which spirits acquire control of previously unknown natural laws varies far more than among individuals on earth.

"These forms of organic life do not disintegrate till after death; here in the natural state they break down and dissolve into their structural elements in full bloom, as was done by the fungi. The poisonous element in the deadly gust, against which I warned you, came from the gaseous ingredients of toadstools, which but seldom, and then only when the atmosphere has the greatest affinity for them, dissolve automatically, producing a death-spreading wave, against which your meteorological instruments in future can warn you. The slight fall you noticed in temperature was because the specific heat of these gases is high, and to become gas while in the solid state they had to withdraw some warmth from the air. The fatal breath of the winged lizards--or dragons, as you call them--results from the same cause, the action of their digestion breaking up the fungus, which does not kill them, because they exhale the poisonous part in gaseous form with their breath. The mushrooms dissolve more easily; the natural separation that takes place as they reach a certain stage in their development being precipitated by concussion or shock.

"Having seen that, as on earth, we gain control of the material first, our acquisitiveness then extends to a better understanding and appreciation of our new senses, and we are continually finding new objects of beauty, and new beauties in things we supposed we already understood. We were accustomed on earth to the marvellous variety that Nature produced from apparently simple means and presented to our very limited senses; here there is an indescribably greater variety to be examined by vastly keener senses. The souls in hell have an equally keen but distorted counterpart of our senses, so that they see in a magnified form everything vile in themselves and in each other. To their senses only the ugly and hateful side is visible, so that the beauty and perfume of a flower are to them as loathsome as the appearance and fumes of a toadstool. As evolution and the tendency of everything to perpetuate itself and intensify its peculiarities are invariable throughout the universe, these unhappy souls and ourselves seem destined to diverge more and more as time goes on; and while we constantly become happier as our capacity for happiness increases, their sharpening senses will give them a worse and worse idea of each other, till their mutual repugnance will know no bounds, and of everything concerning which they obtain knowledge through their senses. Thus these poor creatures seem to be the victims of circumstances and the unalterable laws of fate, and were there such a thing as death, their misery would unquestionably finally break their hearts. That there will be final forgiveness for the condemned, has long been a human hope; but as yet they have experienced none, and there is no analogy for it in Nature.

"But while you have still your earthly bodies and the opportunities they give you of serving God, you need not be concerned about hell; no one on earth, knowing how things really are, would ever again forsake His ways. The earthly state is the most precious opportunity of securing that for which a man would give his all. Even from the most worldly point of view, a man is an unspeakable fool not to improve his talents and do good. What would those in sheol not give now for but one day in the flesh on earth, of which you unappreciatives may still have so many? The well-used opportunities of even one hour might bring joy to those in paradise forever, and greatly ease the lot of those in hell. In doing acts of philanthropy, however, you must remember the text of the sermon the doctor of divinity preached to Craniner and Ridley just before they perished at the stake: 'Though I give my body to be burned, and have not charity, it profiteth me nothing'--which shows that even good deeds must be performed in the proper spirit.

"A new era is soon to dawn on earth. Notwithstanding your great material progress, the future will exceed all the past. Man will find every substance's maximum use, thereby vastly increasing his comfort. Then, when advanced in science and reason, with the power of his senses increased by the delicate instruments that you, as the forerunners of the coming man, are already learning to make, may he cease to be a groveller, like our progenitors the quadrupeds, and may his thoughts rise to his Creator, who has brought him to such heights through all the intricacies of the way. Your preparation for the life to come can also be greatly aided by intercourse with those who have already died. When you really want to associate spiritually with us, you can do so; for, though perhaps only one in a hundred million can, like me, so clothe himself as to be again visible to mortal eyes, many of us could affect gelatine or extremely sensitive plates that would show interruptions in the ultra-violet chemical rays that, like the thermal red beyond the visible spectroscope, you know exist though you can neither see nor feel them. Spirits could not affect the magnetic eye, because magnetism, though immaterial itself, is induced and affected only by a material substance. The impression on the plate, however, like the prismatic colours you have already noticed, can be produced by a slight rarefaction of the hydrogen in the air, so that, though no spirit could be photographed as such, a code and language might be established by means of the effect produced on the air by the spirit's mind. I am so interested in the subject of my disquisition that I had almost forgotten that your spirits are still subject to the requirements of the body. Last time I dined with you; let me now play the host."

"We shall be charmed to dine with you," said Ayrault, "and shall be only too glad of anything that will keep you with us."

"Then," said the spirit, "as the tablecloth is laid, we need only to have something on it. Let each please hold a corner," he continued, taking one himself with his left hand, while he passed his right to his brow. Soon flakes as of snow began to form in the air above, and slowly descended upon the cloth; and, glancing up, the three men saw that for a considerable height this process was going on, the flakes increasing in size as they fell till they attained a length of several inches. When there was enough for them all on the table-cloth the shower ceased. Sitting down on the ground, they began to eat this manna, which had a delicious flavour and marvellous purity and freshness.

"As you doubtless have already suspected," said the spirit, "the basis of this in every case is carbon, combined with nitrogen in its solid form, and with the other gases the atmosphere here contains. You may notice that the flakes vary in colour as well as in taste, both of which are of course governed by the gas with which the carbon, also in its visible form, is combined. It is almost the same process as that performed by every plant in withdrawing carbon from the air and storing it in its trunk in the form of wood, which, as charcoal, is again almost pure carbon, only in this case the metamorphosis is far more rapid. This is perhaps the natural law that Elijah, by God's aid, invoked in the miracle of the widow's cruse, and that produced the manna that fed the Israelites in the desert; while apergy came in play in the case of the stream that Moses called from the rock in the wilderness, which followed the descendants of Abraham over the rough country through which they passed. In examining miracles with the utmost deference, as we have a right to, we see one law running through all. Even in Christ's miracle of changing the water to wine, there was a natural law, though only one has dwelt on earth who could make that change, which, from a chemist's standpoint, was peculiarly difficult on account of the required fermentation, which is the result of a developed and matured germ. Many of His miracles, however, are as far beyond my small power as heaven is above the earth. Much of the substance of the loaves and fishes with which He fed the multitude--the carbon and nitrogenous products--also came from the air, though He could have taken them from many other sources. The combination and building up of these in the ordinary way would have taken weeks or months, but was performed instantaneously by His mighty power."

"What natural laws are known to you," asked Bearwarden, "that we do not understand, or concerning the existence of which we are ignorant?"

"Most of the laws in the invisible world," said the spirit, "are the counterpart or extension of laws that appear on earth, though you as yet understand but a small part of those, many not having come to your notice. You, for instance, know that light, heat, and motion are analogous, and either of the last two can be converted into the other; but in practice you produce motion of the water molecules by the application of heat, and seldom reverse it. One of the first things we master here is the power to freeze or boil water, by checking the motion of the molecules in one case, and by increasing it, and their mutual repulsion, in the other. This is by virtue of a simple law, though in this case there is no natural manifestation of it on earth with which to compare it. While knowledge must be acquired here through study, as on earth, the new senses we receive with the awakening from death render the doing so easy, though with only the senses we had before it would have been next to impossible.

"At this moment snow is falling on the Callisto; but this you could not know by seeing, and scarcely any degree of evolution could develop your sight sufficiently, unassisted by death. With your instruments, however, you could already perceive it, notwithstanding the intervening rocks.

"Your research on earth is the best and most thorough in the history of the race; and could we but give you suggestions as to the direction in which to push it, the difference between yourselves and angels might be but little more than that between the number and intensity of the senses and the composition of the body. By the combination of natural laws you have rid yourselves of the impediment of material weight, and can roam through space like spirits, or as Columbus, by virtue of the confidence that came with the discovery of the mariner's compass, roamed upon and explored the sea. You have made a good beginning, and were not your lives so short, and their requirements so peremptory, you might visit the distant stars.

"I will show you the working of evolution. Life sleeps in minerals, dreams in plants, and wakes in you. The rock worn by frost and age crumbles to earth and soil. This enters the substance of the primordial plant, which, slowly rising; produces the animal germ. After that the way is clear, and man is evolved from protoplasm through the vertebrate and the ape. Here we have the epitome of the struggle for life in the ages past, and the analogue of the journey in the years to come. Does not the Almighty Himself make this clear where He says through his servant Isaiah, 'Behold of these stones will I raise up children'?--and the name Adam means red earth. God, having brought man so far, will not let evolution cease, and the next stage of life must be the spiritual." "Can you tell us anything," asked Ayrault, "concerning the bodies that those surviving the final judgment will receive?"

"Notwithstanding the unfolding of knowledge that has come to us here," replied the spirit, "there are still some subjects concerning which we must look for information to the inspired writers in the Bible, and every gain or discovery goes to prove their veracity. We know that there are celestial bodies and bodies terrestrial, and that the spiritual bodies we shall receive in the resurrection will have power and will be incorruptible and immortal. We also know by analogy and reason that they will be unaffected by the cold and void of space, so that their possessors can range through the universe for non-nillions and decillions of miles, that they will have marvellous capacities for enjoying what they find, and that no undertaking or journey will be too difficult, though it be to the centre of the sun. Though many of us can already visit the remote regions of space as spirits, none can as yet see God; but we know that as the sight we are to receive with our new bodies sharpens, the pure in heart will see Him, though He is still as invisible to the eyes of the most developed here as the ether of space is to yours."

CHAPTER VIII
CASSANDRA AND COSMOLOGY

The water-jug being empty, Ayrault took it up, and, crossing the ridge of a small hill, descended to a running-brook. He had filled it, and was straightening himself, when the stone on which he stood turned, and he might have fallen, had not the bishop, of whose presence he had been unaware, stretched out his hand and upheld him.

"I thought you might need a little help," he said with a smile, "and so walked beside you, though you knew it not. Water is heavy, and you may not yet have become accustomed to its Saturnian weight."

"Many thanks, my master," replied Ayrault, retaining his hand. "Were it not that I am engaged to the girl I love, and am sometimes haunted by the thought that in my absence she may be forgetting me, I should wish to spend the rest of my natural life here, unless I could persuade you to go with me to the earth."

"By remaining here," replied the spirit, with a sad look, "you would be losing the most priceless opportunities of doing good. Neither will I go with you; but, as your distress is real, I will tell you of anything happening on earth that you wish to know."

"Tell me, then, what the person now in my thoughts is doing."

"She is standing in a window facing west, watering some forget-me-nots with a small silver sprinkler which has a ruby in the handle."

"Can you see anything else?"

"Beneath the jewel is an inscription that runs:

 'By those who in warm July are born
 A single ruby should be worn;
 Then will they be exempt and free
 From love's doubts and anxiety.'"

"Marvellous! Had I any doubts as to your prescience and power, they would be dispelled now. One thing more let me ask, however: Does she still love me?"

"In her mind is but one thought, and in her heart is an image--that of the man before me. She loves you with all her soul."

"My most eager wish is satisfied, and for the moment my heart is at rest," replied Ayrault, as they turned their steps towards camp. "Yet, such is my weakness by nature, that, ere twenty-four hours have passed I shall long to have you tell me again."

"I have been in love myself," replied the spirit, "and know the feeling; yet to be of the smallest service to you gives me far more happiness than it can give you. The mutual love in paradise exceeds even the lover's love on earth, for it is only those that loved and can love that are blessed."

"You can hardly realize," the bishop continued, as they rejoined Bearwarden and Cortlandt, "the joy that a spirit in paradise experiences when, on reopening his eyes after passing death, which is but the portal, he finds himself endowed with sight that enables him to see such distances and with such distinctness. The solar system, with this ringed planet, its swarm of asteroids, and its intra-Mercurial planets--one of which, Vulcan, you have already discovered--is a beautiful sight. The planets nearest the sun receive such burning rays that their surfaces are red-hot, and at the equator at perihelion are molten. These are not seen from the earth, because, rising or setting almost simultaneously with the sun, they are lost in its rays. The great planet beyond Neptune's orbit is perhaps the most interesting. This we call Cassandra, because it would be a prophet of evil to any visitor from the stars who should judge the solar system by it. This planet is nearly as large as Jupiter, being 80,000 miles in diameter, but has a specific gravity lighter than Saturn. Bode's law, you know, says, Write down 0, 3, 6, 12, 24, 48, 96. Add 4 to each, and get 4, 7, 10, 16, 28, 52, 100; and this series of numbers represents very nearly the relative distances of the planets from the sun. According to this law, you would expect the planet next beyond Neptune to be about 5,000,000,000 miles from the sun. But it is about 9,500,000,000, so that there is a gap between Neptune and Cassandra, as between Mars and Jupiter, except that in Cassandra's case there are no asteroids to show where any planet was; we must, then, suppose it is an exception to Bode's law, or that there was a planet that has completely disappeared. As Cassandra would be within the law if there had been an intermediary planet, we have good prima facie reason for believing that it existed. Cassandra takes, in round numbers, a thousand years to complete its orbit, and from it the sun, though brighter, appears no larger than the earth's evening or morning star. Cassandra has also three large moons; but these, when full, shine with a pale-grey light, like the old moon in the new moon's arms, in that terrestrial phenomenon when the earth, by reflecting the crescent's light, and that of the sun, makes the dark part visible. The temperature at Cassandra's surface is but little above the cold of space, and no water exists in the liquid state, it being as much a solid as aluminum or glass. There are rivers and lakes, but these consist of liquefied hydrogen and other gases, the heavier liquid collected in deep Places, and the lighter, with less than half the specific gravity of ether, floating upon it without mixing, as oil on water. When the heavier penetrates to a sufficient depth, the interior being still warm, it is converted into gas and driven back to the surface, only to be recondensed on reaching the upper air. Thus it may happen that two rains composed of separate liquids may fall together. There being but little of any other atmosphere, much of it consists of what you might call the vapour of hydrogen, and many of the well-known gases and liquids on earth exist only as liquids and solids; so that, were there mortal inhabitants on Cassandra, they might build their houses of blocks of oxygen or chlorine, as you do of limestone or marble, and use ice that never melts, in place of glass, for transparence. They would also use mercury for bullets in their rifles, just as inhabitants of the intra-Vulcan planets at the other extreme might, if their bodies consisted of asbestos, or were in any other way non-combustibly constituted, bathe in tin, lead, or even zinc, which ordinarily exist in the liquid state, as water and mercury do on the earth.

"Though Cassandra's atmosphere, such as it is, is mostly clear, for the evaporation from the rivers and icy mediterraneans is slight, the brightness of even the highest noon is less than an earthly twilight, and the stars never cease to shine. The dark base of the rocky cliffs is washed by the frigid tide, but there is scarcely a sound, for the pebbles cannot be moved by the weightless waves, and an occasional murmur is all that is heard. Great rocks of ice reflect the light of the grey moons, and never a leaf falls or a bird sings. With the exception of the mournful ripples, the planet is silent as the grave. The animal and plant kingdoms do not exist; only the mineral and spiritual worlds. I say spiritual, because there are souls upon it; but it is the home of the condemned in hell. Here dwell the transgressors who died unrepentant, and those who were not saved by faith. This is the one instance in which I do not enjoy my developed sight, for I sometimes glance in their direction, and the vision that meets me, as my eyes focus, distresses my soul. Their senses are like an imperfect mirror, magnifying all that is bad in one another, and distorting anything still partially good when that exists. All those things that might at least distract them are hollow, their misery being the inevitable result of the condition of mind to which they became accustomed on earth and which brought them to Cassandra. But let us turn to something brighter.

"Though the solar system may seem complex, the sun is but a star among the millions in the Milky Way, and, compared with the planetary systems of Sirius, the stars of the Southern Cross, and the motions of the nebula, it is simplicity itself. Compared with the splendour of Sirius, with its diameter of twelve million miles, the sun, measuring but eight hundred and forty thousand, becomes insignificant; and this giant's system includes groups and clusters of planets, many with three times the mass of Jupiter, five and six together, each a different colour, revolving about a common centre, while they swing about their primary. Their numerous moons have satellites encircling them, with orbits in some cases at right angles to the plane of the ecliptic, so that they shine perpendicularly on what correspond to the arctic and antarctic regions, while their axes are so inclined that the satellites turn a complete somersault at each revolution, producing glistening effects of ice and snow at the poles. Some of the moons are at a red or white heat, and so prevent the chill of night on the planets, while they shine with more than reflected light. In addition to the five or six large planets in each group, which, however, are many millions of miles apart, there is in some clusters a small planet that swings backward and forward across the common centre, like a pendulum, but in nearly a straight line; and while this multiplicity of motion goes on, the whole aggregation sweeps majestically around Sirius, its mighty sun. Our little solar system contains, as we know, about one thousand planets, satellites, and asteroids large enough to be dignified by the name of heavenly bodies. Vast numbers of the stars have a hundred and even a thousand times the mass of our sun, and their systems being relatively as complex as ours--in some cases even more so--they contain a hundred thousand or a million individual bodies.

"Over sixty million bright or incandescent stars were visible to the terrestrial telescopes a hundred years ago, the average size of which far exceeds our sun. To the magnificent telescopes of to-day they are literally countless, and the number can be indefinitely extended as your optical resources grow. Yet the number of stars you see is utterly insignificant compared with the cold and dark ones you cannot see, but concerning which you are constantly learning more, by observing their effect on the bright ones, both by perturbing them and by obscuring their rays. Occasionally, as you know, a star of the twelfth or fifteenth magnitude, or one that has been invisible, flares up for several months to the fourth or fifth, through a collision with some dark giant, and then returns to what it was in the beginning, a gaseous, filmy nebula. These innumerable hosts of dark monsters, though dead, are centres of systems, like most of the stars you can see.

"A slight consideration of these figures will show that, notwithstanding the number of souls the Creator has given life on earth, each one might in fact have a system to himself; and that, however long the little globe may remain, as it were, a mint, in which souls are tried by fire and moulded, and receive their final stamp, they will always have room to circulate, and will be prized according to the impress their faces or hearts must show. But Sirius itself is moving many times faster than the swiftest cannon ball, carrying its system with it; and I see you asking, 'To what does all this motion tend?' I will show you. Many quadrillions of miles away, so far that your most powerful telescopes have not yet caught a glimmer, rests in its serene grandeur a star that we call Cosmos, because it is the centre of this universe. Its diameter is as great as the diameter of Cassandra's orbit, and notwithstanding its terrific heat, its specific gravity, on account of the irresistible pressure at and near the centre, is as great as that of the planet Mercury. This holds all that your eyes or mine can see; and the so-called motions of the stars--for we know that Sirius, among others, is receding--is but the difference in the rate at which the different systems and constellations swing around Cosmos, though in doing so they often revolve about other systems or swing round common centres, so that many are satellites of satellites many times repeated. The orbits of some are circular, and of others elliptical, as those of comets, and some revolve about each other, or, as we have seen, about a common point while they perform their celestial journey. A star, therefore, recedes or advances, as Jupiter and Venus with relation to the earth. The planet in the smaller orbit moves faster than that in the larger, so that the intervening distances wax and wane, though all are going in the same general direction. In the case of the members of the solar system, astronomical record can tell when even a most distant known planet has been in opposition or conjunction; but the earth has scarcely been habitable since the sun was last in its present position in its orbit around Cosmos. The curve that our system follows is of such radius that it would require the most precise observations for centuries to show that it was not a straight line.

"We call this the universe because it is all that the clearest eyes or telescopes have been able to see, but it is only a subdivision--in fact, but a system on a vaster scale than that of the sun or of Sirius. Far beyond this visible universe, my intuition tells me, are other systems more gigantic than this, and entirely different in many respects. Even the effects of gravitation are modified by the changed condition; for these systems are spread out flat, like the rings of this planet, and the ether of space is luminous instead of black, as here. These systems are but in a later stage of development than ours; and in the course of evolution our visible universe will be changed in the same way, as I can explain.

"In incalculable ages, the forward motion of the planets and their satellites will be checked by the resistance of the ether of space and the meteorites and solid matter they encounter. Meteorites also overtake them, and, by striking them as it were in the rear, propel them, but more are encountered in front--an illustration of which you can have by walking rapidly or riding on horseback on a rainy day, in which case more drops will strike your chest than your back. The same rule applies to bodies in space, while the meteorites encountered have more effect than those following, since in one case it is the speed of the meteor minus that of the planet, and in the other the sum of the two velocities. With this checking of the forward motion, the centrifugal force decreases, and the attraction of the central body has more effect. When this takes place the planet or satellite falls slightly towards the body around which it revolves, thereby increasing its speed till the centrifugal force again balances the centripetal. This would seem to make it descend by fits and starts, but in reality the approach is nearly constant, so that the orbits are in fact slightly spiral. What is true of the planets and satellites is also true of the stars with reference to Cosmos; though many even of these have subordinate motions in their great journey. Though the satellites of the moons revolve about the primaries in orbits inclined at all kinds of angles to the planes of the ecliptics, and even the moons vary in their paths about the planets, the planets themselves revolve about the stars, like those of this system about the sun, in substantially the same plane; and what is true of the planets is even more true of the stars in their orbits about Cosmos, so that when, after incalculable ages, they do fall, they strike this monster sun at or near its equator, and not falling perpendicularly, but in a line varying but slightly from a tangent, and at terrific speed, they cause the colossus to rotate more and more rapidly on its own axis, till it must become greatly flattened at the poles, as the earth is slightly, and as Jupiter and Saturn are a good deal. Even though not all the stars are exactly in the plane of Cosmos's equator, as you can see they are not there are as many above as below it, so that the general average will be there; and as all are moving in the same direction, it is not necessary for all to strike the same line, those striking nearer the poles, where the circles are smaller, and where the surface is not being carried forward so fast by the giant's rotation, will have even more effect in increasing its speed, since it will be like attaching the driving-rods of a locomotive near the axle instead of near the circumference, and with enough power will produce even greater results. As Cosmos waxes greater from the result of these continual accretions, its attraction for the stars will increase, until those coming from the outer regions of its universe will move at such terrific speed in their spiral orbits that before coming in contact they will be almost invisible, having already absorbed all solid matter revolving about themselves. These accessions of moving matter, continually received at and near its equator, will cause Cosmos to spread out like Saturn's rings till it becomes flat, though the balance of forces will be so perfect that it is doubtful whether an animal or a man placed there would feel much change.

"But these universes--or, more accurately, divisions of the universe--already planes, though the vast surfaces are not so flat as to preclude beautiful and gently rolling slopes, are spirit-lands, and will be inhabited only by spirits. Then there are great phosphorescent areas, and the colour of the surface changes with every hour of the day, from the most brilliant crimson to the softest shade of blue, radiant with many colours that your eyes cannot now see. There are also myriads of scented streams, consisting of hundreds of different and multi-coloured liquids, each with a perfume sweeter than the most delicate flower, and pouring forth the most heavenly music as they go on their way. But be not surprised at the magnitude of the change, for is it not written in Revelation, 'I saw a new heaven and a new earth; for the first heaven and the first earth were passed away'? Nor can we be surprised at vastness, sublimity, and beauty such as never was conceived of, for do we not find this in His word, 'Eye hath not seen, nor ear heard, neither have entered into the heart of man, the things which God hath prepared for them that love Him'? In this blissful state, those that feared God and obeyed their consciences will live on forever; but their rest can never become stagnation, for evolution is one of the most constant laws, and never ceases, and they must always go onward and upward, unspeakably blessed by the consciences they made their rule in life, till in purity and power they shall equal or exceed the angels of their Lord in heaven.

"But you men of finite understanding will ask, as I myself should have asked, How, by the law of hydrostatics, can liquids flow on a plane? Remember that, though these divisions are astronomical or geometrical planes, their surfaces undulate; but the moving cause is this: At the centre of these planes is a pole, the analogue, we will say, of the magnetic pole on earth, that has a more effective attraction for a gas than for a liquid. When liquids approach the periphery of the circle, the rapid rotation and decreased pressure cause them to break up, whereupon the elementary gases return to the centre in the atmosphere, if near the surface, forming a gentle breeze. On nearing the centre, the cause of the separation being removed, the gases reunite to form a liquid, and the centrifugal force again sends this on its journey."

"Is there no way," asked Bearwarden, "by which a man may retrieve himself, if he has lost or misused his opportunities on earth?"

"The way a man lays up treasures in heaven, when on earth," replied the spirit, "is by gladly doing something for some one else, usually in some form sacrificing self. In hell no one can do anything for any one else, because every one can have the semblance of anything he wishes by merely concentrating his mind upon it, though, when he has it, it is but a shadow and gives him no pleasure. Thus no one can give any one else anything he cannot obtain himself; and if he could, since it would be no sacrifice on his part, he would derive no great moral comfort from it. Neither can any one comfort any one else by putting his acts or offences in a new light, for every one knows the whole truth about himself and everybody else, so that nothing can be made to appear favourably or unfavourably. All this, however, is supposing there is the desire to be kind; but how can spirits that were selfish and ill-disposed on earth, where there are so many softening influences, have good inclinations in hell, where they loathe one another with constantly increasing strength?

"Inasmuch as both the good and the bad continue on the lines on which they started when on earth, we are continually drawing nearer to God, while they are departing. The gulf may be only one of feeling, but that is enough. It follows, then, that with God as our limit, which we of course can never reach, their limit, in the geometrical sense, must be total separation from Him. Though all spirits, we are told, live forever, it occurs to me that in God's mercy there may be a gradual end; for though to the happy souls in heaven a thousand years may seem as nothing, existence in hell must drag along with leaden limbs, and a single hour seem like a lifetime of regret. Since it is dreadful to think that such unsoothed anguish should continue forever, I have often pondered whether it might not be that, by a form of involution and reversal of the past law, the spirit that came to life evolved from the mineral, plant, and animal worlds, may mercifully retrace its steps one by one, till finally the soul shall penetrate the solid rock and hide itself by becoming part of the planet. Many people in my day believed that after death their souls would enter stately trees, and spread abroad great branches, dropping dead leaves over the places on which they had stood while on earth. This might be the last step in the awful tragedy of the fall and involution of a human soul. In this way, those who had wasted the priceless opportunities given them by God might be mercifully obliterated, for it seems as if they would not be needed in the economy of the universe. The Bible, however, mentions no such end, and says unmistakably that hell will last forever; so that in this supposition, as in many others, the wish is probably father of the thought."

"But," persisted Bearwarden, "how about death-bed repentances?"

"Those," replied the spirit, "are few and far between. The pains of death at the last hour leave but little room for aught but vain regret. A man dies suddenly, or may be unconscious some time before the end. But they do occur. The question is, How much credit is it to be good when you can do no more harm? The time to resist evil and do that which is right is while the temptation is on and in its strength. While life lasts there is hope, but the books are sealed by death. The tree must fall to one side or the other--there is no middle ground--and as the tree falleth, so it lieth.

"This, however, is a gloomy subject, and one that in your heart of hearts you understand. I would rather tell you more of the beauties and splendours of space--of the orange, red, and blue stars, and of the tremendous cyclonic movements going on within them, which are even more violent than the storms that rage in the sun. The clouds, as the spectroscope has already shown, consist of iron, gold, and platinum in the form of vapour, while the openings revealed by sun-spots, or rather star-spots, are so tremendous that a comparatively small one would contain many dozen such globes as the earth. I could tell you also of the mysteries of the great dark companions of some of the stars, and of the stars that are themselves dark and cold, with naught but the faraway constellations to cheer them, on which night reigns eternally, and that far outnumber the stars you can see. Also of the multiplicity of sex and extraordinary forms of life that exist there, though on none of them are there mortal men like those on the earth.

"Nature, in the process of evolution, has in all these cases gone off on an entirely different course, the most intelligent and highly developed species being in the form of marvellously complex reptiles, winged serpents that sing most beautifully, but whose blood is cold, being prevented from freezing in the upper regions of the atmosphere by the presence of salt and chemicals, and which are so intelligent that they have practically subdued many of these dark stars to themselves. On others, the most highly developed species have hollow, bell-shaped tentacles, into which they inject two or more opposing gases from opposite sides of their bodies, which, in combination, produce a strong explosion. This provides them with an easy and rapid locomotion, since the explosions find a sufficient resistance in the surrounding air to propel the monsters much faster than birds. These can at pleasure make their breath so poisonous that the lungs of any creatures except themselves inhaling it are at once turned to parchment. Others can give their enemies or their prey an electric shock, sending a bolt through the heart, or can paralyze the mind physically by an effort of their wills, causing the brain to decompose while the victim is still alive. Others have the same power that snakes have, though vastly intensified, mesmerizing their victims from afar.

"Still others have such delicate senses that in a way they commune with spirits, though they have no souls themselves; for in no part or corner of the universe except on earth are there animals that have souls. Yet they know the meaning of the word, and often bewail their hard lot in that no part of them can live when the heart has ceased to beat. "Ah, my friends, if we had no souls--if, like the æsthetic reptilia, we knew that when our dust dissolved our existence would be over--we should realize the preciousness of what we hold so lightly now. Man and the spirits and angels are the only beings with souls, and in no place except on earth are new souls being created. This gives you the greatest and grandest idea of the dignity of life and its inestimable value. But it is as difficult to describe the higher wonders of the stellar worlds to you as to picture the glories of sunset to a blind man, for you have experienced nothing with which to compare them. Instead of seeing all that really is, you see but a small part."

CHAPTER IX
DOCTOR CORTLANDT SEES HIS GRAVE

"Is it not distasteful to you," Cortlandt asked, "to live so near these loathsome dragons?"

"Not in the least," replied the spirit. "They affect us no more than the smallest micro-organism, for we see both with equal clearness. Since we are not obliged to breathe, they cannot injure us; and, besides, they serve to illustrate the working of God's laws, and there is beauty in everything for those that have the senses required for perceiving it. A feature of the spiritual world is, that it does not interfere with the natural, and the natural, except through faith, is not aware of its presence."

"Then why," asked Cortlandt, "was it necessary for the Almighty to bring your souls to Saturn, since there would have been no overcrowding if you had remained on the earth?"

"That," replied the spirit, "was part of His wisdom; for the spirit, being able at once to look back into the natural world, if in it, would be troubled at the mistakes and tribulations of his friends. Now, as a rule, before a spirit can return to earth, his or her relatives and friends have also died; or, if he can return before that happens, he is so advanced that he sees the ulterior purpose, and therefore the wisdom of God's ways, and is not distressed thereby. Lastly, as their expanding senses grew, it would be painful for the blessed and condemned spirits to be together. Therefore we are brought here, where God reveals Himself to us more and more, and the flight of the other souls--those unhappy ones--does not cease till they reach Cassandra."

"Can the souls on Cassandra also leave it in time and roam at will?" asked Cortlandt.

"I have seen none of them myself in my journeys to other planets; but as the sun shines upon the just and the unjust, and there is no exception to Nature's laws, I can reply that in time they do, and with equal powers their incentive to roam would be greater; for we are drawn together by common sympathy and pure, requited love, while they are mutually repelled. Of course, some obtain a measure of freedom before the rest, and these naturally roam the farthest, and the more they see and the farther they go, the stronger becomes their abhorrence for everything they meet."

"Cannot you spirits help us, and the mortals now on earth, to escape this fate?"

"The greatest hope for your bodies and souls lies in the communion with those that have passed through death; for the least of them can tell you more than the wisest man on earth; and could you all come or send representatives to the multitudes here who cannot as yet return to you, but few on earth would be so quixotically sinful as to refuse our advice. Since, however, the greatest good comes to men from the learning that they make an effort to secure, it is for you to strive to reach us, who can act as go-betweens from God to you."

"It seems to me," said Bearwarden, "that people are better now than formerly. The sin of idolatry, for instance, has disappeared--has it not?"

"Men still set up idols of wealth, passion, or ambition in their hearts. These they worship as in days gone by, only the form has changed."

"Could the souls on Cassandra do us bodily or mental injury, if we could ever reach their planet?" asked Bearwarden. "They might oppress and distress you, but your faith would protect you wherever you might go."

"Can you give us a taste of your sense of prescience?" asked Bearwarden again; "for, since it is not clear in what degree the condemned receive this, and neither is it by any means sure that I shall be saved, I should like for once in my history to experience this sense of divinity, before my entity ends in stone."

"I will transfer to you my sense of prescience," replied the spirit, "that you may foresee as prophets have. In so doing, I shall but anticipate, since you will yourselves in time obtain this sense in a greater or less degree. Is there any event in the future you would like to see, in order that, when the vision is fulfilled, it may tend to stablish your faith?"

"Since I am the oldest," replied the doctor, "and shall probably die before my friends, reveal to us, I pray you, the manner of my death and the events immediately following. This may prove an object-lesson to them, and will greatly interest me."

"Your death will be caused by blood-poisoning, brought on by an accident," began the spirit. "Some daybreak will find you weak, after a troubled night, with your bodily resources at a low ebb. Sunset will see you weaker, with your power of resistance almost gone. Midnight will find you weaker still, and but little removed from the point of death. A few hours later a kind hand will close the lids of your half-shut eyes, which never again will behold the light. The coffin will inclose your body, and the last earthly journey begin. Now," the spirit continued, "you shall all use my sight instead of your own."

The walls of the cave seemed to expand, till they resembled those of a great cathedral, while the stalactites appeared to be metamorphosed into Gothic columns. They found themselves among a large congregation that had come to attend the last sad rites, while the great organ played Chopin's "Funeral March." The high vault and arches received the organ's tone, and a sombre light pervaded the interior. There was a slight flutter and a craning of necks among those in the pews, as the procession began to ascend the aisle. While the slow step of the pallbearers and those carrying the coffin sounded on the stone floor, the clear voice of the clergyman that headed the procession sounded these words through the cathedral: "I know that my Redeemer liveth, and that He shall stand at the latter day upon the earth." As the bier advanced, Bearwarden and Ayrault recognized themselves among the pallbearers--the former with grey mustache and hair, the latter considerably aged. The hermetically sealed lead coffin was inclosed in a wooden case, and the whole was draped and covered with flowers.

A look into the future

"Oh, my faith!" cried Cortlandt, "I see my face within, yet it is but a decomposing mass that I once described as I."

Then again did the minister's voice proclaim, "I am the resurrection and the life, saith the Lord; he that believeth in me, though he were dead, yet shall he live; and whosoever liveth and believeth in me shall never die."

The bearers gently set down their burden; the minister read the ever-impressive chapter of St. Paul to the Corinthians; a bishop solemnly and silently sprinkled earth on the coffin; and the choir sang the 398th hymn, beginning with the words, "Hark, hark my soul! angelic songs are swelling," which had always been Cortlandt's favourite, and the service was at an end. The bearers again shouldered all that was left of Henry Cortlandt, and his relatives accompanied this to the cemetery.

Then came a sweeping change of scene. A host of monuments and gravestones reflected the sunlight, while a broad river ebbed and flowed between high banks. A sexton and a watchman stood by a granite vault, the heavy door of which they had opened with a large key. Hard by were some gardeners and labourers, and also a crowd of curiosity-seekers who had come to witness the last sad rites. Presently a funeral procession appeared. The hearse stopped near the open vault, over the door of which stood out the name of CORTLANDT, and the accompanying minister said a short prayer, while all present uncovered their heads. After this the coffin was borne within and set at rest upon a slab, among many generations of Cortlandts. In the hearts of the relatives and friends was genuine sorrow, but the curiosity-seekers went their way and gave little thought. "To-morrow will be like to-day," they said, "and more great men will die."

Then came another change of scene, though it was comparatively slight. The sun slowly sank beyond the farther bank of the broad river, and the moon and stars shone softly on the gravestones and crosses. Two gardeners smoked their short clay pipes on a bench before the Cortlandt vault, and talked in a slow manner.

"He was a great man," said one, "and if his soul blooms like the flowers on his grave, he must be in paradise, which we know is a finer park than this."

"He was expert for the Government when the earth's axis was set right," said the second gardener, "and he must have been a scholar, for his calculations have all come true. He was one of the first three men to visit the other planets, while the obituaries in the papers say his history will be read hereafter like the books of Caesar. After burying all these great people, I sometimes wish I could do the same for myself, for the people I bury seem to be remembered." After this they relapsed into their meditations, the silence being broken only by an occasional murmur from the river's steady flow.

Hereupon the voyagers found they were once more in the cave. The fire had burned low, and the dawn was already in the east. Cortlandt wiped his forehead, shivered, and looked extremely pale.

"Thank Heaven," he cried, "we cannot ordinarily foresee our end; for but few would attain their predestined ending could they see it in advance. May the veil not again be raised, lest I faint before it! I looked in vain for my soul," he continued, "but could see it nowhere."

"The souls of those dying young," replied the spirit, "sometimes wish to hover near their ashes as if regretting an unfinished life, or the opportunities that have departed; but those dying after middle age are usually glad to be free from their bodies, and seldom think of them again."

"I shall append the lines now in my head to my history," said Cortlandt, "that where it goes they may go also. They can scarcely fail to be instructive as the conclusions of a man who has seen beyond his grave." Whereupon he wrote a stanza in his note-book, and closed it without showing his companions what he had written.

"May they do all the good you hope, and much more!" replied the spirit, "for the reward in the resurrection morning will vastly exceed all your labours now.

"O, my friends," the spirit continued most earnestly, addressing the three, "are you prepared for your death-beds? When your eyes glaze in their last sleep, and you lose that temporal world and what you perhaps considered all, as in a haze, your dim vision will then be displaced by the true creation that will be eternal. Your unattained ambitions, your hopes, and your ideals will be swallowed in the grave. Your works will secure you a place in history, and many will remember your names until, in time, oblivion covers your memory as the grass conceals your tombs. Are you prepared for the time when your eyes become blind, and your trusted senses fail? Your sorrowing friends will mourn, and the flags of your clubs will fly at half-mast, but no earthly thing can help you then. In what condition will the resurrection morning find you, when your sins of neglect and commission plead for vengeance, as Abel's blood from the ground? After that there can be no change. The classification, as I have already told you, is now going on; it will then be finished."

"We are the most utterly wretched sinners!" cried Ayrault. "Show us how we can be saved."

"As an inhabitant of spirit-land, I will give you worldly counsel," replied the bishop. "During my earthly administration, as I told you, people came from far to hear me preach. This was because I had eloquence and earnestness, both gifts of God. But I was a miserably weak sinner myself. That which I would, I did not, and that which I would not that I did; and I often prayed my congregation to follow my sermons rather than my ways. I seemed to do my followers good, and Daniel thus commends my way in his last chapter: 'They that turn many to righteousness shall shine as the stars forever and ever,' and the explanation is clear. There is no surer way of learning than trying to teach. In teaching my several flocks I was also improved myself. I was sown in weakness, but was raised in power, strength being made perfect in weakness. Therefore improve your fellows, though yourself you cannot raise. The knowledge that you have sent many souls to heaven, though you are yourself a castaway, will give you unspeakable joy, and place you in heaven wherever you may be. Yet remember this: none of us can win heaven; salvation is the gift of God. I have said as much now as you can remember. Farewell. Improve time while you can. Fear God and keep His commandments. This is the whole duty of man."

So saying, the spirit vanished in a cloud that for a time emitted light. "I am not surprised," said Bearwarden, "that people took long journeys to hear him. I would do so myself."

"I have never had much fear of death," said Cortlandt, "but the mere thought of it now makes my knees shake, and fills my heart with dread. I thought I saw the most hateful forms about my coffin, and imagined that they might be the personification of doubt, coldness, and my other shortcomings, which had come perhaps from sympathy, in invisible form. I was almost afraid to ask the spirit for the explanation."

"I saw them also," replied Bearwarden, "but took them to be swarms of microbes waiting to destroy your body, or perhaps trying in vain to penetrate your hermetically sealed coffin." Cortlandt seemed much upset, and spent the rest of the day in writing out the facts and trying to assign a cause. Towards evening Bearwarden, who had recovered his spirits, prepared supper, after which they sat in the entrance to the cave.

CHAPTER X
AYRAULT

As the night became darker they caught sight of the earth again, shining very faintly, and in his mind's eye Ayrault saw his sweetheart, and the old, old repining that, since reason and love began, has been in men's minds, came upon him and almost crushed him. Without saying anything to his companions, Ayrault left the cave, and, passing through the grove in which the spirit had paid them his second visit, went slowly to the top of the hill about half a mile off, that he might the more easily gaze at the faint star on which he could picture Sylvia.

"Ah!" he said to himself, on reaching the summit, "I will stay here till the earth rises higher, and when it is far above me I will gaze at it as at heaven."

Accordingly, he lay down with his head on a mound of sod, and watched the familiar planet.

"We were born too soon," he soliloquized; "for had Sylvia and I but lived in the spiritual age foretold by the bishop, we might have held communion, while now our spirits, no matter how much in love, are separated absolutely by a mere matter of distance. It is a mockery to see Sylvia's dwelling-place, and feel that she is beyond my vision. O that, in the absence of something better, my poor imperfect eyes could be transformed into those of an eagle, but with a million times the power! for though I know that with these senses I shall see the resurrection, and hear the last trump, that is but prospective, while now is the time I long for sight."

On the plain he had left he saw his friends' camp-fire, while on the other side of his elevation was a valley in which the insects chirped sharply, and through which ran a stream. Feeling a desire for solitude and to be as far removed as possible, he arose and descended towards the water. Though the autumn, where they found themselves, was well advanced, this night was warm, and the rings formed a great arch above his head. Near the stream the frogs croaked happily, as if unmindful of the long, very long Saturnian winter; for though they were removed but about ten degrees from the equator, the sun was so remote and the axis of the planet so inclined that it was unlikely these individual frogs would see another summer, though they might live again, in a sense, in their descendants. The insects also would soon be frozen and stiff, and the tall, graceful lilies that still clung to life would be withered and dead. The trees, as if weeping at the evanescence of the life around them, shed their leaves at the faintest breeze. These fluttered to the ground, or, falling into the tranquil stream, were carried away by it, and passed from sight. Ayrault stood musing and regretting the necessity of such general death. "But," he thought, "I would rather die than lose my love; for then I should have had the taste of bliss without its fulfilment, and should be worse off than dead. Love gilds the commonplace, and deifies all it touches. Love survives the winter, and in my present frame of mind I should prefer earth and cold with it to heaven and spring. Oh, why is my soul so clogged by my body?"

A pillar of stone standing near him was suddenly shattered, and the bishop stood where it had been. "Because," said the spirit, answering his thought, "it has not yet power to be free."

"Can a man's soul not rise till his body is dead?" asked Ayrault.

The spirit hesitated.

"Oh, tell me," pleaded Ayrault. "If I could see the girl to whom I am engaged, for but a moment, could be convinced that she loves me still, my mind would be at rest. Free my soul or spirit, or whatever it is, from this body, that I may traverse intervening space and be with her."

"You will discover the way for yourself in time," said the spirit.

"I know I shall at the last day, in the resurrection, when I am no longer in the flesh. Then I shall have no need of your aid; for we know that in the resurrection they neither marry nor are given in marriage, but are like the angels of God in heaven. It is while I am mortal, and love as mortals do, that I wish to see my promised bride. A spirit may have other joys, and perhaps higher; but you who have lived in the world and loved, show me that which is now my heart's desire. You have shown us the tomb in which Cortlandt will lie buried; now help me to go to one who is still alive." "I pray that God will grant you this," said the spirit, "and make me His instrument, for I see the depth of your distress." Saying which, he vanished, leaving no trace in his departure except that the pillar of stone returned to its place. With this rather vague hope, Ayrault set off to rejoin his companions, for he felt the need of human sympathy. Saturn's rapid rotation had brought the earth almost to the zenith, the little point shining with the unmistakably steady ray of a planet. Huge bats fluttered about him, and the great cloud-masses swept across the sky, being part of Saturn's ceaseless whirl. He found he was in a hypnotic or spiritualistic state, for it was not necessary for him to have his eyes open to know where he was. In passing one of the pools they had noticed, he observed that the upper and previously invisible liquid had the bright colour of gold, and about it rested a group of figures enveloped in light.

"Why do you look so sad?" they asked. "You are in that abode of departed spirits known as paradise, and should be happy."

"I suppose I should be happy, were I here as you are, as the reward of merit," he replied. "But I am still in the flesh, and as such am subject to its cares."

"You are about to have an experience," said another speaker. "This day your doubts will be at rest, for before another sunset you will know more of the woman you love."

The intensity of the spiritualistic influence here somewhat weakened, for he partially lost sight of the luminous figures, and could no longer hear what they said. His heart was in his mouth as he walked, and he felt like a man about to set out on his honeymoon, or like a bride who knows not whether to laugh or to cry. An indescribable exhilaration was constantly present.

"I wonder," thought he, "if a caterpillar has these sensations before becoming a butterfly? Though I return to the rock from which I sprang, I believe I shall be with Sylvia to-day."

Footprints formed in the soft ground all around him, and the air was filled with spots of phosphorescent light that coincided with the relative positions of the brains, hearts, and eyes of human beings. These surrounded and often preceded him, as though leading him on, while the most heavenly anthems filled the air and the vault of the sky.

"I believe," he thought, with bounding heart, "that I shall be initiated into the mysteries of space this night."

At times he could hear even the words of the choruses ringing in his ears, though at others he thought the effect was altogether in his mind.

"Oh, for a proof," he prayed, "that no sane man can doubt! My faith is implicit in the bishop and the vision, and I feel that in some way I shall return to earth ere the close of another day, for I know I am awake, and that this is no dream."

A fire burned in the mouth of the cave, within which Bearwarden and Cortlandt lay sleeping. The specks of mica in the rocks reflected its light, but in addition to this a diffused phosphorescence filled the place, and the large sod-covered stones they used for pillows emitted purple and dark red flames.

"Is that you, Dick?" asked Bearwarden, awaking and groping about. "We built up the fire so that you should find the camp, but it seems to have gone down." Saying which, he struck a match, whereupon Ayrault ceased to see the phosphorescence or bluish light. At that moment a peal of thunder awakened Cortlandt, who sat up and rubbed his eyes.

"I think," said Ayrault, "I will go to the Callisto and get our mackintoshes before the rain sets in." Whereupon he left his companions, who were soon again fast asleep.

The sky had suddenly become filled with clouds, and Ayrault hastened towards the Callisto, intending to remain there, if necessary, until the storm was over. For about twenty minutes he hurried on through the growing darkness, stopping once on high ground to make sure of his bearings, and he had covered more than half the distance when the rain came on in a flood, accompanied by brilliant lightning. Seeing the huge, hollow trunk of a fallen tree near, and not wishing to be wet through, Ayrault fired several solid shots from his revolver into the cavity, to drive out any wild animals there might be inside, and then hurriedly crawled in, feet first. He next drew in his head, and was congratulating himself on his snug retreat, when the sky became lurid with a flash of lightning, then his head dropped forward, and he was unconscious.

CHAPTER XI
DREAMLAND TO SHADOWLAND

As Ayrault's consciousness returned, he fancied he heard music. Though distant, it was distinct, and seemed to ring from the ether of space. Occasionally it sounded even more remote, but it was rhythmical and continuous, inspiring and stirring him as nothing that he had ever heard before. Finally, it was overcome by the more vivid impressions upon his other senses, and he found himself walking in the streets of his native city. It was spring, and the trees were white with buds. The long shadows of the late afternoon stretched across the way, but the clear sky gave indication of prolonged twilight, and the air was warm and balmy. Nature was filled with life, and seemed to be proclaiming that the cold was past.

As he moved along the street he met a funeral procession.

"What a pity," he thought, "a man should die, with summer so near at hand!"

He was also surprised at the keenness of his sight; for, inclosed in each man's body, he saw the outline of his soul. But the dead man's body was empty, like a cage without a bird. He also read the thoughts in their minds.

"Now," said a large man in the carriage next the hearse, "I may win her, since she is a widow."

The widow herself kept thinking: "Would it had been I! His life was essential to the children, while I should scarcely have been missed. I wish I had no duties here, and might follow him now."

While pondering on these things, he reached Sylvia's house, and went into the little room in which he had so often seen her. The warm southwesterly breeze blew through the open windows, and far beyond Central Park the approaching sunset promised to be beautiful. The table was covered with flowers, and though he had often seen that variety, he had never before noticed the marvellous combinations of colours, while the room was filled with a thousand delicious perfumes. The thrush hanging in the window sang divinely, and in a silver frame he saw a likeness of himself.

"I have always loved this room," he thought, "but it seems to me now like heaven."

He sat down in an arm-chair from force of habit, to await his *fiancee*.

"Oh, for a walk with Sylvia by twilight!" his thoughts ran on, "for she need not be at home again till after seven."

Presently he heard the soft rustle of her dress, and rose to meet her. Though she looked in his direction, she did not seem to see him, and walked past him to the window. She was the picture of loveliness silhouetted against the sky. He went towards her, and gazed into her deep-sea eyes, which had a far-away expression. She turned, went gracefully to the mantelpiece, and took a photograph of herself from behind the clock. On its back Ayrault had scrawled a boyish verse composed by himself, which ran:

> "My divine, most ideal Sylvia,
> O vision, with eyes so blue,
> 'Tis in the highest degree consequential,
> To my existence in fact essential,
> That I should be loved by you."

As she read and reread those lines, with his whole soul he yearned to have her look at him. He watched the colour come and go in her clear, bright complexion, and was rejoiced to see in her the personification of activity and health. Beneath his own effusion on the photograph he saw something written in pencil, in the hand he knew so well:

> "Did you but know how I love you,
> No more silly things would you ask.
> With my whole heart and soul I adore you--
> Idiot! goose! bombast!"

And as she glanced at it, these thoughts crossed her mind: "I shall never call you such names again. How much I shall have to tell you! It is provoking that you stay away so long."

He came still nearer--so near, in fact, that he could hear the beating of her heart--but she still seemed entirely unconscious of his presence. Losing his reserve and self-control, he impulsively grasped at her hands, then fell on his knees, and then, dumfounded, struggled to his feet. Her hands seemed to slip through his; he was not able to touch her, and she was still unaware of his presence.

Suddenly a whole flood of light and the truth burst upon him. He had passed painlessly and unconsciously from the dreamland of Saturn to the shadowland of eternity. The mystery was solved. Like the dead bishop, he had become a free spirit. His prayer was answered, and his body, struck by lightning, lay far away on that great ringed planet. How he longed to take in his arms the girl who had promised herself to him, and who, he now saw, loved him with her whole heart; but he was only an immaterial spirit, lighter even than the ether of space, and the unchangeable laws of the universe seemed to him but the irony of fate. As a spirit, he was intangible and invisible to those in the flesh, and likewise they were beyond his control. The tragedy of life then dawned upon him, and the awful results of death made themselves felt. He glanced at Sylvia. On coming in she had looked radiantly happy; now she seemed depressed, and even the bird stopped singing.

"Oh," he thought, "could I but return to life for one hour, to tell her how incessantly she has been in my thoughts, and how I love her! Death, to the aged, is no loss--in fact, a blessing--but now!" and he sobbed mentally in the anguish of his soul. If he could but communicate with her, he thought; but he remembered what the departed bishop had said, that it would take most men centuries to do this, and that others could never learn. By that time she, too, would be dead, perhaps having been the wife of some one else, and he felt a sense of jealousy even beyond the grave. Throwing himself upon a rug on the floor, in a paroxysm of distress, he gazed at Sylvia.

"Oh, horrible mockery!" he thought, thinking of the spirit. "He gave me worse than a stone when I asked for bread; for, in place of freedom, he sent me death. Could I but be alive again for a few moments!" But, with a bitter smile, he again remembered the words of the bishop, "What would a soul in hell not give for but one hour on earth?"

Sylvia had seated herself on a small sofa, on which, and next to her, he had so often sat. Her gentle eyes had a thoughtful look, while her face was the personification of intelligence and beauty. She occasionally glanced at his photograph, which she held in her hand.

"Sylvia, Sylvia!" he suddenly cried, rising to his knees at her feet. "I love, I adore you! It was my longing to be with you that brought me here. I know you can neither see nor hear me, but cannot your soul commune with mine?"

"Is Dick here?" cried Sylvia, becoming deadly pale and getting up, "or am I losing my reason?"

Seeing that she was distressed by the power of his mind, Ayrault once more sank to the floor, burying his face in his hands.

Unable to endure this longer, and feeling as if his heart must break, he rushed out into the street, wishing he might soothe his anguish with a hypodermic injection of morphine, and that he had a body with which to divert and suppress his soul.

Night had fallen, and the electric lamps cast their white rays on the ground, while the stars overhead shone in their eternal serenity and calm. Then was it once more brought home to him that he was a spirit, for darkness and light were alike, and he felt the beginning of that sense of prescience of which the bishop had spoken. Passing through the houses of some of the clubs to which he belonged, he saw his name still upon the list of members, and then he went to the places of amusement he knew so well. On all sides were familiar faces, but what interested him most was the great division incessantly going on. Here were jolly people enjoying life and playing cards, who, his foresight showed him, would in less than a year be under ground--like Mercutio, in "Romeo and Juliet," to-day known as merry fellows, who to-morrow would be grave men.

While his eyes beheld the sun, he had imagined the air felt warm and balmy. He now saw that this had been a hallucination, for he was chilled through and through. He also perceived that he cast no shadow, and that no one observed his presence. He, on the other hand, saw not only the air as it entered and left his friends' lungs, but also the substance of their brains, and the seeds of disease and death, whose presence they themselves did not even suspect, and the seventy-five per cent of water in their bodies, making them appear like sacks of liquid. In some he saw the germs of consumption; in others, affections of the heart. In all, he saw the incessant struggle between the healthy blood-cells and the malignant, omnipresent bacilli that the cells were trying to overcome. Many men and women he saw were in love, and he could tell what all were about to do. Oh, the secrets that were revealed, while the motives for acts were now laid bare that till then he had misunderstood! He had often heard the old saying, that if every person in a ball-room could read the thoughts of the rest, the ball would seem a travesty on enjoyment, rather than real pleasure, and now he perceived its force. He also noticed that many were better than he had supposed, and were trying, in a blundering but persevering way, to obey their consciences. He saw some unselfish thoughts and acts. Many things that he had attributed to irresolution or inconsistency, he perceived were in reality self-sacrifice. He went on in frantic disquiet, distance no longer being of consequence, and in his roaming chanced to pass through the graveyard in which many generations of his ancestors lay buried. Within the leaden coffins he saw the cold remains; some well preserved, others but handfuls of dust.

"Tell me, O my progenitors," he cried, "you whose blood till this morning flowed in my veins, is there not some way by which I, as a spirit, can commune with the material world? I have always admired your judgment and wisdom, and you have all been in Shadowland longer than I. Give me, I pray you, some ancestral advice."

The only sound in answer was the hum of the insects that filled the evening air. The moonlight shone softly, but in a ghastly way, on the marble crosses of his vault and those around, and he felt an unspeakable sadness within this abode of the dead. "How many unfinished lives," he thought, "have ended beneath these sods! Unimproved talents here are buried in the ground. Unattained ambitions, and those who died before their time; those who tried, in a half-hearted way, to improve their opportunities, and accomplished something, and those who neglected them, and did still less--all are together here, the just with the unjust, though it be for the last time. The grave absorbs their bodies and ends their probationary record, from which there is no appeal."

Near by were some open graves, ready to receive their occupants, while a little farther on he recognized the Cortlandt mausoleum, looking exactly as when shown him, through his second sight, by the spirit on the previous day.

From the graves filled recently, and from many others, rose threads of coloured matter, in the form of gases, the forerunners of miasma. He now perceived shadowy figures flitting about on the ground and in the air, from whose eyes poured streams of immaterial tears. Their brains, hearts, and vertebral columns were the parts most easily seen, and they were filled with an inextinguishable anguish and sorrow that from its very intensity made itself seen as a blue flame. The ruffles and knickerbockers in which some of these were attired, evidently by the effects of the thoughts in their minds, doubtless from force of habit from what they had worn on earth while alive, showed that they had been dead at least two hundred years. Ayrault also now found himself in street clothes, although when in his clubs he had worn a dress suit.

"Tell me, fellow-spirits," he said, addressing them, "how can I communicate with one that is still alive?"

They looked at him with moist eyes, but answered not a word.

"I attributed the misery in my heart," thought Ayrault, "entirely to the distress at losing Sylvia, which God knows is enough; but though I suspected it before, I now see, by my companions, that I am in the depths of hell."

CHAPTER XII
SHEOL

Failing to find words to convey his thoughts, he threw himself into an open grave, praying that the earth might hide his soul, as he had supposed it some day would hide his body. But the ground was like crystal, and he saw the white bones in the graves all around him. Unable to endure these surroundings longer, he rushed back to his old haunts, where he knew he should find the friends of his youth. He did not pause to go by the usual way, but passed, without stopping, through walls and buildings. Soon he beheld the familiar scene, and heard his own name mentioned. But there was no comfort here, and what he had seen of old was but an incident to what he gazed on now. Praying with his whole heart that he might make himself heard, he stepped upon a foot-stool, and cried:

"Your bodies are decaying before me. You are burying your talents in the ground. We must all stand for final sentence at the last day, mortals and spirits alike--there is not a shadow of a shade of doubt. Your every thought will be known, and for every evil deed and every idle word God will bring us into judgment. The angel of death is among you and at work in your very midst. Are you prepared to receive him? He has already killed my body, and now that I can never die I wish there was a grave for my soul. I was reassured by a vision that told me I was safe, but either it was a hallucination, or I have been betrayed by some spirit. Last night I still lived, and my body obeyed my will. Since then I have experienced death, and with the resulting increased knowledge comes the loss of all hope, with keener pangs than I supposed could exist. Oh, that I had now their opportunities, that I might write a thesis that should live forever, and save millions of souls from the anguish of mine! Inoculate your mortal bodies with the germs of faith and mutual love, in a stronger degree than they dwelt in me, lest you lose the life above."

But no one heard him, and he preached in vain.

He again rushed forth, and, after a half-involuntary effort, found himself in the street before his loved one's home. Scarcely knowing why, except that it had become nature to wish to be near her, he stood for a long time opposite her dwelling.

"O house!" he cried, "inanimate object that can yet enthral me so, I stand before your cold front as a suppliant from a very distant realm; yet in my sadness I am colder than your stones, more alone than in a desolate place. She that dwells within you holds my love. I long for her shadow or the sound of her step. I am more wretchedly in love than ever--I, an impotent, invisible spirit. Must I bear this sorrow in addition to my others, in my fruitless search for rest? My life will be a waking nightmare, most bitter irony of fate." The trees swayed above his head, and the moon, in its last quarter, looked dreamily at him.

"Ah," thought Ayrault, "could I but sleep and be happy! Drowsiness and weariness, fatigue's grasp is on me; or may Sylvia's nearness soothe, as her voice has brought me calm! Quiet I may some day enjoy, but slumber again, never! I see that souls in hades must ever have their misdeeds before them. Happy man in this world, the repentant's sins are forgiven! You lose your care in sleep. Somnolence and drowsiness--balm of aching hearts, angels of mercy! Mortals, how blessed! until you die, God sends you this rest. When I recall summer evenings with Sylvia, while gentle zephyrs fanned our brows, I would change Pope's famous line to 'Man never is, but always HAS BEEN blessed.'"

A clock in a church-steeple now struck three, the sound ringing through the still night air.

"It will soon be time for ghosts to go," thought Ayrault. "I must not haunt her dwelling."

There was a light in Sylvia's study, and Ayrault remained meditatively gazing at it.

"Happy lamp," he thought, "to shed your light on one so fair! She can see you, and you shine, for her. You are better off than I. Would that her soul might shine for me, as your light shines for her! The light of my life has departed. O that the darkness were complete! I am dead," his thoughts ran on, and when the privilege--bitter word!--that permits me to remain here has expired, I must doubtless return to Saturn, and there in purgatory work out my probation. But what comfort is it that a few centuries hence I may be able to revisit my native earth?--

> *The flowers will bloom in the morning light,*
> *And the lark salute the sun,*
> *The earth will continue to roll through space,*
> *And I may be nearer my final grace,*
> *But Sylvia's life-thread will be spun.*

"Even Sylvia's house will be a heap of ruins, or its place will be taken by something else. If I had Sylvia, I should care for nothing; as I have lost her, even this sight, though sweet, must always bring regret. I wish, at all events, I might see Sylvia, if only with these spirit-eyes, since, as a mortal, she may never gladden my sight again."

To his surprise, he now perceived that he could see, notwithstanding the drawn shades. Sylvia was at her writing-desk, in a light-coloured wrapper. She sat there resting her head on her hand, looking thoughtful but worried. Though it was so late, she had not retired. The thrush that Ayrault had often in life admired, and that she had for some reason brought up-stairs, was silent and asleep.

"Happy bird!" he said, "you obtain rest and forgetfulness on covering your head; but what wing can cover my soul? I used to wish I might flutter towards heaven on natural wings like you, little thrush. Now I can, indeed, outfly you. But whatever I do I'm unhappy, and wherever I go I'm in hell. What is man in his helpless, first spiritual state? He is but a flower, and withers soon. Had I, like the bishop, been less blind, and obeyed my conscience clear, I might have returned to my native earth while Sylvia still sojourns here; and coming thus by virtue of development, I should be able to commune with her.

"What is life?" he continued. "In the retrospect, nothing. It seems to me already as but an infinitesimal point. Things that engrossed me, and seemed of such moment, that overshadowed the duty of obeying my conscience--what were they, and where? Ah, where? They endured but a moment. Reality and evanescence--evanescence and reality."

The light in Sylvia's room was out now, and in the east he beheld the dawn. The ubiquitous grey which he saw at night was invaded by streams of glorious crimson and blue that reached far up into the sky. He gazed at the spectacle, and then once more at that house in which his love was centred.

"Would I might be her guardian angel, to guide her in the right and keep her from all harm!

"*Sleep on, Sylvia. Sweet one, sleep.*
Yon stars fade beside your eyes.
Your thoughts and your soul are fairer far
than the east in this day's sunrise."

I know what I have lost. Ah, desolating knowledge! for I have read Sylvia's heart, and know I was loved as truly as I loved. When Bearwarden and Cortlandt break her the news--ah, God! will she live, and do they yet know I am dead?"

Again came that spasm to shed spirit tears, and had he not known it impossible he would have thought his heart must break.

The birds twittered, and the light grew, but Ayrault lay with his face upon the ground. Finally the spirit of unrest drove him on. He passed the barred door of his own house, through which he had entered so often. It was unchanged, but seemed deserted. Next, he went to the water-front, where he had left his yacht. Invisibly and sadly he stood upon her upper deck, and gazed at the levers, in response to his touch on which the craft had cleft the waves, reversed, or turned like a thing of life. "'Twas a pretty toy," he mused, "and many hours of joy have I had as I floated through life on board of her."

As he moped along he beheld two unkempt Italians having a piano-organ and a violin. The music was not fine, but it touched a chord in Ayrault's breast, for he had waltzed with Sylvia to that air, and it made his heart ache.

"Oh, the acuteness of my distress," he cried, "the utter depth of my sorrow! Can I have no peace in death, no oblivion in the grave? I am reminded of my blighted, hopeless love in all kinds of unexpected ways, by unforeseen trifles. Oh, would I might, indeed, die! May obliteration be my deliverer!"

"Poor fellows," he continued, glancing at the Italians, for he perceived that neither of the players was happy; the pianist was avaricious, while the violinist's natural and habitual jealousy destroyed his peace of mind.

"Unhappiness seems the common lot," thought Ayrault. "Earth cannot give that joy for which we sigh. Poor fellows! though you rack my ears and distress my heart, I cannot help you now."

CHAPTER XIII
THE PRIEST'S SERMON

It being the first day of the week, the morning air was filled with chimes from many steeples.

"Divine service always comforted in life," thought Ayrault, "perchance it may do so now, when I have reached the state for which it tried to prepare me."

Accordingly, he moved on with the throng, and soon was ascending the heights of Morningside Park, after which, he entered the cathedral. The priest whose voice had so often thrilled him stood at his post in his surplice, and the choir had finished the processional hymn. During the responses in the litany, and between the commandments, while the congregation and the choir sang, he heard their natural voices as of old ascending to the vaulted roof and arrested there. He now also heard their spiritual voices resulting from the earnestness of their prayers. These were rung through the vaster vault of space, arousing a spiritual echo beyond the constellations and the nebulae. The service, which was that of the Protestant Episcopal Church, touched him as deeply as usual, after which the rector ascended the steps to the pulpit.

"The text, this morning," he began, "is from the eighth chapter of St. Paul's Epistle to the Romans, at the eighteenth verse: 'For I reckon that the sufferings of this present time are not worthy to be compared to the glory that shall be revealed in us.' Let us suppose that you or I, brethren, should become a free and disembodied spirit. A minute vein in the brain bursts, or a clot forms in the heart. It may be a mere trifle, some unexpected thing, yet the career in the flesh is ended, the eternal life of the liberated spirit begun. The soul slips from earth's grasp, as air from our fingers, and finds itself in the frigid, boundless void of space. Yet, through some longing this soul might rejoin us, and, though invisible, might hear the church-bells ring, and long to recall some one of the many bright Sunday mornings spent here on earth. Has a direful misfortune befallen this brother, or has a slave been set free? Let us suppose for a moment that the first has occurred. 'Vanity of vanities,' said the old preacher. 'Calamity of calamities,' says the new. That soul's probationary period is ended; his record, on which he must go, is forever made. He has been in the flesh, let us say, one, two, three or four score years; before him are the countless æons of eternity. He may have had a reasonably satisfactory life, from his point of view, and been fairly successful in stilling conscience. That still, small voice doubtless spoke pretty sharply at first, but after a while it rarely troubled him, and in the end it spoke not at all. He may, in a way, have enjoyed life and the beauties of nature. He has seen the fresh leaves come and go, but he forgot the moral, that he himself was but a leaf, and that, as they all dropped to earth to make more soil, his ashes must also return to the ground. But his soul, friends and brethren, what becomes of that? Ah! it is the study of this question that moistens our eyes with tears. No evil man is really happy here, and what must be his suffering in the cold, cold land of spirits? No slumber or forgetfulness can ease his lot in hades, and after his condemnation at the last judgment he must forever face the unsoftened realities of eternity. No evil thing or thought can find lodgment in heaven. If it could, heaven would not be a happy place; neither can any man improve in the abyss of hell. As the horizon gradually darkens, and this soul recedes from God, the time spent in the flesh must come to seem the most infinitesimal moment, more evanescent than the tick of a clock. It seems dreadful that for such short misdoings a soul should suffer so long, but no man can be saved in spite of himself. He had the opportunities--and the knowledge of this must give a soul the most acute pang.

"In Revelation, xx, 6, we find these words, 'Blessed and holy is he that hath part in the first resurrection: on such the second death hath no power.' I have often asked myself, May not this mean that those with a bad record in the general resurrection after a time cease to exist, since all suffer one death at the close of their period here? "This is somewhat suggested by Proverbs, xii, 28. 'In the way of righteousness is life, and in the pathway thereof there is no death.' This might limit the everlasting damnation, so often repeated elsewhere, to the lives of the condemned, since to them, in a sense, it would be everlasting.

"Let us now turn to the bright picture--the soul that has weathered the storms of life and has reached the haven of rest. The struggles, temptations, and trials overcome, have done their work of refining with a rapidity that could not have been equalled in any other way, and though, perhaps, very imperfect still, the journey is ever on. The reward is tenfold, yet in proportion to what this soul has done, for we know that the servant who best used his ten talents was made ruler over ten cities, while he that increased his five talents by five received five; and the Saviour in whom he trusted, by whose aid he made his fight, stands ready to receive him, saying, 'Enter thou into the joy of thy Lord.'

"As the dark, earthly background recedes, the clouds break and the glorious light appears, the contrast heightening the ever-unfolding and increasing delights, which are as great as the recipients have power to enjoy, since these righteous souls receive their rewards in proportion to the weight of the crosses that they have borne in the right spirit. These souls are a joy to their Creator, and are the heirs of Him in heaven. The ceaseless, sleepless activity that must obtain in both paradise and hades, and that must make the hearts of the godless grow faint at the contemplation, is also a boundless promise to those who have Him who is all in all.

"Where is now thy Saviour? where is now thy God? the unjust man has asked in his heart when he saw his just neighbour struggling and unsuccessful. Both the righteous and the unrighteous man are dead. The one has found his Saviour, the other is yearly losing God. What is the suffering of the present momentary time, eased as it is by God's mercy and presence, compared with the glories that await us? What would it be if our lives here were filled with nothing else, as ye know that your labour is not vain in the Lord? Time and eternity--the finite and the infinite. Death was, indeed, a deliverer, and the sunset of the body is the sunrise of the soul."

The priest held himself erect as a soldier while delivering this sermon, making the great cathedral ring with his earnest and solemn voice, while Ayrault, as a spirit, saw how absolutely he meant and believed every word that he said.

Nearly all the members of the congregation were moved--some more, some less than they appeared. After the benediction they rapidly dispersed, carrying in their hearts the germs he had sown; but whether these would bear fruit or wither, time alone could show.

Ayrault had noticed Sylvia's father and mother in church, but Sylvia herself was not there, and he was distressed to think she might be ill.

"Why," pondered Ayrault, "am I so unhappy? I was baptized, confirmed, and have taken the sacrament. I have always had an unshaken faith, and, though often unsuccessful, have striven to obey my conscience. The spirits also on Saturn kept saying I should be happy. Now, did this mean it was incumbent upon me to rejoice, because of some blessing I already had, and did not appreciate, or did their prescience show them some prospective happiness I was to enjoy? The visions also of Violet, the angel, and the lily, which I believed, and still believe, were no mere empty fancies, should have given me the most unspeakable joy. It may be a mistake to apply earthly logic to heavenly things, but the fundamental laws of science cannot change.

"Why am I so unhappy?" he continued, returning to his original question. "The visions gave promise of special grace, perhaps some special favour. True, my prayer to see Sylvia was heard, but, considering the sacrifice, this has been no blessing. The request cannot have been wrong in itself, and as for the manner, there was no arrogance in my heart. I asked as a mortal, as a man of but finite understanding, for what concerned me most. Why, oh why, so wretched?"

CHAPTER XIV
HIC ILLE JACET

At daybreak the thunder-shower passed off, but was followed by a cold, drenching rain. Supposing Ayrault had remained in the Callisto, Bearwarden and Cortlandt did not feel anxious, and, not wishing to be wet through, remained in the cave, keeping up a good fire with the wood they had collected. Towards evening a cold wind came up, and, thinking this might clear the air, they ventured out, but, finding the ground saturated, and that the rain was again beginning to fall, they returned to shelter, prepared a dinner of canned meat, and made themselves as comfortable as possible for the night.

"I am surprised," said Cortlandt, "that Dick did not try to return to us, since he had the mackintoshes."

"I dare say he did try," replied Bearwarden, "but finding the course inundated, and knowing we should not need the mackintoshes if we remained under cover, decided to put back. The Callisto is, of course, as safe as a church."

"I hope," said Cortlandt, "no harm has come to him on the way. It will be a weight off my mind to see him safely with us."

"Should he not turn up in the morning," replied Bearwarden, "we must begin a search for him bright and early."

Making up the fire as near the entrance of the cave as they could find a dry place, so that Ayrault should see it if he attempted to return during the night, they piled on wood, and talked of their recent experiences.

"However unwilling I was," said Cortlandt, "to believe my senses, which I felt were misleading me, I can no longer doubt the reality of that spirit bishop, or the truth of what he says. When you look at the question dispassionately, it is what you might logically expect. In my desire to disprove what is to us supernatural, I tried to create mentally a system that would be a substitute for the one he described, but could evolve nothing that so perfectly filled the requirements, or that was so simple. Nothing seems more natural than that man, having been evolved from stone, should continue his ascent till he discards material altogether. The metamorphism is more striking in the first change than in the second. Granted that the soul is immaterial, and that it leaves the body after death, what is there to keep it on earth? Gravitation cannot affect it. What is more likely than that it is left behind by the earth in its orbit, or that it continues its forward motion, but in a straight line, till, reaching the paths of the greater planets, it is drawn to them by some affinity or attraction that the earth does not possess, and that the souls held in that manner remain here on probation, developing like young animals or children, till, by gradually acquired power, resulting from their wills, they are able to rise again into space, to revisit the earth, and in time to explore the universe? It might easily come about that, by some explainable sympathy, the infant good souls are drawn to this planet, while the condemned pass on to Cassandra, which holds them by some property peculiar to itself, until perhaps they, too, by virtue of their wills, acquire new power, unless involution sets in and they lose what they have. The simplicity of the thing is what surprises me now, and that for ages philosophers have been racking their brains with every conceivable fancy, when, by simply extending and following natural laws, they could discern the whole."

"It is the old story," said Bearwarden, "of Columbus and the egg. Schopenhouer and his predecessors appear to have tried every idea but the right one, and even Darwin and Huxley fell short in their reasoning, because they tried to obtain more or less than four by putting two with two."

Thus they sat and talked while the night wore on. Neither thought of sleeping, hoping all the while that Ayrault might walk in as he had the night before.

At last the dawn began to tint the east, and the growing light showed them that the storm had passed. The upper strata of Saturn's atmosphere being filled with infinitesimal particles of dust, as a result of its numerous volcanoes, the conditions were highly favourable to beautiful sunrises and sunsets. Soon coloured streaks extended far into the sky, and though they knew that when the sun's disc appeared it would seem small, it filled the almost boundless eastern horizon with the most variegated and gorgeous hues.

Turning away from the welcome sight--for their minds were ill at ease--they found the light strong enough for their search to begin. Writing on a sheet of paper, in a large hand, "Have gone to the Callisto to look for you; shall afterwards return here," they pinned this in a conspicuous place and set out due west, keeping about a hundred yards apart. The ground was wet and slippery, but overhead all was clear, and the sun soon shone brightly.

Looking to right and left, and occasionally shouting and discharging their revolvers, they went on for half an hour.

"I have his tracks," called Bearwarden, and Cortlandt hastened to join him.

In the soft ground, sure enough, they saw Ayrault's footprints, and, from the distance between them, concluded that he must have been running or walking very fast; but the rain had washed down the edges of the incision. The trail ascended a gentle slope, where they lost it; but on reaching the summit they saw it again with the feet together, as though Ayrault had paused, and about it were many other impressions with the feet turned in, as if the walkers or standers had surrounded Ayrault, who was in the centre.

"I hope," said Cortlandt, "these are nothing more than the footprints we have seen formed about ourselves."

"See," said Bearwarden, "Dick's trail goes on, and the others vanish. They cannot have been made by savages or Indians, for they seem to have had weight only while standing."

They then resumed their march, firing a revolver shot at intervals of a minute. Suddenly they came upon a tall, straight tree, uprooted by the wind and lying diagonally across their path. Following with their eyes the direction in which it lay, they saw a large, hollow trunk, with the bark stripped off, and charred as if struck by lightning. Obliged to pass near this by the uprooted tree-whose thick trunk, upheld by the branches at the head, lay raised about two feet from the ground--both searchers gave a start, and stood still as if petrified. Inside the great trunk they saw a head, and, on looking more closely, descried Ayrault's body. Grasping it by the arms, they drew it out. The face was pale and the limbs were stiff. Instantly Cortlandt unfastened the collar, while Bearwarden applied a flask to the lips. But they soon found that their efforts were vain.

"The spirit!" ejaculated Cortlandt. "Dick may be in a trance, in which case he can help us. Let us will hard and long." Accordingly, they threw themselves on their faces, closing their eyes, that nothing might distract their concentration. Minutes, which seemed like ages, passed, and there was no response.

"Now," said Bearwarden, "will together, hard."

Suddenly the stillness was broken by the spirit's voice, which said:

"I felt more than one mind calling, but the effect was so slight I thought first I was mistaken. I will help you in what you want, for the young man is not dead, neither is he injured."

Saying which, he stretched himself upon Ayrault, worked his lungs artificially, and willed with an intensity the observers could feel where they stood. Quickly the colour returned to Ayrault's cheeks, and with the spirit's assistance he sat up and leaned against the tree that had protected him from the storm.

"Your promise was realized," he said, addressing the spirit. "I have seen what I shall never forget, and lest the anguish--the vision of which I saw--come true, let us return to the earth, and not leave it till I have tasted in reality the joys that in the spirit I seemed to have missed. I have often longed in this life to be in the spirit, but never knew what longing was, till I experienced it as a spirit, to be once more in the flesh."

"You see the mercy of God," said the spirit, "in not ordinarily allowing the spirits of the departed to revisit earth until they are prepared--that is, until they are sufficiently advanced to go there unaided--by which time they have come to understand the wisdom of God's laws. In your case the limiting laws were partially suspended, so that you were able to return at once, with many of the faculties and senses of spirits, but without their accumulated experience. It speaks well for your state of preparation that, without having had those disguised blessings, illness or misfortune, you were not utterly crushed by what you saw when temporarily released. While in the trance you were not in hell, but experienced the feelings that all mortals would if allowed to return immediately. Thus no lover can return to earth till his *fiancee* has joined him here, or till, perceiving the benevolence of God's ways, he is not distressed at what he sees, and has the companionship of a host of kindred spirits.

"The spirits you saw in the cemetery were indeed in hell, but had become sufficiently developed to revisit the earth, though doing so did not relieve their distress; for neither the development of their senses, which intensifies their capacity for remorse and regret, nor their investigations into God's boundless mercies, which they have deliberately thrown away, can comfort them.

"Some of your ancestors are on Cassandra, and others are in purgatory here. Though a few faintly felt your prayer, none were able to return and answer beside their graves. It was at your request and prayer that He freed your spirit, but you see how unhappy it made you."

"I see," replied Ayrault, "that no man should wish to anticipate the workings of the Almighty, although I have been unspeakably blessed in that He made an exception--if I may so call it--in my favour, since, in addition to revealing the responsibilities of life, it has shown me the inestimable value and loyalty of woman's love. I fear, however, that my return to earth greatly distressed the waterer of the flowers you showed me."

"She already sleeps," replied the spirit, "and I have comforted her by a dream in which she sees that you are well." "When shall we start?" asked Bearwarden.

"As soon as you can get ready," replied Ayrault. "I would not risk running short of enough current to generate the apergy needed to get us back. I dare say when I have been on earth a few years, and have done something for the good of my soul--which, as I take it, can be accomplished as well by advancing science as in any other way--I shall pine for another journey in space as I now do to return."

"How I wish I were engaged," said Bearwarden, glancing at Cortlandt, and overjoyed at Ayrault's recovery.

Accordingly, they resumed their march in the direction in which they had been going when they found Ayrault, and were soon beside the Callisto. Cortlandt worked the combination lock of the lower entrance, through which they crawled. Going to the second story, they opened a large window and let down a ladder, on which the spirit ascended at their invitation.

Bearwarden and Ayrault immediately set about combining the chemicals that were to produce the force necessary to repel them from Saturn. Bubbles of hydrogen were given off from the lead and zinc plates, and the viscous primary batteries quickly had the wires passing through a vacuum at a white heat.

"I see you are nearly ready to start," said the spirit, "so I must say farewell."

"Will you not come with us?" asked Ayrault.

"No," replied the spirit. "I do not wish to be away as long as it will take you to reach the earth. The Callisto's atmosphere could not absorb my body, so that, should I leave you before your arrival, you would be burdened with a corpse. I may visit you in the spirit, though the desire and effort for communion with spirits, to be of most good, must needs come from the earth. Ere long, my intuition tells me, we shall meet again.

"The vision of your own grave," he continued, addressing Cortlandt, "may not come true for many years, but however long your lives may be, according to earthly reckoning, remember that when they are past they will seem to have been hardly more than a moment, for they are the personification of frailty and evanescence."

He held up his hands and blessed them; and then repeating, "Farewell and a happy return!" descended as he had come up.

The air was filled with misty shadows, and the pulsating hearts, luminous brains, and centres of spiritual activity quivered with motion. They surrounded the incarnate spirit of the bishop and set up the soft, musical hum the travellers had heard so often since their arrival on Saturn.

"I now understand," thought Ayrault, "why the spirits I met kept repeating that I should be happy. They perceived I was to be translated, and though they doubtless knew what suffering it would cause, they also knew I should be awakened to a sense of great realities, of which I understood but little."

They drew up the ladder and turned on the current, and the Callisto slowly began to rise, while the three friends crowded the window.

"Good-bye!" called the spirit's pleasant voice, to which the men replied in chorus.

The sun had set on the surface of the planet while they made their preparations; but as the Callisto rose higher, it seemed to rise again, making the sides of their car shine like silver, and, carefully closing the two open windows, they watched the fast-receding world, so many times larger and more magnificent than their own.

CHAPTER XV
MOTHER EARTH

"There is something sad," said Cortlandt, "about the end of everything, but I am more sorry to leave Saturn than I have ever been in taking leave of any other place."

When beyond the limits of the atmosphere they applied the full current, and were soon once more cleaving the ether at cometary speed, their motion towards the sun being aided by that great body itself.

They quickly passed beyond the outer edge of the vast silvery rings, and then crossed one after another the orbits of the moons, from the last of which, Iapetus, they obtained their final course in the direction of the earth. They had an acute feeling of homesickness for the mysterious planet on which, while yet mortal, they had found paradise, and had communed with spirits as no modern men ever did.

Without deviating from their almost straight line, they passed within a million miles of Jupiter, which had gained in its smaller orbit on Saturn, and a few days later crossed the track of Mars.

As the earth had completed nearly half a revolution in its orbit since their departure, they here turned somewhat to the right by attracting the ruddy planet, in order to avoid passing too near the sun.

"On some future expedition," said Ayrault, "and when we have a supply of blue glasses, we can take a trip to Venus, if we can find a possible season in her year. Compared with this journey, it would be only like going round the block."

Two days later they had rounded the sun, and laid their course in pursuit of the earth.

That the astronomers in the dark hemisphere were at their posts and saw them, was evident; for a brilliant beam of light again flashed forth, this time from a point a little south of the arctic circle, and after shining one minute, telegraphed this message: "Rejoiced to see you again. Hope all are well."

Since they were not sufficiently near the moon's shadow, they directed their light-beam into their own, which trailed off on one side, and answered: "All well, thank you. Have wonderful things to relate."

The men at the telescopes then, as before, read the message, and telephoned the light this next question: "When are you coming down, that we may notify the newspapers?"

"We wish one more sight of the earth from this height, by daylight. We are now swinging to get between it and the sun."

"We have erected a monument in Van Cortlandt Park, and engraved upon it, 'At this place James Bearwarden, Henry Chelmsford Cortlandt, and Richard Rokeby Ayrault left earth, December 21, A. D. 2000, to visit Jupiter.'"

"Add to it, 'They returned on the 10th of the following June.'"

Soon the Callisto came nearly between the earth and the sun, when the astronomers could see it only through darkened glasses, and it appeared almost as a crescent. The sight the travellers then beheld was superb. It was about 11 A. M. in London, and Europe was spread before them like a map. All its peninsulas and islands, enclosed blue seas, and bays came out in clear relief. Gradually Russia, Germany, France, the British Isles, and Spain moved towards the horizon, as in grand procession, and at the same time the Western hemisphere appeared. The hour of day at the longitude above which they hung was about the same as when they set out, but the sun shone far more directly upon the Northern hemisphere than then, and instead of bleak December, this was the leafy month of June.

They were loath to end the lovely scene, and would fain have remained where they were while the earth revolved again; but, remembering that their friends must by this time be waiting, they shut off the repulsion from the earth.

"We need not apply the apergy to the earth until quite near," said Ayrault, "since a great part of the top speed will be taken off by the resistance of the atmosphere, especially as we go in base first. We have only to keep a sufficiently strong repulsion on the dome to prevent our turning over, and to see that our speed is not great enough to heat the car."

When about fifty miles from the surface they felt the expected check, and concluded they had reached the upper limits of the atmosphere. And this increased, notwithstanding the decrease in their speed, showing how quickly the air became dense.

The return

When about a mile from the earth they had the Callisto well in hand, and allowed it to descend slowly. The ground was already black with people, who, having learned where the Callisto was to touch, had hastened to Van Cortlandt Park.

"I am overjoyed to see you," said Sylvia, when she and Ayrault met. "I had the most dreadful presentiment that something had gone wrong with you. One afternoon and evening I was so perplexed, and during the night had a series of nightmares that I shall never forget. I really believed you were near me, but your nature seemed to have changed, for, instead of its making me happy, I was frightfully distressed. The next day I was very ill, and unable to get up; but during the morning I fell asleep and had another dream, which was intensely realistic and made me believe--yes, convinced me--that you were well. After that dream I soon recovered; but oh, the anguish of the first!"

Ayrault did not tell her then that he had been near her, and of his unspeakable suffering, of which hers had been but the echo.

Three weeks later a clergyman tied the knot that was to unite them forever. While Sylvia and Ayrault were standing up to receive the congratulations of their friends, Bearwarden, in shaking his hand, said:

"Remember, we have been to neither Uranus, nor Neptune, nor Cassandra, which may be as interesting as anything we have seen. Should you want to take another trip, count me as your humble servant." And Cortlandt, following behind him, said the same thing.

Shortly after this, Sylvia went up-stairs to change her dress, and when she came down she and Ayrault set out on their journey together through life, amid a chorus of cheers and a shower of rice.

Cortlandt then returned to his department at Washington, and Bearwarden resumed his duties with the Terrestrial Axis Straightening Company, in the presidential chair.